I0719971

Domestic Threats

Megan Carney

Previous titles by Megan Carney

Sarina, Sweetheart

Navy Trent Series
      Trap and Trace
      From Hackerville with Love
      Humans, Practicing

Learn more about Megan Carney at megancarney.com.

*This book is dedicated to all the community builders.
You are doing the only work that matters.*

Chapter 1

"You know what I miss?" Navy threw the take-out menu on the kitchen table. "Eating burgers in a restaurant."

"I could cook dinner instead." Jackson's smile told Navy the offer wasn't serious.

If she had to choose someone to be stuck in quarantine with, Jackson would be her pick. Nearly three years together and she still caught herself staring at him while he was absorbed in his latest political science book. Six feet and two inches to her five feet six inches. Dark hair to her blond. Green eyes cut like crystals in contrast to her muddy hazel ones. Trim and athletic from their adventures climbing or hiking on the weekends when he wasn't away on assignment.

"Maybe one of us *should* learn how to cook," Navy said. "We're over a year into coronavirus times and our choices for home-cooked dinners are still ramen or peanut butter sandwiches."

Jackson picked up his keys and put on a cloth mask. "They said food would be ready in ten minutes. That's just about how long it will take to walk there."

Navy's phone buzzed. Call me. Now. Sara's message was uncharacteristically serious.

"You look worried. Is something wrong?" Jackson asked.

"Sara wants to talk. Do you mind picking up food on your own?"

"Do I have permission to punch that guy who always gets takeout from Burger Palace and never wears his mask?"

"As long as you don't spill our food." Navy waved at Jackson as he left and then called Sara.

"Navy, I'm so glad you can talk," Sara's words rushed out in one quick breath. The familiar voice immediately conjured Sara's image in Navy's head. Sara was shorter and rounder than Navy but a faster climber on any day. She wore her hair in long braids that swung whenever Sara gestured. Which was almost always when Sara spoke. Navy was consistently amazed at how Sara's energy could fill a room and lift anyone's spirit.

"Well, now you've got me worried. What's going on?" Navy settled cross-legged on the couch. The couch she and Jackson had picked out together in the apartment they now shared. Sometimes the domesticity of that fact comforted her. Sometimes it scared her.

"You and I are going camping."

"Wait, what?" Navy had canceled all of her work trips and most of her personal ones. She hadn't flown on a plane in months.

"You need to come camping with me."

"In Iowa?" Navy and Sara had vented to each other plenty of times about people being careless during the pandemic. Why would Sara want Navy to fly down to Iowa to go camping?

"Yeah. It's about Carrie."

As if that explained everything. "Could you maybe start at the beginning?"

"Right. Sorry. I'm just . . ." Sara took a deep breath.

"Upset. I can tell." One of the many trips Navy had canceled was to see Sara. Navy felt the physical distance between them keenly. "What's going on with Carrie?"

"You're not on Facebook, right?"

"Ugh. No." Navy sometimes wondered if she should reconsider. The social isolation forced on them by the pandemic had shrunk her world down to the few people she texted regularly.

"Right. Little Ms. Paranoid all the time. Anyway, Carrie's been posting some weird stuff recently. About COVID-19 being fake and how it was all planned by Bill Gates . . ."

"But she's an EMT. She's studied medicine."

"She quit two years ago. After her mother and her sister died."

"God, I didn't even know. What happened?"

"Carbon monoxide poisoning. An old space heater or something? I never got the whole story from her. She kind of shut down after that. She lost the house after she quit her job. I'm not even sure where she's staying now. Every time I ask she changes the subject."

Navy wondered what else had happened to the group of friends she had moved away from that she didn't know about. All of the other dramas, big and small, that she had missed by not being there and not calling enough.

"Navy?"

Sara's voice jarred Navy.

"Yeah, yeah. I'm here. I'm sorry. I didn't know Carrie's family had died. Her mother and sister were the only family she had left."

"For a while I thought she was doing better. She found a new job at this gun range. And she started talking about going out and doing some social things."

"So she was doing better," Navy said. "And then?"

"At first she was just posting these weird memes, and then some political stuff criticizing mask mandates and then last week she posted that stupid 'Plandemic' video, and so I called her just to talk and the conversation got weird."

The sound of a TV in the background grew louder than quieter, louder than quieter. Sara was pacing as words continued to tumble out with nervous energy.

"I'm telling Carrie all about how Moss and I are trying to get pregnant, and everything we've been through and how I miscarried again—"

"Oh, Sara. I'm so sorry."

"That's not what I called to talk about."

Navy wondered whether she should press her friend on the topic. Sara tended to focus on saving other people instead of dealing with her own problems. Navy promised herself she would bring it up later. "Okay, so you told Carrie you lost another pregnancy."

"And Carrie says, 'Maybe it's better that way.'"

"What the hell?"

"Exactly. So I asked her what she meant. And she just mumbled something and said she had to go."

"I'm still confused. Why are we going camping with her after she said that to you?"

"I think she's depressed and . . . a little lost. I was reading about how to reach people sucked in by conspiracy theories and someone said familiar environments can remind people of emotional ties."

"You want to recreate the camping trip we did after we graduated college."

"Yeah, do you remember how great the campsite was? Not too far from the city. And there were all those hikes you could paddle to once you set up base camp."

"Look, even if this would help, I'm not sure I want to go camping with someone who doesn't believe COVID-19 is real. Are you willing to risk getting sick? Especially since you're trying to get pregnant?"

"We arrange our own transportation and food. We each sleep in separate tents. And stay six feet apart when we're gathering around the fire."

"Carrie agreed to this?"

"She said she would agree to my 'stupid rules' but only if you come."

"I don't understand. Carrie and I aren't even that close."

"Come on, it'll be like the old days."

"I don't know, Sara."

The apartment door opened and Jackson entered with a large paper bag.

"Think about it?" Sara asked. "Please?"

"I'll think about it."

"You're the best."

"Sara, are you sure you're okay? About the latest miscarriage." Navy watched Jackson unpack food as the silence settled on the other end of the line. Navy didn't want kids and had never wanted them. But Sara did. Badly.

"Some couples try for years," Sara said finally. "We've only been working with the specialist for six months. She said it's still early. I'm okay, I promise."

"Call me if you need if you need to talk."

"I will." Sara hung up.

"Jackson, how would you feel about a road trip to Iowa?" Navy asked.

Chapter 2

Navy checked Meredith's handwritten note again. *1400. US National Arboretum. Holly and Magnolia section. 38.9, -76.9. I'll bring chairs!* If not for the cheery ending and the latitude/longitude numbers, Navy might have felt like she was doing a drill for an undercover op.

She picked the path closest to Meredith's coordinates and entered the grove of trees. Spring in Washington, DC was one of the few pleasant times. Today, the park was nearly empty. It was a weekday, after all. And the cherry blossoms were blooming late this year. The normal swarm of tourists had not yet descended on the National Mall.

Navy hadn't been walking long when she spotted the small clearing, occupied by a woman with long, graying hair. She matched the description Navy had been given. Woman in her sixties, fit, long face, and blue eyes. *After you meet her,* a coworker had told Navy, *you'll wish she was your grandmother.*

As promised, Meredith had brought camp chairs.

Meredith spotted Navy, waved, and then she held a finger up to her lips. Navy slowed her steps to be quieter while Meredith raised a pair of binoculars to her eyes and focused somewhere on the treetops.

Navy didn't mind waiting. She listened to the noisy chatter of the birds, the rustle of the wind, and the squirrels and chipmunks skittering through the leaves on the forest floor.

After several minutes, Meredith lowered her binoculars. She gestured to the empty chair next to her. "Sit. It's an honor, you know."

"An honor?" Navy asked.

"To meet you. I was cheering you on. When you exposed CRYSTAL and went on the run."

Navy had not expected this conversation to start this way. "You've worked at the agency for your entire career and you still feel that way?"

Meredith laughed. "It's been a long marriage. As they say, some good years, some bad years."

Navy wondered if Meredith had conflicting feelings about working for the agency, just as Navy did. She had seen some of the good the CIA could do. She also knew, and had been the target of, some of the CIA's less benevolent operations. "Thank you, for being willing to meet with me."

"Of course," Meredith said. "I read the report on how we tried to catch you. And failed. I sensed a kindred soul."

Navy had been warned Meredith was a hippy. Though, most hippies probably don't know how to forage for poisonous plants almost anywhere in the world.

"You used their own tactics against them. Let them think you didn't know you were being tracked. Lay in wait. Then, confuse and misdirect. Let them find you again but leave a bunch of old scent trails to keep the dogs busy. Very clever, really."

Navy hadn't felt clever. Desperate and cornered, maybe. "I made a bet," she said. "Happened to work, that's all."

"Don't we all?" Meredith smiled. "I remember one operation in the jungles of Panama where I escaped using a poisonous snake that crept into my cell. I tamed it by feeding it rats I caught. Could easily have killed me instead, but I like to think we were friends."

Navy added animals to the list of things Meredith knew how to kill with. "I didn't mean for you to go to all this trouble. We could have met closer to the office."

"Oh, I'm multitasking." Meredith pointed at where she had focused the binoculars. "There's a pair of nesting Rusty Blackbirds there. I like to check on them. Also, your questions." She glanced around the clearing. "I wanted to talk where I didn't have to worry about giving you both opinions and facts."

"You're afraid someone might overhear you saying you don't agree with COVID-19 5G conspiracy theories?"

"You wanted to know if your friend—what did you say her name was?"

Navy smiled. "I didn't." She didn't want Carrie to appear in some CIA file. Not yet, anyway.

"I had to try, anyway. You got my name because you wanted an analyst who understood online conspiracy theories," Meredith continued. "You wanted to know what kind of things your friend might believe. So you can bring her back to reality. I think you should appreciate how dangerous she might be."

"Should I be worried about something other than getting COVID from her?"

"Possibly. Did you browse her social media posts, like I asked?"

Navy had. And felt uncomfortable the whole time. She picked the facts she thought she could share without identifying Carrie. "The posts have almost stopped now. But before she stopped posting . . . her taste in music has changed. She's into a bunch of metal bands with Norse-sounding names. And she got this job at a gun range. Or had a job there? And some of her language, it sounds almost religious. I don't know. Like I said, she hasn't posted much recently."

Meredith's eyes narrowed and her eyebrows gathered in concentration. "Anything else?"

"She lost some close family members a couple years ago. Her posts changed after that. I can't explain it exactly." Like she's still grieving, Navy thought. "I mean, of course she's still grieving. But it's like she hasn't recovered."

"We should start with a history lesson."

Navy wondered if she should have brought a notebook.

"Conspiracy theories have always been a joke for most people. UFOs! Little green men! 5G viruses! Look at how crazy people can be! But they're more dangerous than people appreciate." Meredith pressed her hands into her lap. "Here's the thing. We make fun of people who believe in conspiracy theories, but we don't pay attention to the emotional weight behind them. We don't appreciate how they soften people up to believe in more and more ridiculous things. Especially if that person is vulnerable."

"I—uh—"

"Right, I should slow down."

"Yes, please."

"Grifters use conspiracy theories that reflect the social anxieties of the time. Why did Alex Jones scream about chemicals in the water turning frogs gay? Because changing gender roles make people nervous. He was capitalizing on people's fears to sell water filtration units and nutritional supplements."

Navy tried to follow Meredith's logic. "You mean that we should be paying attention to what the conspiracy theories say because they tell us what anxieties are motivating the believers?"

"Exactly! Take UFO conspiracy theories. The fifties. Height of the Cold War. What are the ufologists saying? Extraterrestrials have come to warn us about the threat of nuclear weapons. Or maybe to help the communists infiltrate the United States using mind control. Reflecting both sides. The sixties. An interracial couple comes out with their alien abduction story featuring an alien who looks like Hitler, but also aliens of different races mixing. What's also happening? The Supreme Court is about to rule on the Loving case. But on the other side you have these ufologists in the 1970s and onward developing racial taxonomies for the aliens they've seen. What's the most 'evolved' race of aliens? The most Aryan looking ones. Clearly some racial anxieties getting mixed in there."

Navy was trying to put together the jumble of historical events as Meredith talked. Clearly, Meredith was passionate about her work. And a little hard to follow.

"But what do UFO conspiracy theories have to do with my friend? And the COVID stuff?"

"I don't mean she's into UFO conspiracy theories. I just mean . . . my friends tell me I get too stuck in the details. I'm just trying to explain—" Meredith stopped herself. "You said she had some posts about 5G cell towers causing COVID."

"Yeah, she did."

"Read between the lines. She's saying she believes that there's a mass government coverup hiding widespread evidence of how harmful 5G is. She's saying she doesn't trust the government. She doesn't trust any establishment authorities like the valid science showing COVID is a respiratory disease."

Navy frowned. "I mean, does anyone really trust the government?"

"You're confusing skepticism and distrust. You and I, we know the government can lie. We know government conspiracies are possible. But we don't automatically disbelieve everything any establishment figure says, right?"

"Sure. I just—"

"To understand her, you have to follow the emotional truth. If the government can't be trusted, if the scientific establishment can't be trusted, then who is she listening to? What community is she trusting? What kind of leaders are in those communities? Who's profiting off these communities? Whose power base is growing?"

Suddenly Carrie's wild suspicions seemed more dangerous. "You're saying I can't consider the COVID conspiracy stuff in isolation."

"Exactly! These communities overlap. They feed on each other. Compete with each other. You have natural health and wellness leaders spreading COVID misinformation and anti-vaccine content rubbing elbows with anti-government elements pushing the idea that COVID is just an excuse for expanded government control. The toxic conspiracy pool seems to be more right-wing than left-wing these days, but it's never completely one or the other."

"That's why you were worried about being overheard. You don't want someone in the office to accuse you of being biased against conservatives in your analysis."

"January 6 was . . ." Meredith let her sentence trail off into the sounds of the birds around them. "We didn't know the scale of the threat because a lot of the FBI's resources to track domestic extremism were cut."

Navy remembered watching the news that day. Her apartment was a twenty-minute drive from where the Capitol Police were being attacked. "If the rioters had succeeded—"

"Not rioters," Meredith said. "Insurrectionists. They were trying to prevent the certification of the election."

"There's been lots of talk around the office about how many paramilitary groups were there," Navy said. "The Proud Boys, Oath Keepers, 1AP. Even some news about the groups 'herding normies' at the protest to get cover for moving around in the crowd."

Meredith snorted. "As if anyone there was normal."

"But that's the problem, isn't it?" Navy would have said Carrie was normal until a few days ago. "Half the people there were normal. The kind of people you meet every day." The newspaper profiles were terrifying in their blandness. A teacher. A veteran. A salon owner. A real estate agent. "They were caught up in a movement."

"Yeah, you're right." Meredith sighed. "This is why I get myself in trouble. But you wanted advice for dealing with your friend."

"I want to—" What did Navy want? To protect Sara. And if Sara was determined to help Carrie, that meant helping Carrie. "Can you get me inside my friend's head? How do you get from normal—whatever that means—to believing that 5G cell towers cause COVID and that vaccines contain microchips and then to preparing for a righteous war against the New World Order?"

Meredith frowned and tapped her fingers against the binoculars. "You said righteous war. And New World Order."

"Yeah?"

"Another history lesson then."

Oh great, Navy thought.

"Nineteen forty-five. End of World War II. J.B. Stoner starts his white supremacist Stoner Christian Anti-Jewish Party. The agenda's right in the name. But Stoner and his followers are getting kicked out of KKK meetings."

"But I thought the KKK was anti-Semitic?" Navy couldn't help being curious.

"They are now," Meredith said. "But 1945, remember? The Allies had just fought the Nazis. The KKK doesn't want to be associated with anti-Semitism and Nazis. It would be *un-American*." Her words rushed on. "So Stoner and his allies try a new tactic. They join groups like the KKK, but they don't talk about being anti-Jewish. Now we're in the 1950s."

At this pace, Navy wouldn't get home until dinner.

"Wesley Albert Swift moves to southern California and starts preaching his white supremacist sermons. He becomes so popular his taped sermons are sent by mail all over the United States—"

"Wait, southern California? Land of hippies?" Navy asked.

"You thought racism was only south of the Mason-Dixon line?" Meredith countered.

"Of course not, just . . ." Just not that out in the open, Navy finished the thought.

"Swift was born in New Jersey. Even Canada has its own fascist and nationalist groups. Anyway." Meredith refilled her lungs for her next torrent of words. "Fifties, sixties, Swift's sermons are going out all over the United States. Some people are hosting Swift parties to share the word. Assholes like Burris Dunn are forcing their wife and children to kneel while listening to them."

Navy knew the history of the United States included violent, racist movements. But she didn't know how recent the history was.

"Meanwhile, the government is getting scared. The FBI is actively using COINTELPRO to infiltrate and discredit these organizations."

Another fact that set Navy's head spinning. "I thought COINTELPRO was used to disrupt civil rights organizations."

"Oh, it was. But it was also used against these right-wing groups. And pretty soon, everyone's paranoid. We get to the mid-to-late 1960s. The big white supremacist groups are splintering. The Voting Rights Act has been around for a few years. Some racists saw the writing on the wall. They lost the war for hearts and minds."

"You mean the less committed racists just gave up," Navy said.

"Right, so who's left in the movement?"

Meredith waited for Navy to answer.

Navy tried to sort through all the groups and names Meredith had thrown at her for the past ten minutes. She tried to imagine them not just as hateful, but as pieces in a game where there were rules and motivations and a goal. "The hardcore supporters and the infiltrators."

"Bingo!" Meredith threw up her hands, nearly dropping her binoculars on the ground. "Swift, Stoner, and all of their friends spent years infiltrating these orgs and pushing them just a little bit further along. They always agreed about the hating non-white people thing, but now they can talk about anti-Semitism openly. Now they can talk about Jews running the world. They can revive the anti-Semitic conspiracy theories that fell out of favor."

By Navy's count, they had fifty more years of history to get through. Why was Meredith taking so long to get to the point?

"Nineteen eighty-two. Louis Beam, a former KKK Grand Dragon, visits the Covenant on a remote farm in Texas. He has a Commodore 64 in his car. And an idea."

"The Commodore 64 was one of the first personal computers," Navy said. "They're museum pieces now. But who are the Covenant?"

"A white supremacist group. They call themselves Covenant, the Sword and the Arm of the Lord."

More religious influences. Navy had an unsettling feeling. "This isn't just a history lesson. You're being evasive."

Meredith pressed her lips together. "I'm trying to prepare you. So you understand the context."

"Fine. Whatever." Navy knew she should be grateful. But this tour of the worst moments in US history was exhausting.

"So Beam's idea is this," Meredith continued. "Organizing in large groups is dangerous. The government will get eyes on us. So let's use this Internet thing. I mean, it wasn't called the Internet then."

"You're talking about dial-up Bulletin Board Systems," Navy said.

"White supremacists were one of the first groups to see how useful online misinformation and hate speech could be. Beam proposed building up a network of small cells of believers all over the US. Decentralized domestic terror cells. Harder to track."

"So people could host their racist bullshit on their own personal computer at home," Navy said. "And other people in the movement could log in to their friends' bulletin boards and download the content and maybe post it on their own bulletin boards."

"And later they evolve, right? BBSes aren't a thing anymore. Now it's Gab, 4chan, 8kun, Parler, YouTube videos, X or Twitter posts, groups on Telegram or Facebook. Wherever these movements can get around platform moderation rules to spread their ideas, they will. This shit has been around on the Internet since day zero. Just waiting for whoever is vulnerable to it."

Navy felt her stomach drop. "What do you mean, whoever is vulnerable to it?"

"You asked how a person could get from normal to believing in any of this. We call it a cognitive opening. There's a personal crisis of some sort. Or maybe a few bad years. And hopefully, the person suffering finds a good community of people who help them through. But sometimes . . . sometimes instead, they find a group who takes advantage of them. These hate groups, they offer people community and purpose."

"I don't understand."

"One more story?" Meredith asked. "Last one. I promise."

"Sure." Navy wished Meredith would get to the point. She was still being evasive.

"Say you're a struggling farmer in the 1940s and a member of the Stoner Anti-Jewish Christian Party wants to recruit you. The recruiter doesn't start out talking about Satanic Jews. They talk about how hard it is to be a farmer. How the banks don't treat you right. How the government screws you over. They earn your trust. Build an emotional connection. Then, when the recruiter thinks you're ready to be radicalized they say they're going to let you in on a secret. There's a reason why you're miserable and everything seems stacked against you. And, oh by the way, guess who runs the banks and the government."

"You're talking a lot about anti-Semitism. Why?"

Meredith looked away. "I—that phrase you used. New World Order. It's often associated with anti-Semitic conspiracy theories. And you said she was into heavy metal now. We keep an eye on the heavy metal genre because there's a persistent subculture of white supremacy. Not everyone. But enough. Particularly bands with 'Norse-sounding names.' Some of those bands overlap with the extremists in the Odinism community."

"Odinism . . ." Navy remembered the prison guard Kevin had framed last year. *Innocent? Hardly. He's part of a racist offshoot of Odinism.* "You're saying my friend is involved with these assholes."

"Maybe, maybe not. I'm saying it's a possibility. The religious language, the idea of a righteous war, the genetic superiority of white people, it's right out of Swift's sermons. These groups don't just commit violent acts. They use violence to provoke conflict. They have a goal. Researchers call it provocative violence."

Navy was afraid to ask. "What goal?"

"They have this idea of the end times, not a rapture as Christianity typically understands it. They think the end times will be a holy race war, where righteous men will be called to be soldiers in the Army of God."

"Jesus," Navy said. Then realized the irony. "I mean—that's fucked up."

"So your friend. Maybe she went through a hard time and this community found her and she doesn't know what the movement leaders really stand for."

"What if she does?" Navy realized she had asked the question out loud.

"Don't be too loyal."

"Too loyal?" An odd description to jump to. That's how Kevin had described her last year. As if the two of them had read the same file on her. "That must be in a psychological profile the company has on me."

Meredith smiled. "They have several. Are you really surprised?"

"I guess not." Navy shouldn't be. "And what's wrong with being loyal to a friend?"

"Look, if you can reach her, great. But these movements—" Meredith closed her eyes and took a deep breath. "I'm a peace, love, and understanding sort. I'm a Christian and at my church we preach respect and tolerance. But we can't tolerate everything. *These movements kill people.*"

Navy shook her head. She knew what Meredith meant and she didn't want to think about it. Would Navy be willing to turn Carrie in? Could Navy hurt Carrie if she had to?

"The Oklahoma City bombing, the Tree of Life shooting, all the other attacks that have happened in the name of hate. We call them lone wolf attacks, but that's bullshit. This is the plan Beam and his contemporaries had all along. Stochastic violence. Create the environment for these ideas to thrive. Inspire people to fight violence with violence."

"I can't imagine she would ever . . ." Navy shook her head again. "She's my friend. We grew up together."

"You were also described as introverted and principled. That's what I'm betting on."

In her own work, Navy had read several psychological profiles. They were clinical yet intimate at the same time. Each element of a person's psyche laid out for examination, like the viscera of a dissected animal. Meredith's casual treatment of Navy's own dissection was unsettling. "Is that supposed to be a compliment?" Navy asked.

"You are motivated by your own internal compass, and you try very hard to do the right thing." Meredith shifted in her chair. "I've made you angry. Of course. Introverts don't like feeling exposed."

Navy got up to leave. "Does anyone?"

"No one warned you, I suppose. You didn't come into your job the normal way." A storm of chattering and churring erupted from the treetops. Meredith closed her eyes to listen. A large reddish bird flew over their heads. "The mating pair just drove off a hawk."

Navy wasn't interested in any more bird facts. Or any more facts from Meredith, really. "Thank you for your time."

"Wait—" Meredith held up a hand. "I was going to say, no one warned you about the sacrifice you make when you join the company. The CIA will keep lots of secrets from you, but you don't get to keep any secrets from them."

Jackson hadn't warned her. But when Navy had been offered the job, the company had already built a file on her and everyone she knew.

"I think that's why I like blackbirds so much." Meredith raised her binoculars again.

Navy tried to imagine what Meredith was seeing. A nest shifting in and out of view as the wind stirred the leaves. Navy could hear the parents calling out defiantly in case the hawk considered returning.

"Blackbirds mean so many things to so many different cultures," Meredith said. "Contradictory things. Death. Rebirth. Lust. A shape-shifter. A protector."

What did this weird woman want from her?

"Of course what I said about you being principled is a compliment. The agency might know everything about you, but only you know who you are."

Thanks for the fortune cookie, Navy thought.

"A bit of advice, if you don't mind." Meredith continued looking through her binoculars. "Having a conscience makes working in this business hard, but not having one will make it harder to sleep after you leave. Take it from someone who's close to retirement."

Meredith sounded very much like the grandmother Navy's coworker had promised. Navy wavered between resentment and curiosity. No one had offered her a survival strategy before. No one else at work had referred to her ethics as anything but a roadblock.

"I know you'll do the right thing." But Meredith's tone didn't sound like praise.

Her tone reminded Navy of the woman who could look a poisonous snake in the eye and charm it into attacking her enemies. What Meredith meant was *I expect you'll do the right thing. And I'll be watching.*

"Oh, and Navy?"

"Yes?"

"You have my number. Call me if you need to."

Navy escaped to the wooded trail. Involving Meredith in Carrie's rescue operation would be a double-edged sword. Any opportunity to help was also an opportunity to control. Would Meredith be keeping tabs on Navy too now? Would Meredith find the social media accounts Navy had created just to see Carrie's timeline? Could Meredith find Carrie through Navy? Had Navy already done the wrong thing?

Chapter 3

Jackson watched the endless fields stretch outside the passenger car window. Corn and soybeans as far as the eye could see. Navy drove with both hands on the wheel, even though the road was clear and there were no other vehicles. She had been quiet since they crossed the Iowa state line an hour ago. He wondered what was stressing her out more, stepping into an old world or the prospect of confronting her friend, Carrie. He wondered if it was worth asking her, or if she'd rather be alone with her thoughts.

"I'm fine," Navy said.

Alone with her thoughts then. "I didn't say anything." Jackson had known from the beginning that being with Navy would never be simple. Even now, after everything they'd been through, he knew that she was careful to keep some emotional distance between them. He'd be lying if he said it didn't hurt.

"You have that expression."

Jackson pretended innocence. "What expression?"

"Like when you want to ask me what's wrong but you're afraid how I'll react."

He smiled slightly and shook his head. "But I knew better than to say anything."

"It's just this drive. The last time I drove these roads . . ."

Jackson thought back. "It was the summer after we got back from Amsterdam." When the people who had sabotaged the CIA operation and gotten Navy kidnapped were threatening her to force her to reveal the government's secrets.

"One trip to see the cherry blossoms."

When Navy had met Jackson, Erin, and Byron briefly in a hotel room to hand them thumb drives full of secrets. "And a second trip," Jackson said. "When you met the president."

"And you and I danced."

Jackson rubbed her leg and felt his hand warm in the patch of sun on her lap. "That's probably the most normal date we've ever had. You know, before you ran off with the government assassin on your trail."

Navy laughed. "What about that romantic stroll we had in Romania among the flowers?"

"You mean when I was pushing you in that wheelchair because you were recovering from being shot in the stomach?"

"You're right. Our most romantic date was obviously when I rescued you on that rainy, cold night on a fishing boat just a few miles off the coast of North Korea."

Jackson smiled. "You and a unit of army soldiers."

Ten more miles passed before Navy spoke again. "I'll make you a deal."

"Okay."

"You're not even going to ask what the deal is?"

Jackson leaned back and closed his eyes. "Nope, I trust you."

"God, you're infuriating."

"What kind of deal are we making?"

Navy glanced at him and then back at the road. "I'll tell you what I'm worried about, if you answer one question honestly."

"Navy, I've always been honest with you about the important things."

"You've been different since you got back from that North Korea op."

"Not that different. A few more nightmares, I guess. Not that surprising, since I was captured."

"You were tortured."

Thanks for reminding me. Jackson pushed the memories away. "What's your question?"

"Have you been keeping the appointments Kevin set up for you? With the psychologist?"

"I—" Jackson sighed. "I canceled a few. But I've kept most of them."

"Reschedule them. You need them." Navy's tone left no room for argument.

"You're right." A large truck piled high with hay passed in the opposite lane. Jackson watched a blade of hay swirl in the turbulent wind and then skip across the windshield. "I've been making excuses. Your turn. What are you really worried about?"

"I don't know what to say to her."

"To Carrie, you mean."

"Yeah, Carrie. I don't know what she wants with me. Or how I'm supposed to be nice to someone who might be giving COVID to everyone she meets."

"You need to gain her trust before you challenge her."

"So if she says some batshit crazy thing about microchips in vaccines . . ."

"Try to redirect the conversation. Remind her of your friendship."

"And if she starts listening to me?"

"Challenge her gently, and don't make it an academic debate. Don't quote sources. Just state truths."

"That's all the advice you have?"

Jackson laughed. "Normally you hate getting my advice. Especially on anything psychological."

"Consider this the exception."

"Helping cult members recover isn't my specialty."

"Cult." The word seemed to shock Navy. "You think she's joined a cult?"

"No, but—" Jackson chose his words carefully. "I know Carrie is your friend and this whole rescue mission is important to Sara."

Navy frowned. "But?"

"Talking to someone who's caught up in any sort of obsessive behavior that distorts reality . . . it's hard to break through. You can nudge someone in the right direction, but you can't save them unless they want to be saved."

Navy's expression turned stony. "You don't think this trip is worth it."

"I didn't say that." Jackson tapped his fingers along the window edge and watched another mile marker pass. "Just don't blame yourself if you and Sara can't reach her."

Navy reached over and squeezed his hand. "I'm glad you're here." When Navy acknowledged his emotional support at all, it was usually with a grimace.

Jackson tried to appreciate the moment of emotional intimacy. He could count on one hand the times she had said 'I love you.' But he knew the odds in this situation were against Navy. And despite his warnings, he knew Navy would blame herself.

Chapter 4

Navy's phone vibrated on the picnic table. A message from Sara.

Accident blocked a lane. Stuck in traffic.

Truthfully, Navy was glad Sara would be late. The longer Navy sat at the rest stop, the longer she could delay meeting Carrie at the campsite.

Navy watched another van arrive. Road trips had come back into style since the coronavirus had made sharing indoor air dangerous. A family emptied out of the van, all wearing matching cloth masks. A man hurried two young kids into the bathrooms. A woman ambled around, yawning as she stretched her legs. A third child, older, walked away while texting and then leaned against a nearby tree. In a few minutes they would all pile back into the van, some in a hurry, some reluctant to get back on the road. A play in three acts that Navy would see repeated when the next car arrived.

Jackson's warnings about Carrie's resistance to help were bringing back images Navy hoped she had forgotten. Nearly two years ago, a crime boss had brought Navy into a room while he was filming child sexual abuse. And she had walked away from both of the victims. Because she couldn't fight that many people and carry away two children who had been groomed so well they didn't want to leave.

The most dangerous thing you can do is rescue someone who doesn't want to be rescued. Kevin's words. Not so different from what Jackson had said.

Practical advice, of course. But it was harder to convince her nagging conscience she had done the right thing. Navy was afraid Carrie would just become another failed task, another name to add to the list of people Navy had hurt by not being strong enough or smart enough or brave enough when it counted. And how would Sara handle it if Carrie couldn't be helped? Navy saw the toll Jackson's failures, real or imagined, took on him. Navy knew what her own failures had cost her.

Sara had less practice than either of them.

"Navy!" Sara dashed from her car. "It's so good to see you!"

Navy stood up to greet her but held her hands up when Sara came in for a hug. "Six feet," Navy reminded Sara.

"You're right." Sara sat on the bench. "These are hard times for huggers."

Navy wasn't much of a hugger herself, but the physical distance hurt her too. She realized it had been months since she had touched anyone but Jackson, even in passing. "Do you remember how we came back from the kidnapping? And for months afterward we could both barely handle standing in a crowded line at the grocery store?"

"You miss crowds, don't you?" Sara said.

"I miss a lot of things." Navy said. "I miss travel. Getting lost in a crowded city . . ."

"Finding the best lunch you've ever eaten . . ." Sara continued.

"And then finding some random gelato place with crazy weird flavors like ginger chocolate matcha that shouldn't work but do." One of many trips Navy had taken with Sara before *that one trip* had upended her life, leading her to moving to DC and sharing an apartment with Jackson. Jackson was the only good thing to come out of the entire experience.

"We should talk strategy." Sara plopped a thick hardcover book on the table. "I read this whole book on how to help loved ones caught up in conspiracy theories."

Navy should have expected Sara to come with a manual. On all of their trips, her backpack was the one weighed down with well-thumbed guidebooks. "Better make sure that Carrie doesn't see that, or you'll lose her right away," Navy said.

"I'll hide it in the trunk. We should arrive separately. Like we didn't meet here."

Navy couldn't help but smile. "You've been plotting."

"This is kind of like what you do, right?" Sara leaned forward. "You'll have to tell me whether I'm secret agent material after this weekend is over."

"My job is mostly office work." Navy couldn't tell Sara anything about Hackerville, or North Korea or . . . well anything about her job. Even the office work parts.

"Anyway, so I've been reading. And the books say first we need to build rapport. Remind Carrie of our friendship."

Navy nodded. "Jackson said we should establish trust before we challenge her on anything."

"I just wish I knew how long that would take." Sara glanced at the open pages of her books. "The books weren't that encouraging."

"We can't fix everything in one weekend, Sara." *We might not be able to fix anything at all.*

Sara drew herself up. "We can start. If you and I get the process started, I can keep checking on her after you leave and . . ."

Should Navy give Sara the same warning Jackson gave her? Navy didn't want to take away Sara's hopes so soon. "We'll do our best."

Sara's eyes shifted focus to something behind Navy. A small child climbing a ladder at the playground.

"What Carrie said about your miscarriage was mean," Navy said.

"There must be some explanation. She's our friend. She wouldn't hurt me like that on purpose."

"Still. If she keeps saying stuff like that, if it gets too hard for you to talk to her. Walk away."

"That's chapter twelve."

Navy shook her head. "Chapter twelve?"

Sara flipped to a page in one of her books and pushed the book in front of Navy. "In this goddamn book. Chapter twelve." Sara had marked one of the passages. *Your loved one may repeatedly lash out at you when they are confronted with information that upsets them. It is up to you whether or not you continue trying to reach them.*

Navy realized that Sara didn't need to hear any of her warnings. Sara was more prepared than she was. Crickets sang from the tall grass at the edge of the cleared picnic area. Warm, humid air ruffled the pages between them. The pages spelling out exactly how difficult their task would be.

"I'm sorry," Navy said. "I'm sorry that you have to deal with this."

"Carrie's your friend too."

"You've always been closer to her than I have. I didn't even know her mother and sister had died." Navy spun her phone on the table, afraid to ask her next question. "Do you know why she asked for me?"

"You were there on the first trip, dummy."

"Moss was there too," Navy pointed out. "And that other woman? What was her name?"

"J-something, Jessica? Jennie? I haven't seen her since."

"Carrie didn't ask for either of them to come," Navy said. "So why me?"

"I don't know. Is it important?"

Navy wondered how much she could say. She didn't like keeping secrets from people close to her. "Ever since my name was in the papers so much, occasionally I run into someone who thinks they know me." Min Gyu had assumed she would sympathize with him, exonerate him. *You and I, we aren't so different.* "They assume I'll justify their actions because they have this version of me in their heads."

Sara looked concerned. "This doesn't sound like it's about Carrie."

"Yeah, you're probably right." Navy untwisted her hands. "We should go."

Sara didn't move. "Five more minutes. If that's okay." Sara's nerves were obvious in the hunch of her back and the slope of her shoulders.

"We can stay as long as you want," Navy said. "I shouldn't have rushed you."

"May you live in interesting times," Sara said softly. "You ever think about that quote?"

Navy kept silent to give Sara space to finish her thought.

"It's not actually a Chinese curse, like some people say. I researched it. The first English reference to it is an American politician quoting a British one. In 1939."

Navy thought about all the nights or weekends she would have been out doing something else and instead had isolated herself at home. "I've also spent too much time looking up useless things on the Internet since COVID started."

"I just . . ." Sara gestured at the parking lot where groups of people passed each other, some masked, some not. "It's dumb, never mind."

"I'm sure it's not," Navy said.

"I have this odd feeling when I listen to the news or when I'm out walking around the neighborhood."

"Like you're anxious," Navy said. "Because you feel disconnected from everyone. I've felt it too."

"And I don't know how to reconcile it. Like the guy at the grocery store who was always so friendly but ended up in a shouting match with the cashier over masking. Sometimes I talk to my friends and it's like we're in different realities. About vaccinations. About masks. About . . . everything."

"You mean more than just Carrie?" Navy asked.

Sara nodded. "Carrie's probably the worst off but she's not the only one. I have other friends posting conspiracy theories from news sites I've never heard of."

Navy knew what she had heard her coworkers talk about. But with Sara, she could only reference what was publicly known. "Misinformation and disinformation."

"What's the difference?" Sara asked. "It's all bullshit."

"Intent," Navy said. "Nation-state actors have learned to use social networks as a weapon to spread disinformation. They create a few news sites. Then a few hundred social media accounts you control link to the articles you post. Rinse and repeat until you get lucky and something goes viral."

"Just to divide us," Sara said.

"It's scary." At work, Navy saw the intel reports that named the actors targeting US citizens. China. Russia. Iran. Before COVID, before a mob had tried to take the Capitol, she had never thought much about the threads binding citizens in a democracy. Now she felt that social fabric tearing in a thousand small ways.

"It's like we don't know how to take care of each other anymore," Sara said.

"I don't we've learned anything," Navy said. "Feels like five years now we'll still be arguing about vaccinations and politicians will still be boosting conspiracy theories for votes."

"God, I hope not." Sara closed the book and gripped it tightly. "Well, we're certainly going to lose Carrie if we never show up."

"See you at the campsite," Navy said.

"I'll be about ten minutes behind you." Sara put on her sunglasses and pulled her cap low over her forehead. She looked dramatically around the now empty playground and parking lot. "And remember, we were never here."

Navy rolled her eyes. "You are having *way* too much fun with this secret agent stuff."

Chapter 5

When Navy pulled into the group campsite, a small camper van was already parked in one of the spaces. The front passenger tire looked a bit low. A kayak was strapped to the top of the van. Slanting afternoon sun made long shadows of the equipment set out on the picnic table, a couple of pots and a two-burner cookstove connected to a fuel canister. Navy's stomach grumbled and reminded her it was nearly dinner time.

The door on the camper opened just enough for a familiar face to appear. "You're here," Carrie said. A mostly familiar face. Carrie had the same light green eyes, the same narrow face and freckled cheeks, but something was different. Last time Navy had seen Carrie, she'd been enjoying a margarita, laughing as she told the latest story about her EMT training. This version of Carrie looked . . . tired. Haunted.

Navy wasn't sure exactly what sort of reunion she'd been expecting, but the lack of enthusiasm in Carrie's voice surprised her. Carrie had specifically asked for Navy to be here. Better to start off on a good foot though. "It's good to see you," Navy said. "I'm excited to get out. I haven't been anywhere in a while."

Carrie's eyes narrowed. "You know, all that COVID stuff is . . . never mind."

And Navy had already said the wrong thing. She forced a smile. "Anyway, should be a fun weekend."

"Sure." Carrie tilted her toward the stove. "Feel free to use the burners if you need to. I brought plenty of fuel. I'll be out in a bit." The door shut and Navy heard a lock click. Carrie had locked the door? When they would be hanging around camp? Carrie hadn't even opened the door wide enough to wave or point to the stove on the picnic table.

Stop being paranoid, Navy told herself. She walked around the campsite to find good places for the tents. Sara's tent was bigger than hers, so Navy took the smaller flat area closer to the fire. But not so close sparks would reach her tent. On the other side of her tent, a small trail led to a spot of shimmering blue. The lake they would paddle across to reach their hiking spot tomorrow. Despite the circumstances, Navy found herself enjoying the familiar routine of laying out her sleeping mat, unpacking the sleeping bag, and hanging the LED lamp from the loop in the center of the tent.

Anything food related she would store in the car. She brought out what she needed for dinner and left her camp stove packed in the car. May as well take Carrie up on her offer.

The water had just reached boiling when Carrie finally came out of her camper.

"I boiled some extra water for you," Navy said. "If you need it."

"I ate already," Carrie said. "Thanks anyway."

Navy poured hot water into her bowl and added the ramen packet. The metal stove ticked as it cooled. *Think of something to say. Don't mention COVID. Don't mention her old job. Don't ask prying questions.* Carrie was silent, staring at the driveway where Sara would arrive any minute.

Navy wondered, again, why Carrie had been so insistent on Navy coming. Carrie didn't seem to have anything to say to her.

"That's a nice camper," Navy said. "I've been tempted to get one."

"I like mine," Carrie said. "Kind of wish I'd gotten something bigger though."

"Looks luxurious next to a tent." Maybe Navy could do this small-talk thing.

"Unless you're downsizing," Carrie snapped.

Or maybe not. Was Carrie living in the camper? "Sara told me you lost the house," Navy said. "I'm really sorry. That's rough."

"It's better this way." Carrie finally made eye contact with her. "I'm less traceable. And I have everything I need to survive, right here with me. You understand."

Three years ago, Navy would have agreed emphatically. She had been hunted by two competing factions in the government, both willing to kill her for what they wanted. Is that how Carrie felt? Hunted? Should Navy pull on this thread or let Carrie reveal more in her own time? "I do like being alone in the woods," Navy said. "Where do you like to camp?"

Carrie's back stiffened. "Here and there. Wherever I feel like it that weekend."

Great. Navy had said the wrong thing. Again. *Redirect.* "I've been enjoying the climbing around DC. It's surprising how many parks there are within a couple hours' drive."

Gravel crunched as Sara pulled in behind Navy's car. *Thank God,* Navy thought. Maybe Sara would be able to have a conversation with Carrie.

"I brought things for s'mores!" Sara announced as she got out of the car.

Sara was definitely doing better at pretending everything was fine on this trip. Navy needed to get in character. To think like she was undercover.

Carrie didn't show any more enthusiasm for Sara's arrival than for Navy's arrival. *Never mind.* Navy was undercover. Navy was a happy, unconcerned camper who had come to spend the weekend with friends. A happy, unconcerned camper with a long list of topics that she shouldn't mention.

"They had firewood for sale down by the ranger station," Navy said. "I could walk down and pick some up after I eat."

"We are having s'mores every night," Sara decreed. "And I want my hair to smell like a campfire by the time I head home."

Carrie stared at Sara with an expression hovering between concern and frustration.

What the hell was going on?

"I have some skewers we can use for marshmallow sticks," Carrie said finally. "In my kitchen."

Sara pretended as if the awkward moment had never happened. "That sounds great. First, I want to get my tent set up though. Before the bugs get worse."

"I put my bug spray on the table," Navy said. "Help yourself."

And, for a second, things almost felt normal.

Chapter 6

The campfire crackled and danced, throwing flickering shadows on the side of Carrie's van. Navy stirred the embers with a long stick and watched glowing sparks float up on the warm air rising from the flames. Sara had gone to her tent already. Navy was alone with Carrie, again. And still unsure what to say.

"That wax firestarter you had sure was handy," Navy said. "Do you make them yourself?"

"I learned from . . . someone at work," Carrie said.

More evasive answers to simple questions.

"I'm trying to make everything I can myself now," Carrie continued. "You never know what's in the stuff you buy at the store."

It was a theme Navy had heard from Carrie a lot over the past couple of hours. Can't trust the government. Can't trust big pharma. On their short hike earlier, Navy had purposefully tripped over a tree root to cut off Carrie's discussion on how you can't trust mainstream media. *Patience,* Navy reminded herself. If not for Carrie, then for Sara.

"I wish I could make more stuff at home," Navy said. "I've always lived mostly on takeout and leftovers and recently I've been thinking I should really learn to cook."

Carrie checked her watch again. She'd been checking the time every few minutes since Sara went to bed.

"Ready to turn in? Should we let the fire burn down?" Navy asked.

Carrie shook her head emphatically. "No, I'll get another log."

Navy gave up trying to figure out what Carrie wanted or needed. Navy was sitting next to a good campfire on a warm summer night. Fireflies blinked around the edges of the campground. Might as well enjoy her time outdoors. If Carrie wanted to talk, she would talk.

The new log Carrie had added blackened as smoke and then flames found it. Sap forced out of the log dripped and sizzled. The bottom log on the fire collapsed and shifted before Carrie spoke again. "I think Sara must be asleep by now. I didn't want to talk in front of her."

So that's why Carrie had been checking her watch every two minutes.

"She practically begged me to go on this trip and then made me agree to all these rules." Carrie gestured to their tents, the campsite. "I mean, you and I know this is all bullshit."

Navy wondered what exactly Carrie was complaining about, Sara's general concern for Carrie or the COVID-19 precautions. "I think Sara was just missing her friends," Navy said finally. "It's been hard for everyone to be so isolated."

"That's the bullshit part." The fire's shifting shadows settled into Carrie's curled lip and angled eyebrows like a Halloween mask. "That's the conspiracy. Some flu vaccines are made from dog cell lines, and dogs get coronaviruses. That's how the Italy outbreak started."

"Carrie, that's—" Navy had to say something to get Carrie to stop talking. "That doesn't make any sense. Lots of flu vaccines are made in chicken eggs, and chickens get coronaviruses too. If that caused the virus, COVID-19 would have appeared way before now."

"That's different because the Wuhan lab wasn't involved." Carrie gestured wildly with her hands. "You see, we paid them millions of dollars. And the government wants us to be sick because big pharma wants us to have to get vaccinated. It's all in Bill Gates' plan. He's been working on it for years."

This is why Jackson told Navy to avoid having an academic debate. Navy could easily get lost in the tangle of theories and misinformation in Carrie's head. Navy tried to say her next words gently. "I don't think that's true."

Carrie shook her head and threw a stick into the fire. "Are you telling me conspiracies don't happen? You were the target of a government conspiracy."

Navy took a deep breath and tried to take comfort in the smell of the campfire, the familiar sounds of the nighttime forest around her. "I don't blindly trust the government just because I work for them," Navy said. "Conspiracies happen. I just don't think COVID-19 is one of them."

"I guess they were right then."

"Who was right?" Navy asked carefully.

"I told them you took a government job to be on the inside. Obviously. I mean, you had to know you couldn't trust the government after what happened. But maybe they were right. Maybe you won't actually help us."

Despite the warm night, Navy shivered. *Don't antagonize her.* "Is there something you need help with?"

Carrie seemed to calm down. For the first time, Navy had said something right. "Well, two things, I guess. I'm worried about Sara," Carrie said.

Sara's the one you're worried about? Was the snark showing on her face? Navy recomposed her expression. "Sara seems to be doing okay. I mean, as well as anyone right now."

"Did she tell you she's trying to get pregnant?"

"Yeah, I know it's been hard for her and Moss." Navy had no idea what had made Carrie's mind jump from COVID-19 conspiracy theories then to some mysterious aid Navy was supposed to provide and then to Sara's miscarriages.

"I was wondering what you know about where Moss comes from."

Now Navy was doubly confused. Carrie, Moss, and Navy had all gone to the same middle school and high school. "He grew up in Cedar Rapids, just like you and me."

"But before then," Carrie insisted. "Where was he born?"

"I don't remember, but he's lived in Iowa all of his life."

"He was adopted, right?"

This conversation was making Navy increasingly uncomfortable. "Yes. That's never been a secret."

"So he doesn't know his real parents."

"He doesn't know his biological parents." *Stop sounding combative,* Navy reminded herself. "I don't know if he's tried looking for them."

"And he has that curly hair."

"Sure." Navy wished Carrie would get to the point.

"Do you know if he dyes his hair that dark red color?"

What the hell was Carrie getting at? "I have no idea."

"It's just, he has that darker complexion and that curly hair. I can't tell if his hair is naturally darker or—"

Navy froze. "You're wondering if Moss is 100 percent white."

"Yes! Exactly." Carrie's eyes shone, reflecting the flames eagerly devouring the new log. "I knew you would understand."

A thousand things rushed into Navy's thoughts at once, but she said none of them. Navy remembered what Carrie had told Sara about her miscarriage. *Maybe it's better that way.* Carrie hadn't just been seduced by COVID-19 conspiracy theories.

"I don't think Sara will listen to me, but maybe she'll listen to you," Carrie said. "Tell her she and Moss should get one of those genetic tests that tells you where you come from."

Navy had been friends with Carrie for years. Surely, the Carrie Navy had grown up with didn't care about whether Moss had non-Caucasian blood in him. Just how far had Carrie sunk into her racist ideas? Could Navy stomach trying to find out? "Those tests aren't always accurate, you know," Navy said. "Determining heritage from DNA isn't as straightforward as they advertise."

"But it's a start. And sometimes our DNA isn't 100 percent pure because of something that happened a long time ago. Like maybe you're mostly Caucasian except your great-great-grandmother was attacked or something."

Navy jabbed her stick into the fire; sparks flew up in a column. So much hatred and ugliness wrapped up in just a few sentences. "If historical rapes are what you're concerned about, maybe you should also worry about the generations of enslaved women who were raped by their owners."

Carrie glanced up, surprised. "Obviously, we don't choose our parents. And I'm not racist. I'm just saying, it's better not to mix DNA. And if you know your DNA is mixed, better not to pass that on."

"That's bullshit." Navy dropped the stick she'd been using to stir the fire, afraid of what she'd do with it. "Sara and Moss will make great parents. Wherever Moss *comes from*."

Slowly, Carrie stood. "You're not going to help us." Carrie had referred to 'us' again. "They were right. I can't rely on Sara. I can't protect her if she doesn't want to do the right thing."

Navy couldn't remember a time in her life when she'd felt angrier or more betrayed. "I don't know what I ever said that makes you think I would sympathize with you." She was talking too loudly now, nearly yelling. "No, I won't help you or 'us' or whatever you've gotten yourself mixed up in."

Carrie was yelling too. "You're going to be sorry. There's a war coming, and you'll be on the wrong side of it. You will not replace us!"

The slogan white supremacists had chanted at the march in Charlottesville.

Carrie was slowly advancing and still yelling, but Navy tuned out most of her words. *Think tactically*, Navy told herself.

Most of the adversaries Navy had faced had known the intimate details of her life and been well-practiced in violence. Carrie had neither of those advantages. Still, Carrie knew a lot about Sara and Moss. The same Carrie who had worked at a gun range, talked about her camper van as a survival vehicle, had been secretive about what she stored inside, and kept talking about some mysterious 'us.'

Navy knew she could easily win hand-to-hand against Carrie. And, as tempting as a skirmish might be, Navy knew it was a bad idea. Physically humiliating Carrie might inspire retaliation with the weapons she could be hiding in her van or from her friends, whoever they were. Sara would be a target long after Navy went back home. Navy stayed where she was, seated in her camp chair.

Carrie stopped right next to her, breathing hard and fast as if they'd already been fighting. Her shoulders were locked into a tight square with her hands squeezed into fists at her sides. An aggressive stance, but an amateur one. Holding that much tension in her shoulders would slow down Carrie's attacks. Navy wondered if the 'us' Carrie referred to had trained her to fight as well as shoot.

Carrie was so angry she was shaking. No, not just angry, Navy saw. Behind all of Carrie's rage and bluster was a deep-seated, misguided fear about her place in the world.

But Navy's sympathy for Carrie didn't change the fact that Carrie was dangerous.

De-escalate, Navy thought. *Disarm her by removing yourself as a target.* Navy kept her breaths calm and even, while Carrie continued to breathe rapidly. Navy let the silence stretch between them, knowing

Carrie's anger would sour into confusion and anxiety. So long as Navy remained calm.

Navy held Carrie's gaze until Carrie's posture began to break down. Then Navy deliberately, slowly, crossed her legs and looked at the fire. "I won't fight you," Navy said. *Yet.*

Carrie's mouth opened as if she was about to speak, but Navy continued.

"You agreed to come on this trip because you wanted to ask for my help. My answer is no. There's no reason for you to stay." Navy watched carefully for any sudden movements in her peripheral vision. Making eye contact with Carrie would only prolong this unfortunate night. "You should leave now. Before anything happens that might get you in trouble. And you should know that if anything happens to Sara or Moss, you will be the first and only suspect."

Carrie made a strangled yell of frustration and then stomped away to her van. The door slammed and then she drove too fast out of the gravel driveway, screeching onto the paved circle around the campsites. Navy stood up and watched the dark driveway, listening for the van's engine, making sure the sound was getting quieter and quieter.

Navy heard rustling noises coming from Sara's tent. She wasn't surprised the argument had woken Sara. Sara came out of her tent and wiggled her feet into her shoes that she had left in the grass outside the zipper door.

When Sara came closer to the fire, Navy could see that she was crying.

"I fucking hate her," Sara said. "I can't believe she thinks that my babies should have . . ." Sara began crying so hard she couldn't talk.

Navy decided the COVID-19 restrictions mattered less than her friend's pain. She hugged Sara while the fire warmed their legs, and the frogs and crickets sang around them. At the same time, Navy was calculating what was necessary to keep them safe tonight.

"We have to break camp tonight," Navy said. "Carrie might come back."

Sara nodded and then jumped back. "Carrie knows where we live. I have to warn Moss. Is it safe for us to be at home?"

"I might have a place for all of us to stay," Navy said. She wondered if Mark would want three new houseguests for the night. Or longer.

Chapter 7

Sara leaned on her car beside the pump at the 24-hour gas station. Navy's car was right in front of hers. Both back seats were full of hastily packed up camping gear. Inside the gas station, the cashier pushed Navy's change across the counter and glanced outside at Sara. Sara understood her suspicion. Two cars had pulled in into the gas station but not to get gas or to use the bathroom. Sara and Navy were both streaked with dirt from hiking and smelled of campfire smoke. Sara turned toward the blurred lights of the highway. If Sara stopped staring at the cashier, maybe the cashier would go back to her magazine.

The truth was, Sara had been staring at Navy. Navy had named the truck stop so quickly after they'd decided to leave. *Had Navy picked the truck stop from memory?* As if Navy had been planning for the possibility of needing to get away quickly. Or maybe Navy always planned that way now. Carrie had changed into a stranger without Sara noticing. Maybe Navy had too.

Navy seemed different. Sara remembered how Navy's tone switched so quickly from curiosity to yelling to an icy, calm contempt. *You should leave now.* And Carrie had. Because Navy's calm was more threatening than Carrie's bluster.

Navy emerged from the gas station with food in one hand and her phone in the other.

"I got you peanut butter M&M's," Navy said. "Jackson texted me they'd be here soon."

Sara checked her phone. "It's just past midnight. Does this count as candy for breakfast?"

"Why do you think I got donuts?" Navy opened her package of chocolate-coated mini donuts and popped one in her mouth.

"I haven't been able to reach Moss yet." Sara kicked at the tire with her heel. "He started silencing his phone at night because he was getting all these stupid prank calls. He's probably just asleep, right? Do you think Carrie would actually do anything?"

"I don't think so." Navy frowned. "I don't know. Predicting people isn't my specialty. There's a reason I work with computers."

"But you knew how to handle her. And you told her she would be the first and only suspect." Sara's tone was more demanding than she had intended. "I just mean . . . it seems like you did know something."

"I know you want better answers." Navy took a blue paper towel from the window washing dispenser and used it to wipe her hands. "And I wish I had them. I wanted to cover the possibility that she would try to hurt you or Moss. But I just don't know."

"I didn't know how far gone she was," Sara said. "The things she said . . ."

"We should check her social media stuff when we back to a computer," Navy said.

"You mean investigate her." Sara felt a mix of shock and resentment. Shocked that Navy would suggest it. Resentful that even after everything Carrie had said, her own first instinct was to defend Carrie.

"Carrie kept referring to other people. Like she's part of a group."

Sara pulled her coat tighter around her. "Like the KKK?"

"There are plenty." Here Navy hesitated. "I might know someone who can help."

"You don't look happy about it." But Sara didn't have the chance to pry any further, because a car pulled into the gas station with a familiar passenger.

Jackson got out of the passenger seat, and another man Sara didn't recognize was in the driver's seat. When Jackson approached them, Navy held up her hands.

"I broke quarantine," Navy said. "I hugged Sara."

Jackson shrugged and held his hand out to Sara. "It's good to see you. Welcome to our bubble."

Sara reluctantly reached out her hand and then wondered why she was so hesitant. She hadn't seen Jackson since the morning she and Navy had left Amsterdam. And Sara had thought Jackson was the enemy because Navy had to make it look like Jackson was the enemy. Despite all the conversations she and Navy had about Jackson since, seeing his face reminded Sara of that morning. "Sorry, I'm just recategorizing your face as a not-an-asshole face."

"Sara—" Navy said.

But Jackson laughed. "I understand."

The second man had parked the car and walked over to them but kept his distance. "Navy, it's been a while." He had a crooked nose and pockmarked face.

"I'm Mark." He held out his hand to Sara. "A friend of Jackson's."

In a brief moment of panic, Sara realized she had shaken hands with Jackson who had been in the car with Mark. By 'our bubble' Jackson had meant Mark too.

"Everyone's welcome to stay with me at my gym for a few days," Mark said.

Correction, Sara had shaken hands with Jackson who had been in the car with Mark, who ran a gym where countless strangers might have been. "How many people go through your gym?" Sara asked, trying to sound neutral.

"Sorry, I should have explained before," Jackson said. "Mark closed the gym to in-person classes months ago."

"Jackson was the first person that's been there in a while," Mark said.

"Do you know what you want to do?" Navy asked Sara.

"I don't know if it's safe at my house," Sara said. "But will it be any more or less safe two days from now? A week from now?"

"I . . . wish I could tell you," Navy said.

Mark cleared his throat. "Might be easier to make decisions after a good night's sleep."

Sara's phone rang and she jumped. *Goddamn nerves.* "It's Moss. Hang on a minute." Sara answered the call as she stepped away from the group. "I've been calling and texting and—" Sara's voice tumbled on the line as she paced.

"I just finished at the police station," Moss said. "I'm sorry, they said they needed my phone for some forensics thing."

"Police!" Sara heard her voice echoing against the concrete. "What happened? Why did they need your phone?"

"Are you close to home?" Moss asked.

"No, I'm with Navy. We're . . ." Sara realized exactly how much she had to explain. "You go first." Sara heard Moss take a deep breath on the other end of the line.

"Someone hung a noose from our tree in the front yard. I heard some honking out front and I looked out the window and saw a rope and this LED portable lamp thing to make sure I could see it." Moss' voice became shaky. "And then I looked at my phone and saw a text message with the picture of the noose in our front yard. You can see me in the window in the picture. The police think all those prank text messages and calls I've been getting might be related."

"Oh, sweetheart." Sara wished Moss were with her, so she could reassure herself that he was safe and whole.

"I don't want to go back to the house tonight," Moss said. "But, fuck them if they think they're going to scare us out of our home."

Sara understood. She volunteered at a domestic violence shelter. She had heard plenty of angry voices while answering the phones. Sara knew it was important not to tell the angry voice on the other end of line who was at the shelter that night. Some battles were worth fighting. Some weren't. "Maybe we could stay somewhere else just for a night or two. Give the police a chance to find something." *Give me a chance to tell you what happened with Carrie.*

"Where would we go anyway? Do you really want to go to a hotel with COVID?" Moss asked. Sara could hear in his voice he was just as tired as she was.

"Jackson has a friend who says we can stay with him a couple nights."

"Jackson? Navy's boyfriend? Why is Jackson with you and Navy? Did something happen to Carrie?"

"Not to Carrie," Sara said bitterly. "Because of Carrie. I'll text you soon with an address."

"How are you training now?" Sara heard Mark asking Navy as Sara turned back to the group. *Training?* Something kept her from taking a step toward them. Navy, smiling and comfortable, was leaning on Jackson. Mark, clearly good friends with both of them, completed the triangle. Sara felt like the odd one out.

"I bought one of those grappling dummies," Navy said. "It's ridiculous, but better than nothing, I guess."

Everything would look better in the morning, Sara told herself. After a bit of sleep, and seeing Moss safe, she could think about what came next. Navy was eating the last donut when Sara walked back to the group.

"I think we will take you up on that offer," Sara said. "Just give me an address and I'll text Moss so he can meet us there."

"Um," Mark hesitated.

"It's still okay if we stay with you, right?" Sara asked.

"You said something about the police having Moss' phone?" Navy asked.

"Yeah, there was . . ." Sara imagined a noose swinging from a tree, as Moss had described. Moss, in the window, photographed by the people who had left the threat. "I'll explain later. Something happened at the house and the police think it might be related to the prank calls he's been getting. He said something about forensics and monitoring his text messages."

"Might be better if Jackson and I meet him here and just lead him to the gym," Mark said.

"Do we need to turn our phones off while we're at your place?" Navy asked.

"Nope. I've got it set up so you can make calls but the location data is obscured," Mark said. "Got a little help from some friends."

"You're running a rogue cell tower." Navy grinned. "You've made some improvements since I was there."

"A *benevolent* rogue cell tower," Mark corrected.

Sara looked between all of them. "What kind of gym is this?"

"A very private gym," Navy said.

Chapter 8

Navy woke up to the smell of cinnamon rolls. She reached out to Jackson's sleeping bag and found it empty. As quietly as her sleeping bag allowed, she sat up. They had all camped out in different corners on the floor of Mark's gym. Sara and Moss were still in their corner, sleeping. Mark and Jackson were closer to the front door, where a table had been set up with food. She eased out of her sleeping bag and grabbed her toiletries. She needed to call someone today, though she didn't feel very much like talking to him.

"Morning," Jackson whispered to her as she made her way to the bathroom near the front door. She kissed him on the cheek and then made a brief bathroom stop to brush her teeth. Navy stared at her tired reflection in the scarred mirror. Bags under her eyes. Hair tangled and sweaty from hiking. As she brushed her hair into submission, she smelled the campfire from last night.

Is there something you need help with? Well, two things, I guess.

Before Navy had pissed Carrie off, Carrie had mentioned two favors. The first was to convince Sara not to pass on Moss' genes. And the second? Navy had no idea. But she knew someone who might.

When Navy came out of the bathroom, Jackson and Mark were sitting cross-legged on the floor eating. Jackson had already loaded a paper plate for her.

"Thanks," she whispered. "I'll be back in a few minutes."

Navy walked across the gym, past Sara and Moss sleeping in their corner, to a hallway that led to the back half of the building. As she had hoped, she found the gun range where Mark had trained her to fire a pistol. The soundproofing would keep her conversation quiet.

Seven in the morning in Des Moines would be eight in the morning in DC. A bit early, but Kevin had woken them up enough times so Navy figured he deserved it.

Kevin answered right away. "Navy." He didn't even sound tired.

"Not even a good morning?" Navy asked.

"Are we exchanging pleasantries again? I was under the impression you didn't like me very much right now."

"I don't," Navy said. "But I—" *Goddamnit.* She didn't like to ask anyone for help. Especially not Kevin. Not after what had happened on the North Korea op. "I need your help with something."

"Okay." Kevin replied without animosity or hesitation.

Navy had expected she would need to convince him. "I'm not asking for myself."

"Okay."

Navy leaned on the counter between her and the shooting targets. She didn't know where to start. Navy hadn't even given Jackson the full account of what had happened last night. Everyone had been so tired by the time they got back to the gym, so they had just gone to sleep.

"I think an old friend of mine might be involved with a dangerous group in Des Moines," Navy said. "One of those white nationalist groups." The soundproofing on the walls swallowed the echoes of Navy's voice. How matter of fact she sounded. How calm. "Sara and Moss might be a target. I need to know how dangerous my friend is. I thought you might be able to help me figure out which group she's involved in. Like with that soldier who was on prison guard duty last year. You knew he was part of that fringe Odinist movement." The soldier that Kevin had framed with dereliction of duty so one prisoner could kill another, and Jackson could be rescued from North Korea.

"Is Jackson with you?" Kevin asked sharply.

"Not right now. I made sure he can't hear me." Jackson wasn't supposed to know that Kevin had arranged for one of the prisoners to die. Navy wasn't supposed to know either, but she had been in the wrong place at the wrong time. "Don't worry, I've kept your secret." Navy couldn't help how bitter her words sounded. She hated keeping this secret from Jackson. She hated that sometimes she thought Kevin had been right.

"Tell me about your friend," Kevin said. "I might be able to help."

"Sara said Carrie's been posting things on Facebook about COVID-19 conspiracy theories and complaining about mask mandates. Sara wanted me to come to Des Moines so all three of us could talk and hopefully bring her back to reality."

"Outdoors, I hope," Kevin said.

"We tried camping. But last night, around the fire, Carrie started talking about race stuff. She asked me for help with two things. She wanted me to convince Sara and Moss to get genetic testing so they don't pass on contaminated genes." Navy had to stop to absorb the last sentence. After a night's rest, Carrie's betrayal seemed more real than it had before. And now that Sara and Moss were temporarily safe, Navy didn't have an immediate crisis to distract herself from the bigger problem.

"What was the second thing?" Kevin asked.

"I . . ." Navy didn't want to tell him she had failed. As if they were on assignment and he was still her handler. "I don't know. I lost my temper. We argued. She yelled, 'You will not replace us' and some bullshit about a war coming. That line she used . . . it's the same thing the right-wing protestors at Charlottesville said. And when she asked for my help, she didn't say 'me.' She said 'us.'"

"I can see why you're worried."

Navy rested her head in one hand. Part of her had been hoping Kevin would tell her she was overreacting. "So how dangerous is she? Which group could she be a part of?"

"Any of the three main groups operating in Iowa, really."

"There are three?!" Navy knew that racism didn't stop at the Mason-Dixon line. But still, it seemed impossible that the state she grew up in had that many hate groups. She hugged herself, suddenly feeling very alone and naïve. Of course the white woman who grew up in Iowa wouldn't know how many hate groups there were. She hadn't been targeted by them.

"National Alliance and Patriot Front both have operations around the state, and Great Millstone has some presence in Des Moines. National Alliance is more neo-Nazi, definitely anti-Semitic, but that line you quoted was from Charlottesville. And the Charlottesville protest was mostly Patriot Front people. Patriot Front is still racist, but it's a white nationalist group more than a neo-Nazi group. Vanguard America has a presence in Iowa too."

Navy was disturbed by how Kevin discussed different kinds of racism as if they were different varieties of wine. In the background, she heard an animatronic voice. "Come! Let Esmeralda tell your future!" A very familiar animatronic voice. That voice sounded exactly like the mildly racist fortune teller game at a coffee shop in Des Moines she had visited exactly once.

"Where are you?" Navy asked.

"Gypsy Joe's Cup of Joe," Kevin said. "And the coffee is terrible. The service too. The guy at the counter disappeared ten minutes ago and just hasn't come back."

"You're . . . in Des Moines?"

"Ah, so you know the place."

"The owner's kind of a jerk." Navy had gone inside expecting to find a hippy vibe, where the owner didn't know that gypsy could be an offensive term. Instead, she'd found a bunch of wall art commemorating the most regrettable SNL skits from the 1980s and 1990s. When she'd ordered her coffee and pastry, the owner had made a joke about her spending her husband's money. She had never been married. She hadn't even been wearing a ring.

"That's why I'm here." Kevin was a lot of things, but he'd never seemed to be that kind of jerk. "A couple years ago, Jackson asked me to find out who hired the guy that attacked you. After you got back from Amsterdam."

"You're referring to the time Jackson asked you for help with my problems and you told him not to bother because I couldn't possibly make it out of that government conspiracy alive."

"Yeah, that time."

Navy shook her head. As was often the case in conversations with Kevin, she was lost. "You're still tracking down that hired thug?"

"No, we found him. I'm tracking his network. He was a member of Vanguard America, but he split off with the Patriot Front group after Charlottesville."

"You're telling me Gypsy Joe's is a front for a domestic terrorist group."

"More like a sympathetic hangout spot."

Navy tried to digest this latest bit of news about the town where she had spent most of her adult life. "There's one more thing. Related to Carrie. Or maybe not. I don't know." Navy listened to the silence on the other end of the line as Kevin waited. "Last night someone hung a noose from a tree at Sara and Moss' house. Sara wasn't there, but Moss was."

Navy heard a clink, as if a cup was being set down.

"A noose with an LED lamp underneath it?" Kevin sounded almost excited.

"Yes, that's what Sara said. And after they left the noose—"

"They took a picture and sent a text message to the person who looked out the window when they honked."

"Yes." Navy shivered. "That's exactly what happened."

"This could be the break we need." Kevin definitely sounded excited.

"Who's we?" Navy asked, suddenly feeling very tired. "Isn't the CIA supposed to not be involved in domestic operations?"

"Oh, I'm not here officially. I'm here as a private citizen volunteering my talents to a friend at the FBI."

"You're using your vacation to track domestic hate groups."

"I'm not much of a beach guy."

Was Carrie really involved with a group like the Patriot Front? Navy felt a pang of guilt. What if Carrie wasn't involved? What if Navy had just put Carrie's name on some government list that would follow Carrie for the rest of her life?

"Navy, if your friend is involved this could be our way in. When Patriot Front split from Vanguard America, I lost track of Adam's network."

"Adam?" Navy asked.

"Adam Berant. Your hired thug."

Navy had never had a name for the man who left her with a black eye and sore ribs that night in the parking lot outside her office. "Can we . . . slow down for a minute? Are you saying that the Patriot Front is targeting Sara and Moss?"

"It's their local M.O. And Carrie being involved would explain the timing of the noose appearing at their house. Unless you know of another reason they would be targeted."

"And you think Carrie could get you inside the group? Why would she cooperate with you?"

"I don't need her to cooperate. From what you said, if she's involved she's a recent recruit. If you and Sara tell me everything you know about her, I can track her from there."

Navy wondered, again, if Carrie really deserved to have her life dissected in the way Kevin was proposing. How would Sara feel about cooperating? Sara had been angry last night. But knowing Sara, Navy suspected that this morning Sara would just want to help Carrie more. And she also had to think about Jackson.

"Even if I were okay with this," Navy said. "How am I supposed to explain to Jackson why you're involved?" Navy stared at the shooting targets waving slightly as the ventilation system kicked on while she waited for Kevin to answer. "You're not comfortable lying to him either."

"I did the right thing, Navy."

"That's debatable." Navy chewed on her lip. "It doesn't matter. We can't change what happened now. Let me feel Sara out to see is she's even interested. I won't be much help without Sara. Carrie and I haven't been close for a long time."

"Thank you, Navy."

Navy hung up the phone without responding; she didn't know what to say. Keeping Sara and Moss safe was the right thing to do. But Navy knew what the cost would be to her relationship with Jackson. More lies. More distance. More guilt.

Navy walked back out to the main gym area. Sara and Moss were eating breakfast with Jackson and Mark. For a second, the scene reminded her of Amsterdam, where she and Sara and Moss and Jackson had explored the city to get tourist photos to sell a cover. Except Mark hadn't been in Amsterdam. Navy only knew Mark because of what happened after she came back. After Navy had been attacked.

Focus, Navy told herself. She got her laptop out and sat down on the floor next to Sara. In between bites of food, Navy pulled up Carrie's social media pages and began printing everything to PDF files on her desktop. It was tedious and slow work since many of the posts had to be expanded or albums opened to see all the photos.

Here was Carrie with a group at a marksmanship competition. Here was Carrie excited about her new job at the gun range. Here was Carrie at a metal concert for "Viking Deployment." Here was Carrie at a community ed class about foraging. Here was Carrie announcing the funeral for her mother and her sister. The posts grew happier and closer together the further Navy went back.

Sara unapologetically watched over Navy's shoulder. "I didn't know Carrie was into death metal. What are you looking for exactly?"

"I don't know yet," Navy said. "Just making sure I record these things in case Carrie decides to roll up her social media accounts."

"You can delete social media accounts?"

"Sort of. Depends on the service. And generally some stuff sticks around anyway. But it's harder to find stuff once people start deleting things." Maybe this was a good opportunity to see how Sara felt about making the investigation into Carrie more official. Navy pushed the laptop away and stretched. "This feels weird," Navy said. Not a lie exactly. A truth shared at a convenient time to achieve her objective. "Treating Carrie like a suspect, I mean."

Sara frowned. "I know."

"What exactly happened last night?" Jackson asked. "At the campground."

"After I went to bed, Carrie asked Navy to convince us to get genetic testing to find out our ancestry." Sara reached for Moss' hand. "Carrie said . . . Carrie said that Moss' blood might not be white enough.

That maybe my miscarriages were a good thing because we shouldn't pass on 'impure' genes." Sara seemed more sad than angry this morning.

"Carrie kept referring to some group, but she never named them," Navy said. "And she wanted to ask me for something else . . . but we never got to that."

Moss turned to Navy. "Do you think Carrie was behind what happened at our house last night?"

"I have no idea." Navy had meant to soften the statement. She was frustrated that Moss was looking to her and also because she didn't have the answer. "I mean, I just don't know. I wish I did."

"We should start with the obvious questions first," Jackson said. "Has anything else happened in your neighborhood recently?"

"Some people with 'Black Lives Matter' signs had death threats left on their cars," Sara said. "But nothing's come of it so far and nobody got hurt. My friend ended up talking to someone at the FBI, but she never heard anything after the interview."

"We have to find out what Carrie's involved in," Moss said. "Otherwise, how will we know when we can go home?"

Jackson frowned. "I guess I could make a couple calls. If you're comfortable with that."

"Why wouldn't we be comfortable with that?" Sara snapped. "Are you saying we shouldn't care?"

"No, I—" Jackson shifted and pushed his plate away. "This will start a file on Carrie. I wasn't sure how you would feel about that. You were kidnapped in that CIA op just like Navy. Would you trust a government agent?"

"I'm sorry," Sara said. "I hadn't thought of it that way."

"These people you might call," Moss said. "Are they friends? Do you trust them?"

Jackson nodded slowly. "They are."

Sara and Moss looked at each other, considering. Navy wondered if she would ever feel that close to Jackson, where for just a moment, they could think as one mind.

"Do it," said Sara.

Were Kevin's FBI friends the same as Jackson's FBI friends? Kevin had been worried about how to get involved without tipping Jackson off. Had Navy solved Kevin's problem for him? *Too many secrets,* Navy thought.

"I'm going to make a few calls then." Jackson kissed Navy on the cheek before he got up. "Mind if I use your office?" Jackson asked Mark. Next to the large area covered with mats for sparring was a small, sparsely furnished office.

"Knock yourself out," Mark said. "Not like I need it to organize classes right now."

"What kind of classes do you do anyway?" Sara asked. "And how do people ever find you with your gym buried in the middle of this warehouse district?"

"Sara—" Navy wasn't sure how much Mark wanted to or could explain about his business. Navy wasn't even sure how Mark's business worked. Navy only knew that she had never seen another student at the gym.

"It's okay," Mark said. "I can explain a little. Mostly, I make my money as a personal trainer for people who have gyms in their own homes. That all moved to virtual sessions recently. Having a few rich clients goes a long way. I also do . . . discreet classes . . . for certain government employees."

"Or friends," Sara said.

"Doesn't everyone do favors for their friends?" Mark asked.

"You trained Navy," Sara said.

Navy felt bad Sara was asking Mark so many questions. Mark hadn't hesitated to let them stay at his gym and Sara was repaying his kindness with prying questions. "We should get our tents hung up," Navy said. "Make sure they're completely dry before we pack them away."

"I know why you hang a tent up after a trip," Sara snapped.

"I didn't mean—" Navy started. It wasn't like Sara to snap at anyone. If anything, Sara was normally too forgiving.

"I'll help bring gear in from the car," Moss said. "Always a pain when you have to pack things up in a hurry."

"No one's going to answer my question then," Sara said.

Navy folded her hands in her lap. "Yes, Mark trained me. I'm not sure why it matters to you so much."

Sara pushed away the arm Moss offered for comfort. "Who are you?" Sara looked at Navy. "You had a truck stop picked out ahead of time in case we had to leave the campsite in the middle of the night. And the way you talked to Carrie. She starts hinting at her racist bullshit and you basically said 'Tell me more' and then you're yelling at her and then you were so calm. Telling Carrie you're not going to fight her and she should just leave because she got her answer." Sara was standing now, gesturing wildly, and nearly yelling. "You knew what to say to keep Carrie talking and you knew what to say to make Carrie leave. And then 'poof!' we're in some *very private* gym and someone's calling their FBI friends and maybe some hate group wants to kill my husband and I don't know when we can go home and I don't know who's targeting us and . . ."

Navy stood and hugged Sara. Sara's anger wasn't about Navy at all. "This whole situation, it's a lot, I know." Navy remembered how overwhelmed she had felt when she realized a shadowy organization was threatening her. "I may have some skills I didn't have before and a few more interesting friends, but I'm going to help any way I can." *I'm still your friend.*

Sara wiped her eyes. "I'm sorry, I didn't mean to yell at you."

"Does this mean you know some secret ninja moves?" Moss asked.

Trust Moss to break the tension. "Yes," Navy said. "Mark specializes in teaching people extra special secret ninja moves."

"Speaking of," said Mark. "After you get your camping gear laid out, let's see how much you've forgotten of what I taught you."

If Navy could, just for a bit, put aside the events that led to spending the night at Mark's gym, maybe she could enjoy a few sparring sessions. Navy hadn't been to her gym in months. "Or maybe, I've learned a few things," Navy said.

Mark grinned. "Bring it on."

Chapter 9

Navy had missed sparring. After half an hour with Mark, her muscles were tired and sore and eager for another hour. Practicing techniques on a live partner was so much better than hitting her punching bag or throwing a grappling dummy.

Jackson interrupted their sparring session with a grim face. "My FBI contacts said the incident at Sara and Moss' house last night matches the local M.O. of the Patriot Front."

"So it's worse than we thought." Navy wiped sweat from her face using a camp towel to hide her expression. Navy already knew what Jackson was telling her from her conversation with Kevin. She felt queasy hiding the conversation from Jackson.

"Do you know anyone working the case down here?" Mark asked.

"Yeah, Kevin," Jackson said. "He's in town right now, apparently. Working with the FBI. While he's on vacation."

Again, Navy hid her face with the towel. Luckily, Mark was as surprised as Jackson.

"Of course he is," said Mark. "Man never knew how to take a break."

"Kevin wants us to meet with the FBI agent on the case," Jackson said. "Where are Sara and Moss?"

"Out getting coffee somewhere," Navy said. "Do we need to call them back right away?"

"I think they could meet us there," Jackson said. "Would give them a little more time to themselves. Sara looked upset this morning."

Navy remembered how it felt to have Sara look at her like a stranger. "I think I scared her. At the campground." Navy felt the sweat drying, cold, on her arms. "When Carrie started hinting at Moss having 'impure' blood, I didn't tell her to fuck off right away."

"If you hadn't played along a little, Carrie wouldn't have told you as much." Jackson rubbed her shoulder. "We have a little time before we need to leave. You want to fill me in on everything that happened?"

Navy did. Sharing all the details about what happened last night made her feel slightly better about hiding her conversation with Kevin. "And then Carrie sped off in her survival camper van and we came to meet you at the spot we arranged just in case."

"You suspected Carrie was dangerous before you came down here?" Mark asked.

Navy shrugged. "I planned for the possibility. I asked around at work about the Plandemic stuff. They told me there's always a risk that conspiracy theorists will escalate. They used some term . . . mental opening? Cognitive opening?"

"Cognitive opening," Jackson said. "A time in someone's life when they're vulnerable to radicalization because of a traumatic event."

"The theory fits," Navy said. "Two years ago Carrie's mother and sister died. That's the only family she had left." And Navy hadn't known. Navy had lost touch with her friend and possibly lost the only opportunity to pull Carrie back to reality. "Anyway, the analysts said someone can start out believing Ebola was created in a US government lab and end up believing anti-Semitic conspiracy theories about Jewish space lasers."

"Navy—"

Navy stood to avoid Jackson's comforting hand. "Or instead of Jewish space lasers they might start believing in an impending race war."

"This isn't your fault," Mark said.

"Don't give me that bullshit." The understanding, sympathetic expressions on Jackson's and Mark's faces only made Navy feel angrier. "I know it's not my fault. The problem is . . ." This is the nagging thought Navy hadn't been able to say in front of Sara. "What if Carrie is involved with the Patriot Front? Once the FBI finds her, she either turns informant or she takes the blame. Either way she's a liability for Patriot Front."

Jackson nodded slowly. "You're not wrong."

"I came down here to help her," Navy said.

"Witness protection isn't the worst thing," Jackson said. "From what you told us earlier, I think Carrie would turn informant."

"Carrie said I was going to end up on the wrong side of a race war."

"Carrie also said she wasn't racist," Jackson said.

Navy stared at him in disbelief. "All that stuff about mixing impure genes is definitely racist."

"Exactly," Jackson said. "Cognitive dissonance. Carrie still thinks being racist is a bad thing. She just hasn't recognized that some of her beliefs are racist."

Mark raised his eyebrows. "Jackson, I know you're the psychologist and all, but she sounds pretty far gone to me. I wouldn't get your hopes up, Navy."

Luckily, a text from Sara interrupted the moment. "Sara says she and Moss can meet us at the FBI offices," Navy said. "I should shower before we go."

The shower in Mark's bathroom was a showerhead and a curtain separating one half of the tiled room from the toilet. Navy was just grateful for a little bit of solitary time. She hadn't been alone since she got in the car to drive down to Iowa for the ill-fated camping trip. Whatever happened at the meeting with Kevin's FBI friend, there were no easy solutions. The 'enemy' was her friend. Navy had spent the past few years sharpening her fighting skills so she could defend herself, but none of the moves she had learned would knock Carrie out of the distorted reality Carrie had chosen.

Navy was thinking of that famously depressing Kissinger quote, ". . . dilemmas cannot be solved. They can only be survived." Would Carrie survive this? Would Sara? Would Moss? Maybe Kissinger's famously cold pragmatism was exactly what Navy needed to channel right now. Or maybe not. Depending on which historian you asked, Kissinger was either an American hero or a war criminal. Or maybe both. Navy hoped that whatever she had to do, she wouldn't have to stack up her good deeds against her bad ones to figure out who she was.

Chapter 10

"You said left on Westown Parkway?" Navy asked Mark as the car approached the corner.

"Yep, left," Mark said from the back seat. "Should be about a mile and then you'll see a brick office park."

"Sure," Navy said.

Navy turned the car left. Her discomfort grew the closer she got to the West Des Moines FBI offices. Here Navy was, in broad daylight, going to an office full of people who might have arrested her three years ago for leaking the details of a classified CIA operation to the press. God knows what the FBI agent they were meeting with thought of her. Generally, people who traded in secrets were suspicious of people who had revealed them.

Despite that, her CIA coworkers had eventually come to trust her. Navy hoped her coworkers saw her as someone who tried to do right thing. She wasn't sure what Jackson's FBI contact would think of her.

"Do you know who we're meeting?" Mark asked Jackson.

"Warren Armstrong," Jackson said. "I've worked with him a couple times."

"Yeah, he seems all right," Mark said. "I took his team through a training exercise last year."

"Do you all know each other?" Navy snapped, sounding angrier than she'd intended. She could feel the walls closing in on her again. Navy was in yet another situation where none of the options were good and she would have to decide who she could trust with Sara and Moss' lives.

Jackson rubbed her hand. "Warren's good people, I promise."

"Sorry, I'm just—" Navy turned off the car. Navy was just what? Tired of having to play will-this-government-agent-like-me-or-hate-me again? Frustrated that none of her skills seemed suited to the moment? Scared because she didn't know what was going to happen? Angry that a bunch of deluded conspiracy theorists had left a trail of bullshit for Carrie to follow? All of the above?

"Let's just go," Navy said.

Jackson looked like he might ask *how she was feeling* but he only said, "Warren said he would meet us outside in the lunch area."

Navy recognized Sara's car in the parking lot. Good, that meant there was already at least one person at this meeting that Navy actually wanted to see. Next to the building, Navy saw a cluster of picnic tables on the green lawn. She recognized Kevin's long-limbed form, Sara's shorter one, and Moss' puff of curly dark red-tinged hair, puffed up a bit because of the humidity. And a stranger, presumably Warren. Warren had the same sharp cheekbones and long nose as Kevin did, but Warren's wide face and even wider smile radiated friendliness. Navy was pretty sure no one had ever described Kevin as friendly.

"Navy!" Sara waved. "We just got here."

"Jackson, Mark, good to see you again." Warren stood up and half held out his hand and then pulled it back. "We're supposed to elbow bump each other now, I guess. I think I'm the only one who misses handshakes."

Jackson smiled warmly, then angled his elbow to meet Warren's. "In a year or so, we'll all be vaccinated and then we can share germs again."

Mark did the same. "How's your team been?" Mark asked. "Did that junior agent of yours pass her shooting qual?"

"She said to send her regards," Warren said. "She's probably my best shot on the team now, thanks to you."

"Navy, Jackson," Kevin nodded to them.

"Crazy how things work out," Jackson said. "I'm glad you ended up being here."

Crazy indeed, Navy thought.

"And you must be Navy," Warren said.

As hard as Navy tried, she couldn't read anything behind Warren's jovial expression. "Jackson and Mark had good things to say about you," Navy said. She realized she sounded skeptical. "I mean . . ." Navy couldn't quite say it was good to meet him. She wasn't sure she trusted Warren yet. "I mean you come highly recommended."

"You as well," Warren said. "I told a couple people you were coming today and they wanted to come ask you some questions on their cybercrime cases."

Navy definitely didn't trust him. Warren was too cheerful and too friendly for her taste.

If Warren read her discomfort, he ignored it. "I'd invite everyone to sit, but the table's a bit too small for us to keep our distance. We'll have to do one of those trendy standing meetings."

"We should start with Sara's and Navy's stories." Kevin leaned against the table, arms and legs crossed. "I only told Warren the broad strokes."

"A few weeks ago I called up Navy and told her we had to go camping," Sara said. "And—"

"Before that," Kevin said. "What made you think Carrie was in trouble in the first place?"

Sara narrowed her eyes. "Interrupt much?"

All the time, Navy thought.

"Forgive him," Warren rested a hand on Kevin's shoulder. Kevin accepted the coaching more gracefully than Navy expected. Navy had never seen Kevin let anyone else order him around. "They don't let him out to deal with normal people much," Warren said. "We want to hear about the camping trip, but what happened before is important too. Radicalization doesn't happen overnight."

Navy listened as Sara repeated the warning signs Sara had told her. Carrie's growing distance from their mutual friends. Carrie's increasingly odd social media posts.

"I archived a bunch of Carrie's social media stuff this morning," Navy said. She fished in her pocket and brought out a thumb drive. "I brought a copy for you."

"I'll have to tell IT I'm going to plug in a thumb drive Navy Trent brought me," Warren said with a wide smile.

"I—" Navy realized Warren was joking. "I can upload files somewhere if that's easier." Her face warmed. Navy hoped Warren would think it was the summer heat coloring her cheeks and not embarrassment.

"Anyway," Kevin said. "That's good background. What about suspicious interests? New things Carrie's been into?"

"Suspicious? Nothing really," Sara said. "Except maybe that job she got at a gun range. But she doesn't work there anymore. I suspect Carrie got fired but she wouldn't say."

"You might want to check out this band I saw in her timeline," Navy said. "Viking Deployment. An analyst at the office said there's been a problem with white supremacy in the death metal community, particularly bands with Nordic themes."

"Good thoughts," Warren said. "Anything else you noticed?"

"Nothing Sara didn't mention," Navy said.

"So I want to hear more about this camping trip," Warren said. "Let's start with Sara."

Sara and then Navy recounted last night's events. Sara sounded just as emotional as this morning. Navy sounded dispassionate, even to herself. As if Navy were giving a field report, rather than talking about something that had happened to her.

"You may want to check out Carrie's van, if you can find it," Navy said. "Carrie seemed to be protective of what was inside. She never opened the door wide enough for us to even glance in. Sounded like she was living in it to avoid having a permanent address."

"We'll see what we can find registered to her," Warren said.

"We saw the police report you filed," Kevin said to Moss. "But—" Kevin glanced at Sara. "If you don't mind, I'd like to hear the story from you."

"If you think it will help," Moss said. "It was around eleven at night. I heard a car honking outside. I ignored it at first, but the honking didn't stop, and it didn't sound like a car alarm or anything." Moss shifted back and forth, focusing on a spot on the brick wall. Sara rubbed his back. "Anyway, I opened the curtains to see what was going on and there's this guy with a mask on standing under our tree in front, holding his phone up."

"What kind of mask?" asked Warren.

"That creepy frog," Moss said. "The green one that became a meme on 4chan."

"Pepe the Frog," Kevin said. "The cartoon character appropriated by the neo-Nazi movement."

"I was so confused I didn't notice right away that the man was standing next to a noose swinging from our tree. I could see other people in the car idling on the curb, at least three of them."

Navy felt Moss' fear keenly. Alone in the house, facing a small group of people threatening him. What would have happened if the four hadn't left? How long could Moss have kept them out if they had tried to get into the house?

Moss took a shaky breath. "So I see the noose swinging and I finally think to call the police, and I pick up my phone and there's a text message with a picture of me. At my window. And another message."

Moss looked at Sara and shoved his hands in his pockets. "I, uh, didn't tell you this part before. The message said, 'Your wife is a race traitor.' I'm glad you weren't home."

Sara was more angry than scared. "If I were home I would have gone outside and—"

"Hopefully not," Kevin said.

"Kevin." Warren shook his head slightly.

"These people are no joke," Kevin said to Sara. "Don't start fights you don't have to."

"Let's go back to what happened," Warren said.

"I . . . froze," Moss said. "When I saw the message about Sara. And by the time I looked up the car was driving away, and the man in the yard was gone. I couldn't see the plates on the car. The car had its lights off and it was too far away anyway."

"The people in the car, did they have masks on?" Warren asked.

"No, but I wouldn't recognize them if I saw them again. It was too dark."

"And the car," Kevin said. "What shape was it? A sedan? SUV?"

"A four-door sedan," Moss said. "Dark colored. I'm not a car guy. I couldn't tell you any more than that."

"The police report says the text messages on your phone came in at 11:04 p.m.," Kevin said. "When did Carrie leave your campsite, Navy?"

"Around 10:45 p.m." Navy had anticipated this question. "I looked at my text messages this morning. I texted Jackson to tell him to meet us at the truck stop at 10:47 p.m."

"Could Carrie have made it from your campsite to Moss and Sara's house in time?" Kevin asked.

"No," Sara said. "Our camp was at least an hour away."

Kevin tapped his fingers on his elbows, arms still crossed. "But Carrie may have sent a message to someone."

"It's a flimsy connection," Warren said.

"Not so flimsy," Kevin said. "Carrie said, 'You will not replace us,' that's a Patriot Front slogan. The noose lawn art is the local Patriot Front group. That band Navy mentioned—Viking Deployment—their flyer was up on Gypsy Joe's bulletin board. Even if Carrie wasn't involved in the attack on the house, she's probably involved with the group."

"But why *them*?" Warren asked. "There are interracial couples all over the city. And Carrie was asking for a DNA test. It doesn't sound like Carrie was even sure Sara and Moss are an interracial couple."

They were right. I can't rely on Sara. Carrie's words, more ominous now, came back to Navy.

"To isolate Carrie," Navy said. "And force a loyalty test. There's no one else in our friend group Carrie talks to anymore besides Sara."

"See?" Kevin said. "Patriot Front gets a two-for-one – terrorize the neighborhood and make sure their new recruit has no one left to run to."

"What—" Sara twisted her hands together and leaned against Moss. "What happens to Carrie if you find her?"

Warren's demeanor reminded Navy of a doctor preparing to give bad news to a patient.

"Depends on what Carrie's involved in," Warren said.

"If Carrie was involved in what happened at our house," Sara said. "What happens then?"

"We bring her in and give her a chance to do the right thing," Warren said. "If Carrie gives us useful information, she might not get charged with anything at all."

"And if Carrie doesn't help?"

"She'll face charges for being an accessory to a hate crime."
Warren watched Sara carefully. "Does that bother you?"

"We'll just have to find Carrie before anything else happens," said
Sara. "How can we help?"

Warren looked nonplussed. "I think it's better if you let us take
things from here. We'll call you every couple of weeks to keep you
updated."

"You expect us to sit around and wait to see what happens," Sara
said. "And hope the extra patrols the police promised to send to our house
are enough in the meantime."

"Navy, help us out here," Kevin said.

Navy felt torn. She knew Kevin wanted her to tell Sara to stay
away from the investigation and wait patiently. Navy also knew how well
Sara would take that suggestion. Navy thought back to the weeks before
she'd gone to Hackerville, how she thought she'd been prepared to go on a
'light' undercover op. How things went wrong and, even with her modest
skills, she barely made it out alive. "You haven't trained for this," Navy
told Sara. *Almost exactly the words Navy had heard from Kevin.* "I
understand how hard it must be—"

"Bullshit," said Sara.

A couple people from the tables around them glanced toward
Sara's raised voice.

"We're trying to start a family and you're going to tell me I should
just plan on bringing a child home and wait to see if a noose shows up on
our tree again?"

Navy blinked. "Sara, are you—"

"Three weeks," Sara said with wet eyes. "It's early. We haven't told anyone yet. Except, I guess, you and Jackson and three almost strangers. No offense, Mark."

"None taken," Mark assured her.

"All the more reason to stay safe," Kevin said. "Mark—are you okay hosting them for a bit?"

"Sure, it's—" Mark started.

"Don't make plans for us," Sara said. "God, you're insufferable."

"Maybe," Kevin said. "But it's still a bad idea for you to get involved."

"Sara's right," Moss said. "It's our house. It's our life. We can run now, but what happens in a couple months? Or after the baby's born? If Carrie gave my number and our address to the Patriot Front, she could tell them a lot more. I grew up with Carrie. She knows my parents. She knows most of our friends. She knows where most of our extended family lives."

Warren widened his stance, as if bracing for a blow. "There aren't any good options here. I'm sorry."

"There are better options," Sara insisted.

"You must have read too many PI novels," Kevin said. "You can't take on a chapter of a nationally-affiliated hate group with amateur sleuth skills."

"Then use us as bait," Moss said.

Jackson frowned. "I don't think you know what you're offering."

Navy could hardly fathom the idea. "It's too dangerous." *Exactly the words Jackson had used when she said she wanted to go undercover.* Later, Jackson had apologized for treating Navy so dismissively. Was she treating her friends the same way?

Warren held his hands up. "Luckily, it's not up to any of you. It's up to me, and my team. And I'm not throwing anyone to the wolves before we've even pursued our first good lead." Warren turned to Sara and Moss. "I've been working this case for weeks now. You aren't the only family I've had to ask to wait. We finally have a good lead—thanks to you. I'm asking you, please, to give us a little time before we resort to desperate measures."

"Can I help in their place?" Navy asked.

"You're too famous around here to go undercover," Kevin said. "Especially since it sounds like Carrie may have told the group you would help them."

"Not in the field," Navy said. "From behind a desk. If Kevin can volunteer, I can too, right? You could probably use an intelligence analyst. I could help dig through public social media profiles. Or whatever information you've gotten via warrants."

"We could use another analyst," Warren said grudgingly. "We are spread thin."

"If we agree to let Navy help," Kevin said to Sara and Moss. "Will that satisfy you?"

"For now," Sara said.

Kevin rolled his eyes. "You're as stubborn as Navy is."

"Don't mind him," Navy said. "We'll figure this out." Sara hugged Navy for a long second. Touching anyone but Jackson still felt odd after so many months stuck in their apartment.

"I want to help," Mark said. "I don't want these neo-Nazi shitheads in my city."

"People know you," Warren said. "Shouldn't be too hard to get permission for you to join too."

"I supposed you want to help too," Kevin said to Jackson.

Jackson put an arm around Navy's shoulders. "I can't let Navy and Mark have all the fun."

"Then it's settled," Warren said.

Mark cleared his throat. "Not trying to make the decision for you," Mark said. "But you're welcome to bring a few things from your house to the gym if you want to stay for a couple weeks."

"Thank you," Moss said. "We'll probably take you up on that. We can work from coffee shops for a bit."

Navy hugged Sara again, "Sounds like Mark, Jackson, and I are going to be here for a couple more hours. See you back at Mark's."

Warren looked at Mark, Jackson, and Navy. "With you three and Kevin, my team is going to be half 'consultants.'"

"Does that mean we're getting paid?" Mark joked.

"Only in donuts and bad coffee," Warren said. "I'll take you in and get you introduced to the team."

"Thank you," Navy said. "For letting us tag along. I hate . . . just waiting on the sidelines."

Warren grinned. "Yeah, Kevin may have mentioned something about that."

Chapter 11

Jackson followed Warren into the office building. Other than a lot of unoccupied desks and everyone wearing masks, the scene looked a lot like most FBI offices Jackson had been in.

"We're rotating shifts," Warren said, his voice slightly muffled by his mask. "And having people work from home that can. We're lucky that most of my team is in today. We can do introductions."

Warren led them into a large conference room. Three other people were there. With Warren, Jackson, Kevin, Navy, and Mark there were eight people in the room. "These are close quarters during COVID," Jackson said, then regretted it. Warren had done them multiple favors this morning. Warren didn't have to let them help. Jackson, Navy, and Mark could have been sent home to wait for news, just like Sara and Moss had been.

"Yeah, I know, sorry about that. I wasn't expecting to double the size of my team this morning." Warren slumped into a chair. "I wasn't kidding about the funding thing. We've been screaming since 2009 that domestic hate groups were on the rise, and this is what I get. Three people and a conference room." Warren gestured at the table piled with papers. One of the other agents glanced up, eyes crinkling above her mask, and then went back to work. "Alicia has heard this speech before," Warren said ruefully.

"Have you made any progress on the local incidents?" Jackson asked.

"Not much," Warren said. "We have seven incidents with nooses on people's lawns so far. Lots of reports of death threats left on people's cars or on people's doors. Some of the death threats are just little shits who thinks it's funny to 'own the libs.' Some are real, local assholes who might actually follow up with violence. And some of them are external assholes who fly in to stoke a race war every time there's a big Black Lives Matter protest. It's a fucking mess." Warren sighed and rubbed his face. "We're trying to sort out who's actually dangerous and who's just a troll, but even that changes day by day."

"Because they get radicalized," Jackson said.

"Yeah, someone starts out as a troll but then listens to some bullshit YouTube video saying Black Lives Matter is a militant movement and white people are a persecuted group and blah-blah-blah, and a few months later the troll is sending death threats to a church because the church helps resettle refugees."

"You put on a brave face for Sara," Navy said. "You don't sound hopeful."

"We do what we can and hope the creek don't rise," Warren said. "Something my dad always said." Warren rapped on the table with his knuckles, and then Warren's eyes crinkled with what was probably a smile. "Let's do some introductions."

Warren's smile seemed forced, but Jackson understood. If you don't believe things might get better, there isn't much point in trying.

The agents who had been typing on their laptops or reading papers looked up.

"Alicia is my partner on this . . . not quite a task force." Warren pointed at a pale, freckled woman with deep brown eyes.

"Unofficial task force." Alicia made a little wave. "Kevin's talked about most of you. Let me see if I can guess." Alicia pointed at Jackson. "CIA field agent extraordinaire Jackson Fletcher." Then Navy. "Gadget Girl CIA analyst Navy Trent."

Gadget Girl was a nickname Navy had picked up last year when she'd talked her way onto Jackson's rescue team. Jackson still had trouble imagining Navy doing a tandem HALO jump with a bunch of Green Berets. Navy continually surprised him. In a good way.

"You Kevin hasn't mentioned," Alicia said to Mark.

"Mark Spademan," Mark introduced himself. "Ex-law enforcement. Firearms and martial arts instructor."

"Lovely to meet you," Alicia said.

"This is Tom, our intel analyst and the only person I know who still reads physical newspapers." Warren pointed at a man sitting at the far edge of the table. Tom was dark-skinned and muscular. Incongruously, he had the hands of a pianist. Of all the agents in the room, Tom had the largest pile of paper in front of him. The pile included several newspapers, some local, some national.

"Analog is underrated," Tom said, eyes crinkling.

"And this is our rookie, Dennis." Warren pointed at a solidly built man who looked like he had been prom king and quarterback at his high school. Dennis also looked too young to have graduated from FBI training, but then all the new recruits at the CIA looked too young to Jackson.

"Thanks for talking me up," Dennis said. "I've been here two years and he still calls me the rookie."

"Maybe I'll stop calling you the rookie when I get younger," Warren joked. "Can you run down what we know about the noose incidents for our new friends?"

Dennis dug under a stack of papers and pulled out some handwritten notes. "Based on interviews so far—the attackers show up late at night in either a dark sedan or a light SUV. Four or five attackers total, but only one comes out on the lawn. They hang the noose, honk when they're done, the victim opens the curtains, the attackers get a picture, and then text a phone number with the image. Sometimes they send an additional message. Does that track with the new incident you learned about today?"

Warren nodded. "Not much new there."

"What about the objects left behind?" Jackson asked. "Have you found any leads there?"

"The LED lamps and rope match common brands available from any of the big hardware stores around here," Dennis said. "We haven't managed to narrow down what store or even a specific day they were purchased. Or if they were even purchased near Des Moines."

"That's . . . not a lot," Jackson said.

"The noose incidents just started a few weeks ago," Dennis said. "We're waiting on some surveillance footage from local businesses that might help."

"I want to check out this gun range Navy and Sara mentioned, On Target Gun Range," Kevin said. "Gypsy Joe's was a bust this morning."

"There might be something in those bulletin board pictures you sent me," Tom said. "I'm still running down the businesses and groups advertising there."

"Even so," Kevin said. "If this gun club is full of second amendment purists with DON'T TREAD ON ME bumper stickers it might be a better lead."

"Sounds fine to me," Warren said. "I need to get started on some paperwork so our new 'consultants' can join the team. Tom, can you get Navy up to speed? Navy has some of Carrie's social media stuff you can go through together. Then you two should do whatever magic intel analysts do and get me some new leads."

"Sure thing," Tom said.

Jackson wasn't as impatient as Kevin was, but Jackson was eager to get out and *do something* that might help Navy and her friends. "I'd like to go to the gun range with Kevin. You coming, Mark?"

"If it's all right with Alicia and Dennis, I'd like to stay and help look through police reports and interview notes. I've lived here most of my life, I might be able to help."

"We'd be happy to have the help. We haven't even finished analyzing all the death threats." Alicia pointed behind her to a map taped to the wall.

Jackson saw a bunch of locations marked in different colored stickers. Each sticker was a scared family waiting on news for when the threat would pass. Each sticker was a symptom of social bonds fraying. Was the United States as different from less wealthy nations as Americans would like to believe? Was the United States actually less tribal? More evolved?

Anti-maskers were protesting at local health departments and school board meetings. Unapologetic racists with weapons were confronting Black Lives Matter protestors. Half of the country was waiting anxiously for a COVID vaccine to be widely available. The other half was anxiously digesting conspiracy theories about the New World Order or biological weapons or QAnon.

Like Warren, Jackson wanted to be optimistic. Jackson was hoping that a few people in an office in the middle of Des Moines could find the rot at the heart of the community. Working in Afghanistan had given Jackson an appreciation for just how fragile democracy could be. Jackson had never expected those lessons to apply closer to home.

Chapter 12

Jackson and Kevin quickly got lost driving around the unmarked rural roads. After driving in circles for an hour, Jackson thought they might have found a highway leading in the right direction to find On Target Gun Range.

"They're either trying to hide, or bad at writing directions," Kevin said. "Their website says, 'Turn at the old Miller farm, then left at the church/schoolhouse.'"

Jackson pulled the car over on a wide, gravel shoulder. "There's some sort of historic site over there." He pointed at a white building with a steeple and a bell tower. All that swung inside the bell tower was a frayed rope.

"May as well try it," Kevin said. "I'm hoping to be back for dinner."

Odd, Jackson thought. Kevin rarely made personal plans when he was working. "You know someone here?"

"I think we found it," Kevin said.

Jackson didn't know if Kevin was dodging the question or not.

Kevin pointed to a fenced area on the right. "The berm and those hay bales look like they're set up to be an archery range. Archery is listed on their site too."

Sure enough, Jackson saw a painted sign with stenciled letters: On Target Gun Range/Archery/Guns/Bachelor parties.

"Not much of a marketing budget," Jackson said.

"It's a good opening for us. Would you like to be the groom or should I?" Kevin asked.

Jackson smiled, trying to think of the last time Kevin had been in a relationship that lasted longer than three weeks. "I'll play the best man. Do they mention the bachelor party thing on their website?"

Kevin scrolled on his phone for a few minutes. "Nothing. You're going to pretend to know Carrie?"

"Casually. See how the owner reacts. What's your meet-cute?"

"My what?" Kevin asked.

"For your cover," Jackson said. "You and your fiancé. How did you meet? How long have you known each other? Do I approve of your engagement or not?"

Kevin rolled his eyes. "You are enjoying this way too much."

"Oh, most definitely. But you should still make up some details."

"How about this? We met at a dog park after our dog's leashes got tangled and then had a romantic dinner at an Italian restaurant where we slurped up a shared plate of spaghetti noodles until we kissed while fireworks exploded overhead."

"Impressive how many movie plots you managed to fit in there, but maybe go for something a little less ostentatious." Jackson parked the car in the gravel lot next to the one lone car. He didn't see any DON'T TREAD ON ME bumper stickers yet.

"We met online, like normal people do," Kevin said. "Her name is Lindsey. It's a second marriage for both of us. We've dated for two years. We both love dogs and are hoping to adopt three foster children."

"You with a dog and children," Jackson shook his head. "Go on."

"You don't approve because you are an unrepentant player and the only dating site you use is Tinder."

"I'll be sure to make lots of jokes about you finding your ball and chain," Jackson said. A squat, long building extended away from the parking lot. A converted pole barn from the looks of the metal siding.

Jackson opened the glass door, noting the bars reinforcing the door and all the windows on the front. The door looked old but the locks were fresh. Boxes of ammunition lined the exterior walls. Guns were mounted on the wall behind a long counter. A flyer next to the register advertised a class to earn your conceal and carry permit.

The man behind the register wore a baseball cap and a scraggly beard. Weathered was the kindest description of his face. He wasn't wearing a mask. Jackson realized how long it had been since he had been inside with a stranger whose face wasn't covered.

"I'm the owner, Bob Millstrom. Can I help you?" the man asked.

Not friendly, Jackson thought. But not unfriendly either. Time to get into character. Jackson clapped Kevin solidly on the back. "My man here has decided to take the plunge and is getting married two months from now. I was hoping to schedule a bachelor party."

"Aren't those normally planned as a surprise?" the man asked.

"Normally," Kevin jumped in. "But I don't like surprises."

Odd how suspicious he is, thought Jackson. By the looks of the place, On Target Gun Range could use some more business.

"I offered strippers and a bar crawl," Jackson said. "But he insisted on something cooler."

Bob didn't look any less suspicious of them. "How'd you hear about us?"

"Last year I ran into someone I went to high school with." That should match up with the timing of Carrie working here. "Carrie said she was working here and you did bachelor parties."

"Carrie hasn't worked here for months."

Jackson feigned innocent confusion. "Oh, well do you have any Friday or Saturday nights open for the next couple months?"

"You know, I think we're all booked up." The owner didn't even pretend to consult a schedule.

"I think my friend may have given you the wrong impression," Kevin said. "About our intentions. My dad used to take me hunting and target shooting. And I just thought it'd be fun for a bachelor party. Something that didn't involve getting drunk and acting stupid."

Jackson played along. "I'm not going to lie. I was a little disappointed when he passed on the strippers. But I've known him since elementary school so if an afternoon of sober target practice is what he wants, that's the bachelor party I'll give him."

Bob's body language softened a little bit. "I've been meaning to change that sign. I thought it would be good business. I know a guy who books parties for people to play with backhoes and cranes. But instead I keep getting yahoos who want to down a six-pack and wave around loaded guns."

Jackson needed to get the topic back to Carrie. What would a shameless player do if he were interested in finding someone? "Did Carrie say where her new job was? She looked good last time I saw her. I was hoping maybe I would run into her here. You know, maybe ask her out."

Kevin made an appropriately disapproving expression.

"I . . . uh . . . don't think you want to get involved with Carrie," Bob said. "She has a boyfriend."

Sara and Navy hadn't mentioned anything about a boyfriend. Jackson decided to be annoyingly persistent. "Do you think she's still with him?"

Bob scratched his neck. "The boyfriend's bad news. He's the reason I had to change the locks around here." Bob paused and nervously shifted some flyers on the counter in front of him. "Look, I probably shouldn't be telling you all this but I don't want you to get hurt. I had to fire Carrie because I found out she was letting her boyfriend and his backyard militia into the shooting range at night."

If only Jackson could directly ask for a name.

"It sucks now," Kevin said. "When I tell people I like to shoot I get this look, like I must be some ride or die second amendment gun asshole. But it's not like that. I grew up hunting and fishing."

Bob leaned his elbows on the counter, clearly warming to Kevin's persona. "Yeah, exactly. I like the sport. The challenge. I didn't want to fire Carrie, but she was starting to talk like Derek."

A first name, Jackson thought. Halfway there.

"So you met the boyfriend a couple times?" Kevin asked.

"Before I figured out Carrie was letting him in to train," Bob said. "He would buy some supplies here. Ammunition, mostly."

"Didn't the neighbors complain about the noise?" Jackson asked.

"They were practicing with silencers," Bob said.

Exactly the information Jackson had hoped to get.

"That's what I mean when I say he's bad news," Bob continued. "A couple months after I fired Carrie, I saw his face on the Jan 6 footage of people who broke into the Capitol building."

Jackson wondered how Sara and Navy would take the news that Carrie was involved with a man who had participated in the attempted coup.

"No way," Kevin said. As if Kevin didn't want to grill Bob Millstrom, unwitting owner of the training grounds for Carrie's militia, on all the details. "And he threatened you?"

"He said he'd have all his friends at the garage wreck the place. And I can't prove it's him, but I had a bunch of bad anonymous reviews posted about the range. It's really hurting business."

"I saw a guy I knew at the Capitol riots," Jackson said. "An old army buddy. I turned him in to that FBI tip line." If Bob had reported Derek, they should be able to find a record in the FBI's database.

"Another friend of mine recognized Derek. They're both ex-military," Bob said. "He's a police officer now. He said he turned Derek in. I'm glad I didn't have to do it."

Jackson was keeping mental notes. A mechanic named Derek whose name should be in the list of people reported to the FBI. The details about the militia's weapons were helpful. They probably weren't going to get any more out of the struggling small business owner Bob Millstrom today. Dragging out the conversation much longer would make it look like they were here to interrogate him.

"Hey man," Kevin said. "Your place looks great to me. I'm going to be out here in a few days just to practice."

Jackson noticed how sad Bob's smile looked. The business must really be in trouble.

"Sure," Bob said. "We'd love to have you. And if your friend wants to practice and you're willing to supervise, I'll throw in one gun rental for free."

Jackson had earned an expert marksmanship badge every year he'd been in the army. "I'd love to learn the basics before the bachelor party," Jackson said.

"Told you I didn't need the meet-cute story." Kevin said once they were outside.

"I'll be sure to work in the details when we come back to practice," Jackson said.

"We need to see where Derek was training," Kevin said. "I'd bet anything his group left casings behind. That'll tell us more about the weapons they're using."

"I'm not sure we're going to be able to find brass from six months ago, especially if they were training on the same ranges that other people use," Jackson said.

"Nothing there is getting used," Kevin said. "Did you see the dust on everything?"

"Well, either way." Jackson steered the car back onto the highway, eager to get back to the office. "I think we can get some more details on

Derek if we get him talking some more. And more on Carrie too. If Carrie and Derek met online, I'll bet Navy can find the trail."

"I'm glad you ignored me when I told you not to get involved with her." Kevin leaned his seat back and closed his eyes.

"Does Warren have you working late nights?" Jackson asked.

"Late nights and early mornings. I've been splitting my time between tutoring Irving online in the afternoons and watching the parking lots of bars, coffee shops, and clubs."

"You suck at vacation," Jackson said. "How is the little brother/big brother thing going?" Jackson asked.

"I feel I am growing as a person because I am learning how to mentor a child." Kevin's characteristic deadpan sarcasm was delivered without even opening his eyes. "That's the answer you wanted, right?"

Jackson grinned. He hadn't expected Kevin to devote so much time to Irving. "I think you might be learning something despite yourself. With Warren's coaching and some more time with Irving, you might even learn how to deal with people who don't have to listen to you."

"You know Sara was being ridiculous this morning," Kevin said.

Jackson parked the car at FBI headquarters. "Even so. Warren got more information out of Sara and Moss than you did."

"I think from now on I'll just try to stay out of her way."

"Probably wise," Jackson said. "I bet she hits as hard as Navy does. When she puts her mind to it."

Kevin put his badge against the card scanner to open the front door. The receptionist at the front had already left. Jackson checked his watch. After six. They had been gone longer than Jackson had expected. Only Warren and Navy were left in the conference room upstairs.

"Learn anything useful at the gun range?" Warren asked.

Jackson glanced at Navy, wondering how she'd take the news. "Carrie has a boyfriend, Derek. Or she did a few months ago. He was in the group that stormed the Capitol building in January. And Carrie was sneaking him and his militia in to train at the gun range. That's why Carrie got fired."

Navy set her pen down carefully. "So she is dangerous."

"We don't know if Derek is with Patriot Front or not," Jackson said.

Warren was taking notes. "Anything else we can use to track down Derek?"

While Kevin was giving Warren all the details, Jackson watched Navy. He knew she was upset by how she seemed almost frozen, staring down at the pages in front of her. He also knew better than to try and discuss it right now. Navy didn't like to be reminded she was human. And she especially didn't like to show emotion in front of other people.

"And he should be on your list already," Kevin told Warren. "The gun range owner said Derek had been reported to the FBI tip line."

Warren pulled his laptop over. "There aren't any reports about a Derek who lives in Iowa. You sure you trust the gun range owner?"

"Bob said he didn't report Derek," Jackson said. "A mutual friend did. Bob said he and Derek both knew a police officer. And the police officer recognized Derek too."

"And this report should have been made months ago?"

Jackson nodded. "Several months ago."

"Someone's lying to you." Warren sounded troubled. "Either the gun range owner . . ."

"Or the police officer is lying," Navy finished. "Moss was working with the police about the incidents at the house. Did you get a name for the police officer?"

"No name yet," Kevin said. "But I promised to come back for practice before we schedule my bachelor party."

"Quick engagement," Navy said. "Do we get to meet her?"

Kevin rolled his eyes. "It was a cover, okay. And it was a good excuse for us to visit again so we can learn more about Carrie and Derek and their military cosplay sessions."

Warren packed up his notes. "I'll have Tom run down the leads tomorrow. I want you back at the gun range as soon as you think you can go without looking suspicious. We need a name for that cop. But for now, little brother, we have dinner with the family."

"Kevin has a brother?" Jackson and Navy asked at the same time.

"Thanks, Warren," Kevin said. "They didn't know."

Warren's forehead creased. "I'm sorry. You just talk about them so much, I assumed."

Kevin brusquely swung the leather strap of his briefcase over his shoulder. "It's fine."

Jackson cleared his throat. "What time should Navy and I be here tomorrow?"

"Early as you like. I'm here by six thirty." Warren locked up the conference room behind Jackson and Navy.

"Do you normally work twelve-hour days?" Navy asked.

"For this case I am. Until I catch these bastards," Warren said.

The physical resemblance between Warren and Kevin wasn't strong. But Jackson recognized Kevin's drive for justice in Warren. Anything for the mission.

"We'll be here too," Navy said. "We need to find her."

Kevin looked like he was about to say something, but instead he just walked away.

"I really didn't know." Warren watched as Kevin turned the corner of the hallway. "I didn't mean to . . ."

"I'm sure he'll be fine tomorrow," Jackson said. "As long as Navy and I don't bring it up."

"So unfair," Navy muttered.

Warren's eyes crinkled. "What's unfair?"

"I've worked with the man for two years now. This is the first hint I get that Kevin is human and I'm not supposed to ask?"

Jackson put an arm around her shoulders. "I know, I know." He pulled off his mask as they left the building, and Warren and Navy took off their masks too.

Navy's mask had been hiding her worried expression. "What am I supposed to tell Sara? About Carrie's boyfriend?"

"Nothing," Warren said. "There's a lot we don't know. And what would Sara do with the information anyway? Other than possibly get herself in trouble."

Jackson was more worried about the police officer who had possibly been covering for Derek. "We do need to tell Sara and Moss to be careful not to tell anyone where they're staying. Not even the police working their case."

"But I can't explain?" Navy asked.

"Nothing specific," Warren said. "We don't have any useful information to share right now anyway."

Navy stepped away from Jackson. "Got it. Tell no one anything. I'm so tired of these fucking secrets."

"I—" Jackson started, but Navy was already walking away.

"Guess it's that kind of day," Warren said. "Welcome to the team."

Welcome to the team indeed, Jackson thought.

Chapter 13

Sara jumped up as soon as she saw the gym door open. "Mark has been back for an hour, where have you two been?"

Navy's smile seemed forced, and Jackson looked tired. "Wrapping up a few things," Navy said.

"Well, you're just in time for pizza," Sara said. "We drove halfway across town to get your favorite."

Navy dropped her backpack near her sleeping bag. "You didn't have to do that."

"It was a good excuse to get out," Sara said. "They started giving us looks at the coffee shop after being there for five hours so we left, and then there was nothing to do but . . . sit here."

"It's not the most exciting place, I know," Mark said. "I have a TV in storage I could pull out."

"Not complaining," Sara said quickly. Sara hadn't meant to sound ungrateful. But spending an afternoon waiting for news had her feeling stir-crazy and frankly, a bit insane.

"I know." Mark didn't seem offended. "I'll go find it."

Sara led Navy and Jackson to the table Sara had set up in one corner of the gym. Some of the mats had been pulled up against the wall to make space for the table and chairs. "Welcome to the dining room."

"Nice redecoration," Navy said. But Navy's enthusiasm from earlier in the day was gone.

Sara was eager to ask for *all* the details on the case, but Navy seemed so tired. Maybe Sara should give Navy a few minutes to eat and relax.

"Let's e—" Sara started but a cacophony of squeaks and rattles interrupted her. Mark was pushing a cart through the hallway off the main gym area. He steered the cart through the narrow strip of concrete not covered by mats.

The cart held a massive TV, the old CRT style now filling up electronic recycling places everywhere. Thick dust caked the screen and all the plastic sides.

Mark coughed, probably from the dust cloud behind the cart. "Found the TV. I'm afraid my movie selection might disappoint you, though. I have some instructional videos and a couple Bruce Lee movies."

"Is that a . . . VCR?" Navy asked, pointing to the other dust-caked piece of equipment on the cart.

"Why throw it away if it works?" Mark asked.

Moss looked closer at the pile of videos. "Half of these are romantic comedies."

"I, uh, forgot," Mark said. "Those must have been left behind by someone else."

Moss put a hand on Mark's shoulder. "Don't be ashamed of being in touch with your feelings."

"Someone said something about pizza?" Mark said, not so gracefully changing the subject.

Sara took a second to enjoy the rare moment of levity. She and Jackson and Moss and Mark, despite looking a bit embarrassed, were all smiling. Then Sara realized someone was missing.

Navy was hunched over pizza and a can of pop, one hand scrolling on her laptop. Navy barely acknowledged the rest of them, even as Navy moved to make space for everyone to sit at the table.

Sara recognized the images on the screen—the PDFs Navy had captured of Carrie's social media feeds earlier.

"In all seriousness," Moss said. "That scene in *Hope Floats* where Sandra Bullock just sits on the steps while her daughter tries to run after the dad's car, because the dad is leaving the daughter behind and the daughter won't listen to her . . . still gets me. Every time."

"I'm sure we'll have plenty of time to rewatch every single movie here," Sara said. The indeterminate, long confinement in their house because of COVID had been bad enough. None of the trips she used to take. Few indoor visits with friends. Now she felt the world shrinking again.

"Yeah, I know." Moss' smile wavered. "Navy, was there any news on our case this afternoon?"

"A couple new leads to look into, but nothing definite yet." Navy didn't look up from her laptop.

Someone who didn't know Navy so well might think Navy was being dismissive. Sara knew differently. Navy was avoiding a difficult conversation.

"That's all you can tell us?" Sara asked carefully. Nerves, fatigue, and impatience were testing Sara's self-control. Sara had agreed to back off because she thought Navy would keep them updated.

"We have some new information," Jackson said. "But nothing definitive yet and—"

Sara cut Jackson off. "Navy, would you shut your laptop for one damn minute and talk to us?"

Navy sighed then wiped her hands clean before she closed her laptop. "It's like Jackson said. We learned a couple new things from a source. But you always want to corroborate new information before you rely on it. And that means—"

"That means you're not going to tell us anything," Sara said.

"When there's information worth sharing with you, I will," Navy said.

"Unbelievable." Sara threw her napkin down on the unfinished pizza slice on her plate. The pizza Sara had gone out of her way to get for Navy. "We're really doing this all over again? Moss and I are in danger and you're going to keep secrets from us."

"Sara, I—" Navy fidgeted with the corner of a pizza box. "I didn't tell you what I knew after Amsterdam because it would have put you in danger too. I was protecting you. I'm still protecting you. I promise."

"By treating us like children," Sara said. "Moss, would you back me up here?"

Moss looked down at the table before answering. "It doesn't feel great, I'll admit."

"Exactly!" Sara said.

"Let me finish," Moss said. "But I see Navy's point."

This was not the backup Sara had been expecting. "You're on Navy's side."

"I'm on our side." Moss glanced at Jackson and Mark. "Navy, do they know about ..."

"Theo?" Navy grimaced. "Mark doesn't. But it's fine."

"I can take a walk," Mark said. "If you want me to."

Navy shook her head. "Really, it's fine. I'm finally over it."

"What does any of this have to do with Theo?" Sara said.

"Just . . . hear me out," Moss said. "Do you remember when Navy was at the shelter you volunteered at? After she left Theo?"

Of course Sara remembered.

"And you told me that Theo kept calling the front desk for days, saying he knew Navy was there. And he said he was going to come break down the door. Or tell you that he was going to kill himself if Navy didn't come back."

Navy's eyes widened. "You never told me any of this."

"Because it didn't matter," Sara said. "Lots of assholes do it. Theo didn't actually know you were at the shelter. He wasn't actually suicidal. He just looked up every shelter in town and said the same thing. I know because we worked with the other shelters. We were lucky because we happened to get the officer who initially arrested Theo when I reported the threatening calls. The officer visited Theo to get him to back off."

"I'm glad you didn't tell me," Navy said. "I might have gone back to him because I didn't want anyone else to get hurt."

Sara dropped back into her chair, stunned. "That's not fair," she told Moss.

"You knew Theo was bluffing, and you knew Navy wouldn't understand that Theo was bluffing," Moss said. "And you didn't tell Navy because you knew what Navy might do."

"This is different," Sara insisted weakly. It was different, Sara thought. Because if Sara couldn't be angry at Navy for keeping secrets, if Sara couldn't do anything but sit around and wait, what the hell was Sara supposed to do? "The people who left the noose on our lawn aren't bluffing."

"I don't think they're bluffing either," Navy said finally. "But that doesn't change anything. None of the details I learned today are going to help you or give you something useful to do. So better not to tell you. I'm not—" Navy stopped herself. The aroma of sausage, pepperoni, and garlic hung in the awkward silence. Navy clearly didn't know what to say, and Sara didn't know what Navy could say that would make Sara feel better.

"I'm not trying to treat you like a child," Navy said. "But I am going to help you, as best I can. And right now, that means I'm not going to tell you everything. I hope you can understand."

"I'll try," Sara said. Navy's friendship meant a lot to Sara. They had managed to remain close even after Navy moved away. "Might take me a bit," Sara added.

"That's fair," Navy said.

"And it would be easier, if you don't shut me out."

"Guess we both have something to work on," Navy said.

Sara looked in surprise at Moss. "Are you . . . tearing up?" she asked.

"In the most manly way possible," Moss said. "Mark understands."

Mark and Jackson both laughed. Navy managed a smile.

"Warren wanted us to pass along one thing," Jackson said. "You should be careful about telling people where you're staying. Even on the local police force."

Jackson hadn't given Sara this warning earlier. "And is this related to something you learned today?" Sara asked.

"Nothing definite," Navy said. "Once we confirm a few details, we may be able to tell you more. But just . . . be careful for now. Even with the police who are working on your harassment case."

"Moss, are you okay?" Sara asked. Moss looked shocked.

"Should I not have reported what happened? What the hell was I supposed to do?" Moss asked.

"Exactly what you did," Jackson said. "How did the police officers you spoke with react?"

"Appropriately horrified," Moss said.

Jackson nodded. "That's a good sign. And everything you told us was in their report. Like I said, I think you did the right thing. We're just being extra cautious."

Sara found herself staring at a streak of dirt on the wall, trying not to be overwhelmed. She felt as if she were on a boat in rocky seas, locked below deck. Sara didn't know what was going to happen or who she should trust or how long the storm would last. She only knew that she felt nauseous and mildly terrified and oh so very, very tired.

Chapter 14

Navy liked working best in the shooting range at Mark's gym. The conversation over dinner had wrung her out emotionally and the soundproofing meant she couldn't hear any of the conversations in the gym. And no one else could hear her clicking away on her keyboard. Or be kept awake by the light of her laptop when they wanted to go to bed.

So stupid, Navy typed into the chat screen open on her computer. A gray set of dots indicated something was being typed in return.

Navy heard a knock on the door and Jackson entered.

"Working late again?" Jackson asked. He leaned on the counter next to her, his arm brushing hers.

Navy had turned one of the shooting stations into a sort of standing desk. "Not that late."

Jackson raised an eyebrow. "It's one a.m."

"I, um, knew that." Navy hadn't noticed. "I think I'm making headway with this Facebook group. It's not just racist bullshit. There's a lot of crossover with the election conspiracy crowd."

"I know better than to try and convince you to stop working on something," Jackson said.

"But?" Navy smiled.

"I'll only point out that last night was a pretty late night too, getting back from the campground and all."

Was it only last night that Navy had sat around the campfire and listened to Carrie's terrifying rhetoric? It must have been. "Tom said if you're only on during work hours people get suspicious."

We don't have to accept a rigged election. A reply had appeared in Navy's chat window.

Jackson read the screen and whistled softly. "Never thought I'd see conspiracy theories like this here."

"I like being undercover this way," Navy said. "I don't have to hide my expression."

It's too late, Navy typed back. Everyone has moved on.

Navy couldn't seem too eager to help. "I hate letting them think I agree. Just like it felt gross to lead Carrie on."

"You okay after all that stuff came up with Sara today?" Jackson asked.

The real ballots will prove we're right, came the reply.

"Sure." Navy leaned into Jackson's arms for a second and watched the cursor on her screen. On the other end of the connection, a probably racist and potentially violent threat waited for her answer.

`Real ballots?` Navy asked.

"I don't believe you," Jackson said.

"Nothing will get better until we find the people threatening them," Navy said. "So I'm going to find them."

Jackson's forehead creased.

"I know what you're going to say, and I don't want to hear it." Navy turned away from Jackson. At the end of the lanes she could see the paper targets where she had practiced her first shots. With a gun Jackson had left for her that she didn't want, but in the end had narrowly saved her life. "Maybe we find them, maybe we don't. But right now, I need to believe we're going to find them."

"Pragmatic optimism, I get it." Jackson looked over the open social media profile page. "What's your cover?"

"Frustrated upper-middle-class white woman and entrepreneur. I own a gym that went out of business during the pandemic." Navy switched over the social media window in the browser and showed Jackson some of the posts. "Tom's a genius at building these profiles but he can't be active on all of them at the same time. He's been posting for weeks as her, complaining about big government killing her business. Rattlesnake has been engaged with her posts since the beginning." Navy clicked into his profile page, with a big banner of the DON'T TREAD ON ME flag.

Jackson rubbed his face. "His nickname is Rattlesnake? Seriously?"

They're hiding them in the statehouse basement, Rattlesnake said in the chat.

"The statehouse is what everybody here calls the Capitol," Navy said. "He asked to move the conversation to Telegram. That means he wants to share more details. This is good."

Why haven't I heard about this????!! Navy replied.

"And you have to have stay up and do this tonight because?" Jackson rubbed her arm lightly.

The touch broke Navy's focus and reminded her she was in fact, a little tired. And maybe sleep would be a good thing. "I can't just ask him to tell me his plan," Navy said. "I have to set the groundwork. Get little bits and pieces."

"Okay," Jackson said. "But staying on too long might be a little suspicious too, don't you think?"

"Touché," Navy said.

WATCH THE VIDEO, Rattlesnake said then posted a link.

With a few quick commands Navy downloaded the video to archive it, then opened the video in a browser. The dramatic music and scenes full of shadow would have been funny if the video weren't so serious. A title appeared on the screen "Crime reenacted by Patriots for youR education."

"Could have used a proofreader," Jackson muttered.

Men in suits with furtive expressions were emptying boxes from a truck. The dark, gritty loading dock could have been any loading dock at any warehouse in town. Then they loaded new boxes into the truck. The stilted dialogue was as terrifying and ridiculous as the opening scenes. The real ballots had been stolen and replaced with ballots that elected the wrong president. The election was stolen by a vast, government conspiracy to control you. COVID-19 was an imaginary disease, a pretext for control, meant to distract from the stolen election.

"People actually believe this shit?" Navy said.

"This is as bad as terrorism propaganda," Jackson said. "Slickly produced too."

`Are you watching?` Rattlesnake asked.

`OMG I can't believe it,` Navy said. And she couldn't, but not in the way Rattlesnake thought she meant.

`BELIEVE IT,` Rattlesnake said.

"He likes his caps lock," Jackson said.

"That's probably enough for tonight," Navy said. "Jane the former gym owner would probably need to think on this conspiracy theory overnight before she commits to the cause."

`After that, I probably won't be able to sleep, but I have to try. Job interview in the morning,` Navy typed.

`Good luck,` Rattlesnake typed. `Hope you don't lose your job to a n*****.`

"Jesus," Jackson said. "The persecution complexes these people have."

Navy stared at the screen. She'd been talking to Rattlesnake for an hour now and probably shouldn't be surprised. But the casual hatred still shook her. Just to be sure, Navy tallied up the technical measures she'd taken to protect her actual location from Rattlesnake. Two proxies so the IP location data would be wrong. Fake profiles. And still, Rattlesnake's hatred left a cold fingerprint on her heart. Navy had spent most of her adult life in Des Moines. And she had never known how deep racism ran in her town.

Chapter 15

Sara looked around the empty gym and sighed. At least when she was working from home, she had her home office. At Mark's gym, she had an uncomfortable chair at a small table. Next to the garbage can full of pizza boxes. She could still smell last night's dinner. And there was the silence.

Navy, Jackson, and Mark were all at the FBI office learning things they wouldn't tell her about when they got back. Moss had gone out for an errand and to pick up takeout for dinner. When had being alone for a couple hours become so difficult?

When you learned you were being hunted and one of your best friends might be involved, Sara answered herself.

Her phone buzzed. Sara reached for it too eagerly. She'd be grateful for any message right now.

Except this one. A text from Carrie.

He's saying he'll hurt me. Because I was too
stupid to get Navy onboard.

Sara stared at her phone. Carrie wanted Sara's help. After everything Carrie had said. After Carrie may have sent four people with a noose to threaten Moss. And who was Carrie talking about anyway? Did she have a boyfriend?

I don't know what to do.

Leave me alone, Sara thought.

I'm at our coffee shop. I can't stay much
longer. If he notices I'm gone . . .

So much like the messages Sara dealt with in her volunteer work. Abuse victims who were just as afraid to leave as they were to stay. Carrie had isolated herself to be with terrible people. But if Sara didn't offer a way out, Carrie would stay because those people were her only support.

Sara yelled in frustration and threw her phone on the floor just as the door opened.

Kevin cleared his throat. "Uh, hi. Jackson here?"

Sara felt her face getting red. "They're all out." Kevin was the last person she wanted to see. Especially right now.

"Okay if I wait for them?" Kevin shifted his feet. As if he actually cared whether or not she wanted him here.

"Whatever," Sara said.

"I can, um, go hang out in back room if you'd rather be alone."

Maybe Sara had misjudged him. "I had a lot of alone time already this afternoon," she said.

Kevin came farther into the room. "Good thing the floor's padded." He picked up her phone and handed it back to her.

There was another unwelcome message.

Pls come. Just want to talk.

She set the phone facedown on the table a little harder than necessary. It vibrated again. Another message. If Kevin weren't here, Sara would have thrown it again.

"Do you want to talk about it?" Kevin asked.

"Not with you." Sara felt bad for being rude, then reminded herself of how Kevin had treated her earlier. Anyway, Kevin didn't seem bothered by it.

"Okay."

Sara tried to go back to working. Two emails left to send and she'd be done. But she couldn't concentrate enough to complete a sentence. She would have blamed it on Kevin, but he was scrolling on his phone and ignoring her. She closed her laptop and read through Carrie's messages again. If it weren't Carrie, Sara would already be on her way.

"It's Carrie," Sara heard herself say.

"She's texting you," Kevin said. His tone was careful, neutral.

"She wants me to come get her. She says someone's threatening to hurt her."

"The boyfriend?" Kevin asked.

"She has a boyfriend?" Sara said. "Navy didn't tell us yesterday."

Kevin nodded. "Not surprising."

Sara narrowed her eyes. She still didn't like Navy being part of this club she couldn't join. Even if Sara understood. "After all the hateful things Carrie said. She wants me to feel sorry for her?"

"Fuck her feelings."

"Exactly," Sara said. "I don't owe her anything." She twirled the corner of her phone on the table. "But if I don't help . . ."

"Oh, we should definitely go get her," Kevin said.

"Wait, what? You just said . . ."

"I said fuck her feelings. We're not going to pick her up for her sake."

Sara tried to push aside the mountain of hurt she felt about Carrie's actions. "Because she could be useful."

"Exactly. She breaks from her boyfriend, maybe she'll tell us more about what's going on."

Sara looked toward the door as it opened again, this time letting in Navy, Jackson, and Mark.

"Don't take your shoes off, Navy," Kevin said. "You and Mark are leaving again."

"I should go," Sara said.

Navy blinked. "Maybe start at the beginning."

"Carrie says she wants to leave her asshole boyfriend and we need to go pick her up," Kevin said. "Carrie can't see me and Jackson because we already have covers."

"She texted me," Sara insisted. "I should go."

"And what if she's lying to draw you out?" Kevin said. "Carrie knows Navy too. And Navy knows how to fight if Carrie tries anything."

"I—" Sara didn't want Kevin's logic to make sense. "She'll think I abandoned her."

"I'll pick her up," Navy said. "But I don't want her here."

"I can get her a hotel room," Mark said. "We can interview her there and she'll be safe for a couple nights."

"Where should Mark and I meet her?" Navy asked Sara.

Sara shook her head to clear it. What had just happened? Would Carrie run if Navy showed up in Sara's place?

"Navy, I don't think Carrie's lying," Sara said. "You might not have enough time to convince her to come with you. You said yourself you're not as close as you used to be."

"What do you mean *not enough time*?" Kevin asked.

"Carrie said her boyfriend's going to come looking for her soon." No time to waste, Sara thought. She stood up.

"Are you trying to get yourself killed?" Kevin said. "If—"

Jackson held up a hand. "I think what Kevin is trying to say is the boyfriend possibly showing up is a good reason for you not to go."

"I don't think you're understanding the situation here," Kevin said.

Sara glared at him. "Just when I was beginning to think you're not an asshole."

"We don't need to convince Carrie to come with us," Kevin continued. "There's a warrant out for her. If she doesn't want to come, we have her arrested."

"Kevin," Navy said. "Would you back off for two seconds?"

"What do you think we should do?" Sara asked Navy. Sara could feel tears pricking at her eyes. The combined frustration of being pushed out of her house plus worrying about her family's safety—family. Could she say family now? Or was it too early? Try not to get attached before three months, someone had warned her. But already she could almost feel the weight of an infant in her arms.

"Remember when I said there are some things I'm not going to tell you?" Navy sighed heavily. "To protect you."

"Yeah." Sara crossed her arms. "Still not wild about that."

"If Carrie's boyfriend is who we think he is, he's more dangerous than the abusive boyfriends you've dealt with before. And I can't tell you why."

Sara weighed her own safety against her obligations to Carrie. She trusted Navy. Right? Yes, she trusted Navy. But she hated being kept in the dark. "Fine. I'll stay here. But you should try to bring Carrie in without arresting her. You don't want to traumatize her."

"I understand," Navy said. "You were a good teacher."

"Teacher?" Sara shook her head.

"At the shelter. I watched you counsel the other women. You have a gift for making them feel safe."

"Carrie's at Java and Namaste," Sara said. "We used to do yoga classes then coffee there most Saturdays. Before COVID."

"I'm coming with as backup." Kevin dug into his pocket. "Here are earpieces for you and Mark."

"You just have earpieces with you all the time?" Navy said.

"Always be prepared," Kevin said. "I'll make a call to have a couple plainclothes officers there just in case."

"I have to text Carrie," Sara said. "Or she won't wait much longer." She stared at her phone. What could she say? *I'm coming* would be a lie. *Navy's coming* might make Carrie leave.

"You'll think of something," Navy said. "You've been helping people like Carrie for forever."

Make Carrie feel safe. Make Carrie feel like she should trust Sara. But above all, make sure Carrie stays put. Sara typed a reply and hit send.

Don't leave.

Guilt roiled Sara's stomach. Yes, Sara was sending help. But the not the kind of help Carrie was expecting. A lie of omission was still a lie.

Chapter 16

Navy noticed Carrie's van in the parking lot of Java and Namaste. The front passenger tire was still low. But the outside was a lot dustier than last time she'd seen it. She wondered what gravel roads Carrie had been on in the past few days. Navy opened her car door but didn't get out yet. Was she really going to do this? Convince an abused women to come with her so Navy could turn her into an asset?

Better for Carrie if she left Derek, certainly. But Navy didn't like having ulterior motives.

"I'm on the patio," Mark said over Navy's earpiece. "You have to walk through the shop to get to the patio." Mark was telling Navy where she would find Carrie.

"Are you having an imaginary conversation on your phone?" Navy asked the empty car.

"Yeah, just waiting for you." But there was a lightness in Mark's tone. Navy imagined Mark smiling from whatever post he'd chosen to watch Carrie.

"Can she see the parking lot from the patio?" Kevin asked.

"No," Mark said.

"Great," Kevin said. "I'm going to check out that van."

"Sure," Mark said to finish his imaginary conversation.

The patio was an odd choice for someone who was worried about a dangerous boyfriend showing up. Was Carrie luring them into a trap? The patio was better for COVID exposure, though. And Navy had Mark and Kevin to back her up. And if Derek did show? Part of her wanted the fight. After two days of talking to racist assholes in chat rooms, it would be nice to have an excuse to punch one.

A group of women in exercise gear was stacked in line at the register when Navy entered the coffee shop. Navy ignored the ordering line and went straight to the patio. Turning Carrie would get infinitely more complicated if Derek arrived.

Mark had come in a few minutes before. He was reading a book in the corner. He didn't exactly fit in. The normal crowd at Java and Namaste was women in their thirties and forties.

"Navy?" Carrie looked around. "Why isn't Sara here?"

Navy tried to think of what Sara would say, if Sara had come in Navy's place. "She wants to help, she just ..." Navy took a deep breath. "She overheard what we were talking about at the campfire."

Carrie grabbed her phone. "So she hates me. I messed up everything. I should go."

"Keep her talking," Kevin said in Navy's ear. "I just got into her van."

"Please don't." Navy knew several different physical restraints that would keep Carrie in place. But right now what she needed were the right words. "If Sara hated you, she wouldn't have sent me."

"I don't know what I was thinking." Carrie's words came out in a rush. "Everything makes sense when I'm with the group but I can't explain it right when I'm talking to someone else. And after I drove away I started thinking about Moss and how we grew up together and so what if he's not from here but then I got back to Derek's and he was so angry I failed."

What about racism makes sense? Navy thought. What explanation would make racism sound better? Had some of Navy's words gotten through? None of those questions mattered right now. *Make her feel safe. Make her trust you.* "And you get scared when he's angry with you."

"He doesn't actually hit me."

Memories of Navy's own experiences twisted her gut. Even after all this time, she could feel the echoes of her fear. "He just yells at you until you cry." Navy had shared too much. But the words had the desired effect on Carrie.

"Exactly. And every couple argues, right?"

"Carrie . . .." Navy didn't know how to sum up what she'd come to understand in the years since she left Theo. "Abuse doesn't have to be physical." *Abuse is about control.*

"I'm not in an abusive relationship!" A couple of the women at another table glanced at them. "Sara would understand."

How is it that the victims always felt more shame than their abusers? "I didn't say you were," Navy said.

"You implied it." Carrie said.

"I'm sorry." Just keep her from leaving, Navy thought. "I just meant that it's not okay for him to do that."

"Navy, there's an AirTag hidden in the dashboard somewhere," Kevin said. "Do you think Carrie would use those?"

How was Navy supposed to work that into conversation? "My wallet." Navy looked in her pack, as if she was worried she had forgotten it. "Oh, good, it's there. Some days I can't keep track of anything. Maybe I should get one of those AirTag things."

"AirTags?" Carrie asked. She seemed relieved the conversation had moved away from her relationship.

"These little tracking devices," Navy explained. "You can put them in your wallet or purse and then if you ever lose it, you know how to find it." *Or put them in your girlfriend's car if you think she's going to leave you and you want to follow her.*

Carrie shrugged. "All I have is this old phone. Probably wouldn't even work with them."

"If Carrie doesn't know, the AirTag is probably Derek tracking her," Kevin said. "He'll know exactly where we are."

Inwardly, Navy groaned. If Derek was using an AirTag to track Carrie, he might be using other tricks. "I try and keep my phones until they die too."

"No, it's not really . . ." Carrie stared at the phone as if it were a coiled snake. "This is a phone I was given. When I spent a night at a shelter. Derek doesn't know I have it."

Navy noticed that Carrie didn't have a purse or any sort of bag with her. Carrie didn't have a cup in front of her either. Did Carrie even have a wallet? "You left in a hurry," Navy said. "That's why all you have is a set of a keys and a phone."

"Not much for him to track her with," Kevin said. "Anything that could be a tracker on her keys?"

Before Navy could think of a way to answer Kevin, Carrie spoke.

"He was just angry that I failed." Carrie was leaning back, putting distance between her and Navy. "When I'm angry, I do things I'm not proud of."

"We got you a hotel room," Navy said. Let Carrie think 'we' meant Sara and Navy. "Sara was hoping you might spend the night there."

"I'm not leaving him." Carrie was angry again. "I told you, I'm not in an abusive relationship."

"Then don't leave him," Navy said. "It's just a hotel room. For one night."

"Maybe for one night. Until he calms down."

"Carrie, I'm not—" *I'm not here to force you into anything*, Navy wanted to say. But wasn't she? Navy wasn't just stalling so Kevin could search Carrie's van.

"Are the plainclothes officers here?" Mark's voice, almost a whisper, in Navy's ear.

Navy's heart twisted imagining Carrie being hauled out of the coffee shop in handcuffs. Carrie would never forgive her or Sara. Navy would be another terrible thing in the list of terrible things that had happened to her.

"Five minutes," Kevin said. "Just keep her talking, Navy."

"Sara cares about you," Navy said. "And I know we're not close but I . . . I care too." *Because if I do the wrong thing here, you'll think I'm the monster.* "We're just trying to help. The best way we know how."

"I don't want to leave him," Carrie said.

"Okay." Navy watched two women, who must be friends, talking a few tables away. They were smiling and relaxed. She wondered when she and Sara would have a conversation like that again. Navy didn't have any guile left. She couldn't trust Carrie, but somehow she needed to get Carrie to trust her. "I was in an abusive relationship."

Carrie's eyes widened. "You? But you're successful. You went to college. You have a career. I became an EMT just to get a job that wasn't a cashier."

"Whenever I did something he didn't like, he would yell at me. At first, I tried to talk things out with him. But that never helped. Then I tried yelling back just so he would listen. But that didn't help either. He would just yell at me until I cried or he got what he wanted." Navy tapped her foot against the table leg. "Took me years after I left to understand. Everything he did, it was about control."

Carrie's shoulders and neck were rigid. Her face was impassive. But she wasn't getting up to leave.

"He yelled at me to make me feel bad so he could control me. He tried to isolate me from my friends so he could control me. He made me feel guilty for his manufactured jealousy so he could control me. And when none of that worked, he hit me."

"It's not . . . it's n-not like that," Carrie stuttered.

Navy wondered what Mark and Kevin must think of her. "I don't know what it's like for you. I can't tell you whether or not you should stay with Derek. But we have a place for you to stay tonight, if you want to use it."

"One night." Carrie frowned then looked past Navy. "Okay. One night."

The thought of having another conversation with Carrie to get her to stay exhausted Navy. But that was a problem for tomorrow. "That's all Sara wanted."

"I'll follow you in my van."

"She can't take her van," Kevin said in Navy's ear. "She'll lead Derek right to her."

"Is it drivable?" Navy asked. "Your front tire looked flat when I came in."

"Nice," Kevin said. "I'll make it happen."

"That stupid tire. It's been a problem since that nail—" Carrie cut herself off. "It's had a slow leak for month. Just won't hold air."

Carrie's secrets would have to wait.

"You can ride with me," Navy said. After a car ride with a COVID denier, Navy would be spending a night in a hotel too.

"That tire's flat," Kevin said "She's not driving the van anywhere. I put my own tracker on it, in case Derek tows it somewhere. And the plainclothes officers are here. They'll follow you to the hotel. Time to leave."

Before Derek shows up, Navy finished the thought.

In the parking lot, Carrie kicked at the now flat tire on her van. "I'm going to grab a few things."

Navy glanced around. A new car was in the parking lot. A plain sedan, with two men in the front seat pretending not to watch them. The plainclothes officers. Thank God Carrie was terrible at looking out for tails.

"Sure," Navy said. "We should get going, though."

Carrie returned with a small plastic shopping bag of toiletries and a change of clothes. Navy unlocked the passenger side and pulled two N95 masks out of the glove compartment. She tossed one to Carrie and put one on herself.

"You know I don't believe in the COVID stuff," Carrie said.

Navy had run out of patience for Carrie's excuses. As a malware analyst who could work remotely, she wasn't on the priority list for vaccinations. "Humor me," she said.

Chapter 17

Kevin met Navy in the parking lot across the street from the hotel after she'd checked Carrie in.

"I got us a room too," Kevin said.

"Us?" Navy asked.

"You have to stay somewhere for a few days. Bad luck you're the one that got exposed when you can't get vaccinated yet." Kevin pulled a small duffel out of his car. "You can get tested soon. Might as well stay here until then."

"With you." Navy leaned against her car. She had known she couldn't go back to Mark's gym right away, but Kevin was the last person she wanted to share a room with. And, yes, she had been cursing her luck. Jackson and Kevin had been on the priority list for vaccination because they did field work. Her desk job meant she had to wait her turn.

"Carrie's boyfriend might track her down, it's safer if we share a room."

Navy didn't like that Kevin was right. "At least tell me we're not next door to Carrie."

Kevin shook his head. "We're next to the other entrance. The officers can only watch the front entrance from the parking lot."

"What happens tomorrow?" Navy asked.

"You convince Carrie to work with us over continental breakfast out on the patio."

Navy sighed. "How did that become my job? Not exactly my skill set."

"You're not my first choice, I'll admit."

"Thanks."

"You said it yourself." Kevin handed her a room key. "I checked us in already. Mark is going to bring your stuff over from the gym."

"Guess you've taken care of everything then."

"Not quite. Did you see anything on Carrie's keys that would let Derek track her?"

Navy shook her head. "Literally just keys on a thin metal ring. I'm guessing she has to keep them hidden. But she did take a bag of stuff from her van." She looked at the large, impersonal hotel with all the curtained windows lined up a in a row. Carrie wouldn't be able to see who they were from this far away, even if any of the curtains were open.

"Must have been hard to have that conversation with Carrie," Kevin said.

"I don't want to talk to you about Theo."

"That's fair." Kevin leaned against the car a couple feet away from where Navy rested. A warm spring wind carried the smell of flowers and a garbage from a nearby dumpster. "Warren's my cousin. Biologically, anyway."

Why was Kevin sharing this with her? Navy was curious, but she didn't want to engage. "Okay."

"But sometimes he calls me little brother because I lived with his family from when I was eleven."

Navy glanced at Kevin. *He's trying to draw you in*, she thought. *Don't fall for it.* But her curiosity won out. "Your parents died?"

"No, worse."

What could be worse?

Kevin cleared his throat. His eyes were focused on the hotel across the street. Was he watching for a person leaving? Or was he avoiding looking at her? "When I was eleven, I had a crush. On this girl who lived on our block. And when my father found out, he was apoplectic."

Navy waited for the explanation.

"She was Black and he was an abusive racist asshole."

"You didn't know?" Navy realized how harsh her words must sound and tried to think of what to say. "I mean—"

"Hindsight is 20/20. You know that better than anyone."

Navy thought of all the signs she had missed before Theo hit her. "Yeah, I do."

"My siblings and I went to a private school, same one my father had gone to. It was a school started in the sixties when public schools were being desegregated. Our school didn't exclude Black people on paper, but tuition was expensive and the school had a reputation. Most Black families couldn't afford it and the rest stayed away. We went to an all-white church that used all the code words people used. About moral superiority and the purity of women and nostalgia for the antebellum South."

Warren had mentioned he grew up in Alabama. So Kevin must have too.

"In retrospect, it's all obvious. We never talked about racism directly, not until my dad discovered I had this crush." Kevin's narrow eyes echoed his bitter words. "But I was always the most difficult one. So when my dad told me I couldn't go near her house or see her I told him to go fuck himself."

"Those were your exact words?" Navy's mind tripped over the image of a young, precocious Kevin swearing like an adult.

"I was the youngest of the five. I learned a lot of things trying to keep up." Again, Kevin stopped and seemed to collect himself. All of the dicey situations they'd been in together, and she'd seen only seen Kevin show vulnerability once. Until now. "He slapped me. He grabbed my arm, twisted it until it nearly broke. My mom intervened." He took a shaky breath. "But not to help, not really. She promised my dad she would talk to me."

"She sent you away," Navy whispered.

"She told me she thought my dad was wrong but she couldn't challenge him. And then I realized how cowed she was by him all the time. How she always deferred to him. He had never threatened her in front of me, but I finally saw how it was."

"God, I'm sorry, Kevin."

"She said if I wasn't willing to make up with my father, I had to leave in the morning. For my safety. I tried to convince her we should all leave. Instead, the next morning, my dad leaves for work, she packs a bag for me and takes me to her sister's house—Warren's mom. And she left me there."

Navy remembered what Kevin had said to her the first time he had pushed her to talk about Theo. *I know what it's like to be betrayed by someone who's supposed to protect you. I know what it's like to have to run away.*

Navy hugged herself against the chill his words left. "You hate her for it."

"Shouldn't I? She abandoned me."

"Maybe she didn't know how to leave. Maybe she would have lost custody of your siblings."

"She never even tried," Kevin said. "She had more support than most women do. My aunt had been keeping a record of all the incidents. My uncle is a family practice lawyer and would have represented her for free."

"Still."

Kevin shook his head. "I don't owe my mom anything. She knew my dad was a bastard when she married him."

"You know it's not that simple. Lots of abuse victims come from abusive households." Navy hadn't, but she had never been taught about emotional or verbal abuse. She hadn't recognized when it started happening to her.

"So she should have stayed and passed it on?" *Thwack, thwack.* The flat, staccato sound of Kevin flicking the room card against his thumb. "My siblings are split now. One's a human rights lawyer and has disavowed the whole family. One's a pastor in a church that preaches tolerance and anti-racism. The other two have spent the pandemic posting racist memes and getting COVID from their megachurch, which has never stopped holding in-person services."

Would Navy have been as angry and unforgiving as Kevin? She didn't know. But, clearly, Kevin wasn't going to find any sympathy for his family.

"Same split happened with my mom and her siblings. My aunt told me the whole story when I was old enough. My aunt disavowed everything my grandparents stood for. But my mom married into a family just like hers." *Thwack, thwack.*

Navy had never seen Kevin with a nervous tic before.

"Both old money families, slave money," Kevin said. "My aunt has an old bible that traced the family tree back to the pre-Civil war days. I'm descended from one of the generals that fought for the South. Some of my distant cousins still own the plantation that made our family rich. A few years ago, they tore down the slave quarters to build a rose garden. They hold weddings and Daughters of the Confederacy meetings there now."

Rushing cars filled the silence that stretched between them.

"I understand why you're still upset I forced you to talk about Theo," Kevin said. "Even though that conversation was years ago. We all come from fucked up places, one way or another. You and I ran. We made something better of ourselves."

You and I, we aren't so different. Another thing Kevin had said to her.

Thwack, thwack. That nervous tic again. "Anyway. Maybe you feel better knowing my story. I've been weak and vulnerable just like you. No shame in it."

Navy bit her lip, wondering if she dared say it. "Would you be telling me that if I had never left?" She was angry that Kevin wasn't extending the same grace to all the other victims who, like his mom, never managed to leave.

"I deal in practicalities," Kevin said. He straightened and shoved the room card into his pocket.

Guess we're done with the touchy-feely part of this conversation then, Navy thought.

"My mom wasn't willing to help me or herself. She's useless to me. You were willing to help yourself. You and I, we can do some good here. If Carrie's willing to help us and leave her asshole boyfriend, she can have a hotel room for as long as she needs. If she's not, we throw her to the cops and let the system lean on her."

"That's pretty harsh." But hadn't Navy thought essentially the same thing a day ago?

"You can't rescue someone who doesn't want to be rescued. I thought you had learned that lesson already."

"I mean, yes, but—"

"But I should feel bad about it? I should torture myself if my words couldn't convince her to leave?" Kevin wasn't just talking about Carrie. "You shouldn't feel bad either. If you can't convince Carrie to help. Be pragmatic. Don't forget what we're here to do."

"I'll go get dinner for us," Navy said. Any excuse to give her some time alone before she shared a room with Kevin for the night. "Be back in an hour or so."

Chapter 18

Kevin pulled his car into the parking lot at On Target Gun Range. Warren's car, actually. This time, Jackson was the passenger. Logistics on this mission were turning into one of those brain teasers: Navy and Jackson both need a car, Jackson and Kevin are vaccinated, Navy isn't vaccinated and was possibly exposed. How do you get everyone to where they need to be?

Kevin turned off the car and waited.

Jackson finished a text and put his phone away. "Sorry, just texting with Navy."

"Take your time," Kevin said. He was staring at his phone too. "Just checking on the van. The bug picked up someone digging through the van last night, but it hasn't moved."

"You think Derek is waiting for Carrie to come back to it?"

Kevin shrugged. "Who knows. Could have been someone breaking in to look for valuables. Is Navy holding up? The conversations with Carrie last night and this morning were hard on her."

"You're talking like you're her handler again," Jackson said. Kevin was often gruff and rude, but he was careful about his agents' mental state when they were in the field.

"Someone had to be. I was coaching her through the conversation with Carrie this morning," Kevin said. "She didn't do half-bad. Convinced Carrie to stay one more night and even meet with Warren."

"Yeah, they're still at the interview. Navy's waiting for Carrie to finish up before they go back to the hotel." Jackson rolled his shoulders back and stretched. "Ready to get into character?"

"Always," Kevin said. He put on his character like shrugging into a skin. Responsible hunter and fisherman and loving fiancée with a best man who was a womanizer. Change the accent a bit, lean on the drawl. Kevin felt for the right muscles around his jaw, in his cheeks. An accent was as much physical as it was mental. Posture, standoffish but not angry or aggressive. Gait, slow and measured. After all these years of putting on new identities and discarding others, he didn't feel any nerves at all.

He was good at lying to people.

Kevin and Jackson put on their cloth masks and walked inside the gun range. Bob Millstrom, the owner, looked the same as Kevin remembered. Tired and stressed.

"We came for some shooting practice," Kevin said. "Hoping to rent a couple guns and buy some ammo."

"You're the groom-to-be from a couple days ago," Bob said.

"We didn't introduce ourselves," Kevin said. "Sorry about that. I'm Russ, and this is my best man Chris."

"Glad to see you back," the owner said. And he did seem glad, very glad.

He must need the business, Kevin thought.

"I don't want to make a fool of myself at his bachelor party," Jackson said. "Maybe I'll even try to beat Russ' score."

"At my own bachelor party." Kevin pretended shock. "A good friend would let me win."

Bob put some papers on the counter next to the register. "Here are our standard waivers. And I'll need to see some IDs."

Kevin and Jackson pulled out the Iowa driver's licenses that Warren had provided for their cover identities. The waiver was fairly standard cover-your-ass language. Kevin signed and pushed the waiver across the counter.

"Here you—" The door slammed open behind Jackson.

"Where is she?" The man yelling at Bob was heavyset and tall. A thick, dark beard covered his tanned face.

By the time Kevin looked back at Bob, Bob had a shotgun pointed at the stranger. "You're not allowed on my property, Derek."

Derek stopped advancing. "You're a fucking coward. You always were."

"I can have you arrested just for showing up here." Bob was remarkably calm.

Kevin backed up to the counter and saw that Jackson had done the same.

"Carrie called you to rescue her when the van broke down, didn't she?" Derek yelled.

So it was Derek who had searched the van last night.

"You're hiding her!" When Derek raised his arm in a fist, his sleeve fell back. Kevin instantly recognized Derek's forearm tattoo of the circle of thirteen stars surrounding a weapon. Patriot Front.

"Carrie's not here," Bob said. "And you need to leave."

Derek looked at Kevin then Jackson, finally noticing that they were there. "If I find out Carrie was here, I'm coming back for you, old man. Hiding behind court orders won't save you."

"Last chance to leave, asshole." The tension in Bob's posture betrayed his fear.

Kevin was still impressed. Plenty of people would have reacted worse or accidentally shot someone.

Derek yelled some more insults at Bob as he left. The door slammed shut again. A sedan backed up to the door then sped away. Kevin had already tucked the license plate away in his mind. Warren could use it to find the owner. Then maybe they would have a last name and address for Derek. Might even be the sedan that had shown up at Moss and Sara's.

"Wow," Jackson said. "You weren't kidding about Derek being bad news."

Bob slowly lowered the gun then stowed it behind the counter. "I'm sorry. You . . . I'm sorry you were here for that." He pushed their signed waivers back to them. "You're probably going to take off now. I understand."

Kevin knew it would be better for their cover to leave. But he was even more eager to know what Derek and his backyard militia had been up to on Bob's gun range. "Naw, man," Kevin said. "He's gone, right? You still good, Chris?"

"For sure," Jackson said.

Kevin took care of picking out guns and ammo. He refused to let Bob give them the second gun rental for free, even though Bob had promised to give them a deal. The back-and-forth was a good way to keep Bob distracted while Jackson texted in the corner. If Kevin had trained Jackson well, Jackson would already have texted Warren the license plate of the sedan and told Warren to keep Carrie at FBI headquarters for a while. And Kevin had trained Jackson well.

Bob locked the front door and hung a sign out saying he'd be back in a few minutes. Kevin followed Bob out a back door to a yard with sparse vegetation and some targets set at various distances. A mound of dirt rose behind the targets. A stand of trees circled the range and formed a 'U' shape behind the building where Bob had just scared off Derek.

"Thanks, man," Kevin said. "We'll probably be here for an hour, if that's okay."

"Stay until you use up the ammo," Bob offered. "You'll go over basic gun safety?" He pointed at Jackson.

"Safety first and safety always," Kevin said. A slogan sometimes used in the military for gun training. Kevin knew it would win Bob's trust.

To keep their cover, Kevin spent the first fifteen minutes going over gun safety with Jackson. As if Jackson didn't know anything. The effort was burning valuable time.

"That's enough, I think," Jackson said. "Bob's not watching at the window anymore. If the shots are fairly constant, he'll leave us alone."

"You stay here," Kevin said. "I'm going to look around. Shoot like a newbie, remember."

Jackson shot and missed his target completely. Kevin knew Jackson could have hit the target dead center. Another shot pinged the dirt. Looking back, Kevin saw Jackson's feigned concentration.

Kevin slipped into the woods. They didn't know exactly when Carrie had been fired. How many months had passed? He kicked at the layer of leaves covering the ground. Would he find anything at all?

Might as well start where he was. He consulted the compass on his watch. This path headed east. Two steps, search. Look around for any structures or targets or the glimmer of metal underneath last fall's leaves. Two more steps, search. Look around again. He couldn't afford to rush. But he couldn't take too long either. Kevin doubted Bob would be happy if he found out his gun range was at the center of an FBI case.

Two steps, search. Look. Birds chattered, hidden by the green canopy. A chipmunk skittered across his path then turned, cheeks full, to make sure Kevin wasn't following. Two steps, search. The chipmunk ran toward a downed tree for cover. No, not a downed tree. The collection of large branches was too orderly for that. A faint path led Kevin to his target. Branches had been arranged into a wall about the height of his waist. A gap in the wall led to a circle of trees. The wall extended in a circle all around him, maybe eighty feet across.

Like a child's fort. But too well-done for that. He ran his fingers over the wall the branches, tugged on the joints. Definitely too well-done to be a children's fort. Someone with survival or military training had built this.

A graying rope twisted in the wind. Kevin followed the rope up the tree. A faded hunting seat was mounted with straps to the trunk. When he surveyed the other trees he saw other hunting seats around the circle. And more gaps in the wall. He took a step to explore, then heard a soft clink of metal under his shoe. Shell casings. Lots of them. From small caliber handgun to large caliber hunting rifle ammunition. He took some pictures with his phone, using his thumb for scale. Then he stuck a handful in his pocket to bring back to Warren.

He walked to the other side of the fort to see what was beyond the other entrances and found more walls forming pathways. Too evenly spaced to be coincidence. Wherever the pathways branched or opened into forest, he found more spent shell casings. As if they had walked the pathway and stopped to shoot into the openings. Not openings, Kevin realized. Doors. This was a mockup of a hallway. Derek's militia was training to breach a building.

He took more pictures and made some notes on his phone with approximate measurements and then hurried back to the range to get Jackson.

Chapter 19

Navy chose an empty office to isolate herself while Warren interviewed Carrie. Four days until she could get tested and hopefully get back to Mark's gym with everyone else. In the meantime, she had work to do. She opened her laptop and set up her proxy connections. Well, Jane's laptop, to be exact. This was the laptop she used when she was masquerading as Jane, the former gym owner. Time to be an asshole again.

She logged into all of Jane's social media accounts to see what new bullshit memes had been posted in the last day. More New World Order stuff. Universal Music Group is actually the Freemasons. Kobe Bryant's death was planned by the elites as a masonic rite. And Corona is the devil's number? All based on numerology?

Corona is 6 letters. A is 1, B is 2, C is 3 and you put Corona lined up is 6-6. So that is 6-6-6 . . .

On another laptop, she opened a chat window with Tom.

What's this numerology stuff I see in some
of the posts? Navy asked.

Most of it is gematria, Tom said. I guess you
could call it Hebrew/Jewish numerology.

Why are these Facebook groups full of anti-
Semitic memes and Hebrew numerology?

Tom sent her a shrug emoji as Jane's laptop chirped with a
notification.

Duty calls, Navy typed. Back in a bit.

How'd the interview go? Rattlesnake asked.

Shitty, Navy said. I overheard someone in the
hallway whispering about the MAGA bumper sticker
on my car. I don't think I'm going to get it.

THAT'S BULLSHIT. Rattlesnake and his caps lock.

JaneOfTheJungle (Navy's screen name) had heard plenty of
ranting from Rattlesnake. But so far, nothing useful in drawing out
Rattlesnake's plans. Maybe JaneOfTheJungle needed to make herself a
better candidate for radicalization. I'll call the bank again.
Maybe they'll give me another extension.

Rattlesnake took a long time answering. Had Navy pushed things
too quickly?

I know a friend who runs a courier service,
Rattlesnake finally said. Decent temp work, if you can be
discreet.

Shit. Navy had been trying to give Rattlesnake an opening for
another diatribe, not fishing for a job opportunity. She had to hide behind a
screen for this entire op. Did Warren have anyone who could go undercover
as Jane? Probably not.

Sounds great but . . . a lot of people know me from the gym. I get recognized at the grocery store all the time. Not exactly discreet.

This would be work on the graveyard shift, Rattlesnake answered. You can wear a mask to blend in with all the sheep.

Midnight deliveries where her employer wanted discretion? Now Navy was getting somewhere. And if she was wearing a mask that covered most of her face, she might just be able to do the work herself. I'll think about it.

Don't think too long. The money's good and he might find someone else.

I'll get back to you this afternoon, Navy promised. *And make sure you have enough rope to hang yourself after we wrap this up.*

Tom knocked on the door and opened it. Navy pushed her chair back as far as she could. The office was small and she had been trying to avoid contact with anyone.

"Jackson and Kevin are back," Tom said. "Warren wants everyone in the conference room. He has someone with Carrie."

"Even if—"

"It's important," Tom said. "We all have N95 masks on. Best we can do."

Whatever Jackson and Kevin had found out at the range must be big. Navy followed Tom to the conference room. The piles of paper around Tom's seat had shifted a bit, but otherwise it was exactly as she remembered it from two days ago. Jackson, Kevin, and Warren were already sitting at the table.

"Good, everyone's here," Warren said. "We can get started."

Navy decided to stay in the corner, as far as she could be from everyone else. A small wave was the only sign of affection she could show Jackson from six feet away.

"Updates from everyone before we get to Kevin's news," Warren said. "Jackson, you're first."

"Derek showed up at the gun range this morning," Jackson said. "He accused the owner of hiding Carrie. Derek knows Carrie's van broke down, but he doesn't know where Carrie is."

Kevin's news was bigger than Derek showing up at the range?

"I think it's safe to assume Derek was the one who searched the van last night," Jackson continued. "And that Derek was the one who planted the AirTag in the van to track Carrie."

"I ran that plate you texted us," Dennis said. "The car Derek arrived in doesn't belong to him. Matches the description of the cars involved in several of the noose incidents, though that's not saying much. Most of the victims could only tell us dark sedan. The car belongs to another mechanic. Who works at this autobody shop on the south side of town. Could be where Derek works."

"Some good news, at least," Warren said. "Alicia?"

"I've been working our contacts at other FBI offices," Alicia said. "Kevin said Derek had a Patriot Front tattoo. We're trying to find links between the Patriot Front here to the groups in other states. The hate crime incidents don't have the same M.O. but it's pretty typical for these groups to operate independently."

Navy remembered what Meredith had said about how white supremacists use propaganda to create small groups . . . *a network of small cells of believers all over the US. Decentralized domestic terror cells.*

A network of domestic terror cells built on social networks amplifying hateful content because those posts trigger strong emotions. Carrie had stumbled onto these posts and been seduced by them. Sara's friend. Moss' friend. Navy's friend, once upon a time. Years of friendship undone by some racist memes and conspiracy theories.

"Navy?" Warren was asking her a question.

Navy tried to focus. "Sorry, what did you say?"

"Your update. What have you found out from the online conversations you've been having?"

That there are entirely too many racist assholes in the world. "Rattlesnake offered me a job as a courier," Navy said. "He says it would be overnight jobs and I should wear a mask so no one will be able to identify me. I need to give him an answer this afternoon."

"Promising," Alicia said. "And we might actually be able to send you with if your face is covered most of the time."

Warren nodded. "Tom, go."

"This Rattlesnake guy sent Navy a video about ballots being stolen," Tom said. "Been seeing a lot about that conspiracy theory. The video says a bunch of ballots for the 2020 election were stolen and replaced by ballots for the Democrats. And the original ballots are hidden in the statehouse basement. But I can't connect any of this to Patriot Front or to Derek or to anyone on our radar. Just a bunch of idiots screaming stupid things online. Nothing concrete enough to go to a judge."

"Iowa's electoral votes went to the Republicans," Alicia said. "Why do they think we're the center of an election conspiracy?"

"Why do they think Chavez is responsible when he died in 2013? Why do they think JFK is alive?" Tom threw up his hands. "Why did they think satanic rituals were happening in the basement of a pizza place? You read this shit long enough you stop trying to make sense of it."

Warren smiled. "Okay, okay. We get it. Mark's out running down some leads . . . so that leaves you, Kevin."

Kevin plugged his laptop in to the projector. "The gun shop owner said Carrie was fired for letting Derek and his friends in at night to train. But we didn't see much interesting in the official shooting range. I found this in the woods near the range. They're training to breach some sort of building." Kevin flipped through several images. Brass on the ground in several calibers. Seats attached to the trees for snipers. A structure of sorts built out of fallen branches and twigs. "I took some measurements in paces. And here's the overall shape."

A sketch of a circle with spokes sticking out of it appeared on screen. Navy immediately had a flashback to a middle school field trip. "The statehouse. That's the rotunda at the statehouse."

Jackson whistled softly. "Derek's militia is planning to breach the statehouse."

"To find the imaginary ballots they think will change the election results," Warren finished his thought. "Christ."

"We need to brief the governor's team on this," Alicia said.

"You need anyone else for that?" Warren asked.

Alicia was thumbing through her phone. "No, best for everyone else to concentrate on fleshing out the details. Especially a timeline." She got up and swept past Navy. Alicia's phone was already up to her ear. "Lieutenant. We have a situation here."

"Navy, tell Rattlesnake you want the job," Warren said. "We'll probably send you, but we can figure out the details later."

"Not too much later," Navy said. "Jane the former gym owner is a brunette. I'll need a hair and makeup artist and a new ride."

Warren nodded. "Understood."

"Tom and Dennis, I need you on details. Now that we have a plausible connection between Derek and Patriot Front and the statehouse conspiracy theory we should be able to connect more of the dots. Dig into the owner of that car. Jackson, I want you to go by that autobody shop and check things out."

Jackson nodded.

"I should work with Navy," Kevin said. "Work on setting up the courier thing."

"What about Carrie?" Navy asked. "Where does she go from here?"

"After I finish interviewing her, you can take her back to the hotel. With a patrol unit in the parking lot, she'll be as safe there as anywhere else."

"But Derek's looking for her," Navy said. "What if he shows up at the hotel?"

"I can't put her in witness protection if she doesn't want to be a witness, Navy," Warren said. "I don't even know if she has anything useful to tell us because she hasn't told me anything I didn't know already. If she has something useful to tell us and she wants to cooperate, I can give her more. Otherwise, my hands are tied."

"Her tire," Navy said.

Warren looked at Navy blankly.

"Her van was muddy and her tire was going flat when I met her at the coffee shop," Navy said. "She was about to tell me why there was a nail in her tire before she cut herself off."

"You think it's important?"

"I think if she ran over a nail on the highway, she wouldn't need to hide it. If she ran over a nail in Derek's hideaway somewhere, maybe she saw something she wouldn't want to talk about. Something *useful*."

"Maybe we can use the AirTag to find Derek," Jackson said. "Get a court order to find out where it's been."

"Both excellent ideas," Warren said. "Junior?"

"On it, geezer," Dennis said.

"Geezer? Really?"

"If you keep me calling me junior."

Navy left the conference room with crowded thoughts. Why was she trying so hard for Carrie? To prove she wasn't as heartless as Kevin? She should probably be nervous about carrying mysterious packages for white supremacists all over Des Moines. But at least it would be a distraction from sitting alone in an impersonal hotel room waiting for disaster to strike.

"Navy." Warren touched Navy's shoulder. "I'm trying with Carrie, I am."

"I know, I didn't mean to. . ." Navy wished she could read Warren's expression better under his mask. "I haven't exactly earned her trust yet either." *I don't know how to help her.*

"You win some, you lose some," Warren said. "When you're trying to uncover domestic terror cells on a shoestring budget in our current political climate, you lose a lot. We do what we can—"

"And hope the creek don't rise," Navy finished.

Warren's mask shifted. A smile or a frown? Navy couldn't tell. She went back to her computer. Somewhere in the cesspool of online hate and conspiracy there was a clue. But it was hard to keep looking through the JaneOfTheJungle's daily reading and find any hope.

Saint Breivik. Anders Breivik. Murdered sixty-nine people at a Norwegian summer camp and eight people with a car bomb.

Saint Tarrant. Brenton Tarrant. Murdered a total of fifty-one people at two mosques in New Zealand.

Saint Bowers. Robert Bowers. Murdered eleven people at a synagogue in Pittsburgh.

Saint Roof. Dylann Roof. Murdered nine people at a black church in Charleston.

Will you make it onto the leaderboard . . . in the fight for white survival?

Even if Warren's team found Derek. Even if they found Derek's whole team. There were thousands of others, inspired by the racist rhetoric people like Rattlesnake spread. Navy, Warren, Alicia, Jackson, Kevin . . . they were all trying to empty the ocean with a spoon.

Chapter 20

Jackson parked in the strip of fast-food restaurants near Road Worthy Autobody. Whoever had driven Derek to the gun range worked here. Jackson would have to keep his distance. Frustrating, but necessary. Derek had seen Jackson at the gun range. Derek seeing Jackson here would jeopardize the operation.

His only companion for the next few hours would be the burger and fries he'd picked up at the drive-through. Surveillance is never exciting, but at least with new toys Jackson would be less conspicuous.

In the back window, Jackson had placed what looked like a cylindrical portable black speaker. The glossy plastic on the ends of the cylinder disguised a long-range lens that Jackson controlled from his phone. On the dashboard, he had placed lights from both Uber and Lyft. If anyone from Road Worthy Autobody even thought to look at him, they would see a ride-sharing driver staring at his phone and waiting for the next fare.

Jackson zoomed in until he could see the entrance of the autobody shop clearly. Between bites of hamburger, he clicked on the app to take pictures as customers came and left. The photos were uploaded as fast as his cell phone allowed, where Dennis and Tom would run facial recognition searches.

Thirty minutes passed. Then an hour. The radio station started repeating the same songs. Jackson changed the frequency. He fought a yawn, took more pictures.

Man in khaki shorts with toddler. *Not a threat.*

Woman in a business suit who caught a rideshare after dropping off her car. *Not a threat.*

He knew the rules of the game were imprecise. Jackson might guess wrong. But instinct was all he had to start with. At this point, they needed leads.

A couple arrived in a truck with a gun rack and a smashed front end. *Threat? Or maybe they just hit a deer on a country road.*

Another hour. More guesses.

The car Jackson had seen at the gun range arrived. Derek got out of the passenger seat, this time wearing the uniform of the shop. Another man got out of the driver's seat, also in uniform. Tap. Tap. More pictures.

`Confirmed Derek works at Road Worthy Autobody,` Jackson texted Dennis.

Jackson switched the radio station again, found the news. More pictures. More guesses.

He heard the motorcycle before he saw it. Aftermarket muffler, most likely. Jackson's interest piqued when the rider parked the motorcycle at the autobody shop. An employee maybe? Not unless the rider was stopping by off-shift. He wore a sleeveless shirt and tactical pants, both black. Motorcycle boots. The shirt was emblazoned with an eagle, a flag, and a gun.

Too obvious, right? Jackson thought. But then Jackson remembered the stories he'd heard from friends who worked undercover in white supremacist groups. Yahoos running around in the forest attempting to slaughter goats, nearly shooting themselves in the process. Bragging openly about their plans. You don't have to be smart to be evil.

Jackson zoomed the camera out a bit to put the rider's bike in frame. Took more pictures. The rider undid a bungee cord on the back of his bike to release a canvas bag. Heavy, by the looks of it. As the rider walked to the entrance, Jackson zoomed in to get his face. But before the rider reached the door, Derek appeared from around the side of the building and waved the rider over.

Shit. Jackson couldn't get close-ups of the rider's face without adjusting the camera. Should he risk it? They wouldn't talk for long. He leaned back and adjusted the hidden camera to point at Derek and the rider. By the time Jackson had a good shot, the rider was already leaving. Jackson only managed to get a picture in profile before the rider was out of the frame.

If he couldn't get a face shot, maybe he could get a license plate. He adjusted the camera again. The rider climbed on his motorcycle and it started with a throaty growl. Jackson recorded the motorcycle making an illegal U-turn, and then the mysterious rider was gone.

Chapter 21

Sara would be lost if she hadn't lived in Des Moines most of her life. The route Mark was driving would have looked like a line of twisted spaghetti on a map. When Sara had asked Mark to take her and Moss back to their house to pick up a few things, Sara hadn't expected the trip to take this long.

"Won't be too much longer." Moss rubbed her hand. "I hope."

"A few more minutes," Mark said. "Haven't seen anyone following us yet."

"Guess I should triple-check the list," Sara said. "Make sure we don't need to come back in a few days." *If it's going to take this long every time.* She pulled up the list on her phone. Medications. Prenatal vitamins. More clothes. Her favorite lotion she'd forgotten to grab in the first hurried trip back to their house.

"Sorry about the extra time," Mark said.

"I don't mean . . ." Sara didn't want to sound ungrateful. "We appreciate it. I'm just not used to all of this, I guess."

"Hope you don't have to get used to it," Mark said. "I promise we have some leads. Just—"

"Nothing you can talk about," Sara finished.

"Yeah, sorry about—" Mark stopped the car outside Sara and Moss' house.

"What the fuck is this?" Sara threw the door open and stepped onto her lawn. "The police said they'd been patrolling and they didn't mention—"

"The three-foot tall graffiti on the front of our house," Moss said.

Better stay gone, was written in spray paint across the front of their house. A painted noose punctuated the sentence. The paint covered the siding they had just replaced last year. The windows. The door. Thousands of dollars of damage, easily. Sara stomped up to the front door and touched the hateful lines. Dry.

What had she been expecting to find? They would have come at night to avoid getting caught. The vandalism could have happened anytime in the past few days.

"These fuckers never would have done this if we'd stayed," Sara said.

"Or they would have hurt us too," Moss said. "I'm glad we weren't here."

"But now they think they're winning. They think we're running. Somehow they know we came back for our stuff and now they think they've scared us away."

"Maybe we should concentrate on the how," Mark said.

Sara looked at him blankly. "How what?"

"How did they know you came back for your stuff?" Mark asked. "We didn't even see any of your neighbors when I drove you back here the first time."

Sara wanted to kick the door out of frustration. "Are you saying our neighbors are spying on us?"

"No," Mark said. "I'm saying we should look around."

"It's a good idea." Moss bent down to examine the lights in the planting beds lining the front sidewalk. Then the lights above the front door. He scanned the yard for any other likely hiding places. "There has to be something."

"Other than our neighbors working with them," Sara finished the thought. "There has to be an explanation." A glint caught Sara's eye in the tree in the front yard. The one the noose had been hung from. "Over here!"

Mark circled the tree and pointed to one of the lower branches. "It's a trail camera watching the front door."

Sara noticed he was standing where the camera couldn't see him. "So what do we do now? Leave it up? Take it down? Call the police?"

"We have to take it down." Mark pointed to the antenna on the corner of the plastic case. "This looks like one of those trail cameras with a cell phone connection. Might even have audio too. They'll see us searching for the camera, if they haven't seen it already. If we leave the camera here, they might come back for it and get rid of the evidence."

"You're saying they can see us and maybe hear us right now," Moss said.

Sara had never heard that tone of voice from Moss before. Quiet. Angry. As fragile as an explosive.

Moss stepped in front of the camera and held up both middle fingers. "Hey, fuckers. You didn't scare us off. We're—" Mark yanked Moss away from the camera.

"We're in the middle of an investigation," Mark whispered. "Two investigations, actually. Let's not fuck everything up."

Moss, still breathing fast, shoved Mark back. But Moss stayed behind the camera.

"I get it, okay?" Moss dropped to a crouch and put his head in hands. He was whispering too. "Just give me a minute."

"Oh, honey." Sara bent down to touch Moss' shoulder. "I wanted to do the same thing."

"I . . . um . . . need to grab something from the car," Mark said softly. "Remember to keep your voices down."

"It's just not fair." Moss stood up and held Sara's hands. "We're hiding and boxing shadows. We don't know anything about them. But they know everything about us. And we just have to . . . wait? I don't know what to do."

"I don't know either," Sara said. "I trust Navy, I do. But this waiting is killing me. I want to go to Carrie and yell at her until she tells me what's going on. And if she's involved I want to—I don't know. But we're just hanging out at this stranger's place, pretending everything's fine and it's not."

Moss swallowed hard. "I should be able to keep you safe. To protect you. And I can't. I don't know how. I don't even know who I need to protect you from."

"Don't be an idiot." Sara smiled. "We aren't that kind of couple. It isn't your job to protect us. It's our job." Sara hugged him tightly and felt their mutual desperation as he hugged her tightly back. She had been this scared once before, in the basement of a mansion in Amsterdam while they waited to be executed. Navy had saved them then. But at least their enemies had been close enough to shoot. They hadn't been fighting a movement.

Would they leave if they had to? She had researched Patriot Front and regretted it. The group was national. Most major cities had chapters. Of course, Sara had known things in the United States weren't perfect. But she had never expected there to be a time when it no longer felt like her country. Or a country that wanted her.

Mark cleared his throat. "We need to get going. Get this camera down. The sooner we get it to Warren the sooner he can find out who's cell phone plan is tied to it. Do you have a ladder?"

Sara tried to clear her head. "We don't need one. Moss, give me a boost." At least her climbing skills could be useful here. Sara lifted herself into the tree and undid the straps holding the camera on. She wanted to smash it against the trunk but knew better. If this could lead back to the people threatening them, maybe, just maybe they could get their life back.

Mark dropped the camera into a cloth bag. The cloth was thick and stiff. Not at all like anything she'd seen before.

"It's a Faraday bag." Mark answered the question she hadn't asked. "The camera won't be able to send photos or location data while it's in the bag."

"And you just have one of those handy in your car?" Moss asked.

Sara jumped down to the ground. "Of course he does. God, let's hope this wraps up before you and I get that paranoid."

Mark was already texting someone on his phone. "I'll get this to Warren after I drop you off. Grab your stuff and let's go."

Sara bristled at what felt like an order, but she knew he was right. Better not to hang out here too long. Still, she stopped before putting her key in the front door. A pleasant afternoon. Sunny but not too warm. The kind of day she might have spent working outside on the patio. Before a racist gang had threatened her husband. And her. Had they gone inside the house while Sara and Moss were gone? Were there other cameras watching her?

"Sara?" Moss asked.

"I know, I know," Sara snapped. She pushed the door open before she apologized. Moss didn't deserve her ire. But she was too angry to manage anything resembling grace.

The house was as they had left it. The living room was cluttered with the contents of the closet—the camping equipment had been buried in the back. How many days ago had that trip been? Four, five? She found her prenatal vitamins in the kitchen. She grabbed her medicine too. The stack of books on the kitchen table taunted her. Books she'd read hoping she could help Carrie. Maybe she should have told Carrie to fuck off instead.

Had Carrie given their address to Patriot Front that night of the camping trip? If Sara hadn't have gone on that camping trip, would things be different? Maybe Sara wouldn't have known what group Carrie was in. Maybe, just this once, blissful ignorance would have been better.

Sara's phone rang. Not Navy's number, like Sara had hoped. It was Carrie. Sara hadn't said anything to Carrie since that last text. *Don't leave.*

"You don't have to answer," Moss said.

"I know." Sara let it ring once, twice more. She'd never been able to leave well enough alone. She tapped the green button. "Hi, Carrie."

Sara could hear a TV commercial in the background. How many hours had it been for Carrie, alone in a hotel room?

"I . . . I didn't think you'd pick up," Carrie said.

Then why did you call? Sara took a deep breath. *Don't be an ass.* "I'm glad you decided to spend a couple nights in the hotel."

"It helps. To clear my head." Carrie's voice was hesitant. As if she was saying what Sara wanted to hear.

Or was that just the morning's paranoia rubbing off on Sara? "Oh." *Say something else. Anything else.*

The TV seemed loud in the background. Sara recognized famous voices. A *Sex and the City* rerun. A show they used to watch together.

"Agent Warren says I have a choice," Carrie said.

Carrie had talked to Warren? Had Navy arranged that? What else was going on that Sara didn't know about? "What kind of choice?"

"He says if I help the FBI find my friends, he can help me."

You're still calling them friends? "And if you don't?"

Carrie sniffled, as if she'd been crying. "I might go to jail for hate crimes. Maybe for years."

Sara dug her fingernails into the table. Carrie had sent those people to her. And Moss. Everything she'd been through in the last few days was Carrie's fault.

"I'm scared." Carrie's words were soft and small. Like a child facing a nightmare.

"We're scared." *Don't tell her that.* Why not tell her? Carrie wasn't an enemy. And if showing vulnerability was a mistake, Sara had already made it. Might as well play it out. "They threatened us with a noose, Carrie. They vandalized our house."

"I never meant . . ." Carrie sniffled in the background. Maybe she was crying.

Sara didn't care.

"I told them not to do anything to you. They didn't listen."

Outside on the patio, their deck furniture was arranged just as Sara had left it. Ready for Sara to spend a morning working from the patio. Now Sara wondered if she would ever be able to relax out there again.

"I told them it was risky because Navy would know it was connected to me. I would get blamed. The police might find our group."

Carrie's new friends had betrayed her. And Carrie still had to be talked into leaving. When had Carrie become so attached to her new racist friends? And how had Sara not noticed? Sara had only seen Carrie's depression, not her vulnerability.

"They wanted the attention. They didn't care what would happen to me."

"You want my sympathy." Sara should have yelled it. Or asked the statement as a question. Instead, Sara felt a cold, hard anger pressing against her ribs. Anger at Carrie for everything that had happened. Anger at herself for feeling conflicted. Carrie didn't deserve her sympathy.

"Say something." Desperation warped Carrie's voice. "Are you still there?"

"I'm here," Sara said flatly.

"If I work with the FBI, it won't be safe for me here."

It's not safe for us here. "What do you mean?" Sara asked.

"I mean, I'd have to leave. For a while."

"Like witness protection?"

"Yeah."

Familiar music in the background tugged on Sara. Popcorn and late nights. Conversations that lasted hours. Sara had known Carrie longer than she'd known Moss. "I'm sorry." Sara couldn't quite say she'd miss Carrie. She would, but not this Carrie. She missed the Carrie she'd known. The Carrie she'd trusted.

"Do you think I should do it?" Carrie asked.

This is your fucking mess. Of course you should do it. "Who gets hurt if you don't stop them?" Sara asked. *How bad are your new friends exactly?*

"I—They didn't tell me all the details. That's why it's dangerous for me. Agent Warren says I have to wear a wire."

Sara thought of all the cop movies she'd seen. All the times when the person undercover was nearly discovered. Or was. Did she really want Carrie to take that risk? Did she really want Carrie to go back to her abusive boyfriend for long enough to get a confession? Sara heard an interrupted sob on the other end of the line.

"If I don't do this, are we still friends?" Carrie was almost begging.

Was it fair to ask Carrie to risk her life then abandon everything she knew? It was a steep price to pay for friendship. Was it a fair price to ask for redemption? "I don't know." Sara wasn't sure she would ever trust Carrie again.

Another hiccuped sob from Carrie. "You don't know what it was like on the farm. You don't know what they do to people who betray them."

Mark appeared in the kitchen doorway. "Hey, we—"

Moss held up his hand and pointed to the phone. "Carrie," he mouthed.

The farm? Sara turned her back to both of them. She needed to think. What should she be here? Friend? Counselor? Instead, her instincts had shifted to interrogator. She wanted to ask where and how and what. Where were the people threatening her? How could she find them? What would it take to stop them?

"I don't want you to get hurt," Sara said. "But this isn't just about you."

"You hate me, don't you." Carrie punctuated the sentence with more sniffles.

"Goddamnit, Carrie. Don't you get it?" Sara's anger was a relief. She was tired of holding it in. "It would be easier if I hated you."

"Just tell me what to do," Carrie pleaded. "I don't have anyone."

Sara kicked at a chair and it spun to the floor. "After what you've put us through, you're pushing this decision on me?" The Carrie she knew free climbed. The Carrie she knew helped people. "Make your own goddamn decisions." She hung up, then instantly regretted it. "Oh, god."

Sara turned and found Moss right there. "I screwed everything up. Carrie asked me if she should cooperate and I just . . . yelled at her."

"You don't know that," Moss said.

"Don't fucking patronize me," Sara snapped. The wounded look on Moss' face soured her anger. "I'm sorry."

"It's okay." Moss touched her shoulder. "I guess I meant . . . you're only human."

"You talked for a while," Mark said. "Did Carrie tell you anything new?

Once Sara had been Carrie's friend. During their talk, she had felt like Carrie's interrogator. Now she would be an informant. "Something about a farm. That's all."

Mark took Sara's phone and dialed it. "This is Warren's number. Call him right now so he can debrief you while your memory is fresh."

Sara followed Mark out to the car as the phone rang. Was this really her life now? Running from her house while she dialed the FBI?

"Sara." Warren answered with her name. Of course he knew it was her number. Her life was being dissected too. "Mark told me what happened with your house. We're getting closer to finding these guys, I promise."

"Carrie just called me," Sara said. "I might have fucked everything up."

Warren chuckled. "Well, how about we start with what she said."

Sara remembered his warm demeanor from when Warren had first interviewed her. He was good at putting people at ease. It was his job. She let herself believe, just for a few minutes, that everything might be all right. Sara knew the feeling wouldn't last.

Chapter 22

"I hate them." Navy looked at the bangs covering her forehead in the mirror. Her light blond hair had been covered by a dark brown wig cut to hide most of her face. "But thank you."

The stylist's eyes crinkled, the only part of her face Navy could see around the mask. "You're welcome."

"You have the color contacts?" Kevin asked.

"Yeah," the stylist said. "What color do you want her eyes to be?"

Navy bristled at being dressed like a doll. "Her profile doesn't really say."

"Brown," Kevin said. "You have brown eyes in your profile picture when you zoom in. Also, thicker eyebrows. Paint them in a bit, if you can. And narrow the nose."

"A photo would help," the stylist said. Kevin held out his phone and the stylist examined it. "Nice. This doesn't look like an AI fake."

Kevin shook his head. "It's a real image. Altered a bit."

"Please don't tell me we're using stock photos," Navy said.

"Those are too easy to search." Kevin was sitting on the hotel bed, surrounded by electronics equipment. He paused to consider his words. "Let's just say we never use someone's photo without their permission."

The colored contacts were just as uncomfortable as Navy remembered. She looked in the mirror and felt disoriented. A new haircut, a different color, a little makeup. Just a few changes, and she was no longer herself.

Kevin tucked an earpiece in her ear. "This is for our comms." He put a burner phone on the table in front of her. "This is the phone you'll talk to Snakecharmer on. I'm getting copies of all the text messages sent or received."

Navy nodded. "Anything else?"

Kevin handed her a set of keys. "There's a rusted Dodge Caravan in the back parking lot. The fob doesn't work, so you'll have to use the physical key. And you have a stowaway. Don't be surprised."

"A stowaway?" Navy asked.

Kevin was already pushing her out the door. "You don't want to miss your date with Snakecharmer."

Rattlesnake. Snakecharmer. Navy wondered if online trolls chose their ridiculous screen names ironically.

When Navy climbed into the van, she found a petite woman crouched on the floor tightening a bolt attached to a black box the size of a refrigerator. Bright warning labels in yellow and red covered one side of it.

Navy wasn't sure what the social protocol was for meeting a stranger working on dangerous equipment in a van.

"A couple last adjustments," the woman said. "We had to rush to get it installed in your, uh, lovely ride."

Navy turned the key and spoke to the windshield as she drove, as if she was already being watched. "Can we start over? Assume I know nothing."

The woman laughed. "For sure. I'm Kaitlyn, with the FBI bomb squad."

Navy was glad they were stopped at a red light. "The bomb squad." Kevin had neglected to mention explosives might be involved.

"Warren said one of the informants had mentioned a farm where they were making pipe bombs. He thinks Snakecharmer might be using you to deliver them."

The nail in Carrie's flat tire. Pipe bombs. Navy's mind spun. Pipe bombs created shrapnel all on their own. But if you really wanted to make a statement. If you really wanted to kill or maim as many people as possible. What was the phrase Meredith had used? *Provocative violence.*

"Anything I should know about handling these packages?"

"Don't drop them!" Kaitlyn said with a laugh. She didn't even look up from her socket wrench.

Great, Navy thought. *A comedian.*

Kaitlyn stowed her tools and sat back against the machine. "Sorry, gallows humor. Occupational hazard."

What answer had Navy expected, really? "Probably a stupid question," Navy said. "Feeling some nerves, I guess. I've never dealt with explosives before." Navy turned the van as gently as she could. Kaitlyn still had to brace with her feet to avoid sliding.

"Drive like you normally would," Kaitlyn advised. "I'm not here, remember?"

"Right," Navy said. "Apologies in advance for any bruises."

"I think you and I will get along fine." Kaitlyn's broad smile exposed both rows of her teeth. "And it's not a stupid question. Not really. Just . . . hard to answer."

Under orders from Kevin, Navy was driving a circuitous route away from the hotel before heading toward the city park where Snakecharmer's directions started.

"There are a thousand different ways to make an initiator for an IED. The trigger might be a call from the right cell phone or pressing a button or releasing a button or moving the bomb too quickly or not moving it all for a certain period of time or moving the bomb into the right area or away from the right area."

"Like code," Navy said.

"Yeah, exactly. Especially with the more sophisticated attackers using microcontrollers." Kaitlyn braced again as Navy made a final turn into the city park where the directions from Snakecharmer started.

Navy's instructions were to park and wait.

"Do you see anyone?" Kevin said in Navy's earpiece. "And before you answer, remember that from here on out always assume they're watching."

Navy leaned forward as if she were adjusting the radio, where no one outside the car could see her face. "Not my first rodeo."

"And on your first rodeo," Kevin snapped. "What did I tell you there?"

Râmnicu Vâlcea. Hackerville. The first time Navy had gone undercover. "Don't be cocky." She looked up to scan the parking lot and the tree line before ducking down again. "There's no one here."

"We're five minutes early," Kevin said. "Hold tight."

"What if the packages are bombs," Navy said. "Do I still deliver them?" Would she if those were her orders? She didn't think she could.

"Only if we can disarm them," Kevin said.

"And if we can't?" Navy asked.

"You'll lose employee of the month status."

Navy might have laughed if she wasn't going to be the one in the small metal box with all the explosives. "You mean I just run away with their bombs."

"Yep."

"Christ, K—" *No names*, Navy reminded herself. "You could have warned me."

"Would you have changed your mind?"

It would have strengthened her resolve. But Kevin had no right to assume. "No."

Kaitlyn cleared her throat. "This big fancy machine is also used for containment. It's meant to absorb the energy from small explosions."

Navy nodded, knowing that only Kaitlyn could see her response. Let Kevin wonder. Or not wonder. He was annoyingly good at predicting what people would do. It's how he made unpredictable situations somewhat predictable.

Her burner phone chimed with a message.

You're on time. Good.

Should I continue following the directions? Navy texted back.

Follow the route exactly, Snakecharmer replied. Wait for my text when you get there.

"How does he know you're there?" Kevin asked. "No one's made contact."

Navy started the car and consulted the directions she'd printed out. "Maybe a trail camera in the trees, like they left at the house," she said. "Or there's a camera on the corner of the maintenance building."

"We were assuming Rattlesnake wasn't that sophisticated," Kevin said. "Maybe Snakecharmer is."

"When do we get the packages?" Kaitlyn asked.

"Don't know yet," Kevin said. "Snakecharmer's directions take us to a mall parking lot. I doubt the exchange is there."

"Snakecharmer is trying to make sure we're not followed?" Kaitlyn asked.

"Likely," Kevin said. "But I've looked at his comms and I get the sense it's more than that. He likes the control. A bunch of these psychopaths do."

Navy shivered. She was following a twisted game of Simon Says to possibly deliver weapons to a violent group of racists. She thought of Wesley Swift's taped sermons, hate translated into signals on a magnetic strip and delivered all over the United States. If she were delivering hard drives loaded with the Christchurch manifesto, was that any less incendiary? A different sort of danger maybe. A longer term threat.

She had always imagined social networks as computers connected by fiber and Ethernet cables. Now when she imagined social networks she saw humans sitting at screens. She saw them as if they were a crowd at a concert. She had seen video of the Woodstock 1999 crowd jumping at the command of rock stars screaming into the mic. A quarter of a million humans pulsing like one organism. And the most chilling part. What the lead singer of Korn said afterward. *There's no drug, there's nothing on this planet that can give you that fucking feeling of having a crowd in your hand like that . . .*

"What if Snakecharmer's name isn't just a bad joke?" Navy said. "What if he really is pulling the strings?"

"Do you mean he's the group leader?" Kevin asked.

Navy tried to figure out how she could summarize everything Meredith had told her in a few sentences. "No, I mean . . . what if he's running an influence operation. Like the Russians did with the IRA but on a smaller scale."

"The Internet Research Agency that spread disinformation during the 2016 election," Kaitlyn said.

"Yeah," Navy said. "That kind of pull . . . you want control of multiple accounts. You want bandwidth."

"Okay?" Kevin said. "I don't understand where you're going."

"The farm, headquarters, whatever. If Snakecharmer is operating out of there, he wants bandwidth. Have we found it yet?"

"No . . . still waiting on warrants to get the AirTag owner."

"Fiber," Navy said, trying to hide her excitement.

"Translate, please," Kevin said in a clipped tone.

"If Snakecharmer wants a high-bandwidth connection in a rural area, the only choice is fiber. Which the ISP doesn't run for free. The property owner has to pay to dig the trench to the pull box then work with the ISP to get service."

"Which leaves a paper trail," Kevin finished. "Good lead. Can we focus now? You're almost there."

Snakecharmer's directions specified which spot she had to park in. Unlike where she started, there were people all over. Navy waited. Again.

You were talking to someone, SnakeCharmer texted. I told you to leave your personal phone at home.

"Shit." Kevin said. "He couldn't tell that from just from a surveillance camera. He has eyes on you here."

Just singing along to the radio, Navy texted back.

Turn the radio off.

"Be my eyes, stowaway," Kevin said. "Tell me what's going on."

"On it," Kaitlyn said. "She just pretended to turn the radio off."

Good, SnakeCharmer texted. No more distractions.

Fuck off, Navy thought. At least she could count on the mask hiding most of her expression.

I'm going to send you an address and a route. Follow the route exactly. Do not use GPS. You will be given the packages there.

Would Snakecharmer have eyes on her at every corner? Okay, Navy replied. The familiar streets felt threatening now. Any car parked on the street, any car following her, might be one of Snakecharmer's friends. Watching.

The directions, Navy told herself. *Focus on the list.* But she forgot the next turn and had to fumble with the the phone. Only two more turns. One more turn. She was at a gas station. No, a mechanic and autobody shop that also sold gas. Road Worthy Autobody. The place Jackson had staked out. She bent down, as if picking something up from the floor. "This is place where the motorcyclist delivered the bag," Navy said into the floormats.

"I know," Kevin said tersely. "Tracking you on the map."

Navy heard whistling and footsteps. "Stowaway, you should hide."

But Kaitlyn already had. Navy didn't even have time to figure out where before someone knocked on the window.

"JaneOfTheJungle?" asked a man holding a canvas bag bulging with square packages. The fabric stretched around the corners of the objects of whatever the bag held.

"Yeah." Navy didn't know what she had expected a domestic terrorist to look like. But it wasn't this man. Clean-shaven. Khakis and a business casual shirt. No tattoos she could see. If she'd met him on the street or seen his picture on a dating app, she would have no idea how dangerous he was.

"Open up the back," he said.

Where was Kaitlyn hiding exactly? Would he drop the bag right on top of her? Would he see the portable X-ray machine she'd installed?

"The door sticks," Navy said. "I'll get it."

Dusk was setting in. Navy hoped the dying light would make her ruse more believable. She pretended to turn the key in the back door. She jerked on the handle a couple times. "Goddamn door." This time she actually turned the key, but held on the door as she lifted it. As if she needed to pull it open. "Could you work just this once?" she muttered, for the khaki terrorist's benefit.

When the door was halfway up, Navy stopped it. "It won't go any higher," she said apologetically. The bag would fit under the door, but he couldn't see much inside the van. "This good enough? Otherwise we can throw it in the passenger seat."

"Guess it'll have to be." He slid the bag in the opening.

Not gently enough, Navy thought. If there were explosives in there. She shut the door and heard it click.

"Rattlesnake said you were having money troubles," the khaki terrorist said.

Was she being tested? "I used to run a gym," Navy said. "Government forced me to close because of COVID, and then we went out of business. Been looking for work for a while."

"The government never wastes a good crisis," he said. "Bring your van in next week. We'll take a look at that door. No charge."

"Thanks." Navy could see how Carrie got sucked in. A strategic act of kindness when you felt like you were drowning. Like Meredith had talked about. Had Derek rescued Carrie before he had abused her?

"You'll get directions on your phone," the khaki terrorist said. "The movement appreciates your help."

And having someone to blame, Navy thought. Khaki terrorist or Derek or Snakecharmer or Rattlesnake could have delivered these packages. They were paying her so it would be harder to trace the packages back to them.

"See you next week," Navy said. A message was waiting on her phone when she got back in the van. Another address. Another route. And she still had no idea where Kaitlyn was hiding.

"Don't worry about me," Kaitlyn's muffled voice said in Navy's earpiece. "Just get back on the road."

Sure, fine. I'll just keep driving around with what might be bombs. She hated silently following Snakecharmer's directions. It felt like letting him win and she didn't know what was coming next.

"I want to see if you're alone at the next stopping point," Kevin said. "Then we'll make a plan."

Navy almost nodded, then remembered that Kevin couldn't see her and Snakecharmer might be watching. She stopped in another parking lot outside another building on the outskirts of town. Her fourth parking lot of the night. But this one was empty of both cars and people. The building was dark. Navy turned off the headlights and let her eyes adjust. A large, faded sign had fallen at one end and blocked the front door. Neon beer signs behind dusty windows. A bar that had closed because of COVID, maybe. Or maybe long before. She looked for any security cameras that might be hidden along the front of the building.

There are directions in the bag, Snakecharmer texted. You have ten minutes to read them. Then get on the road.

"If you're alone, we'll let Kaitlyn out," Kevin said.

Navy turned away from the windshield before she spoke. "No one I can see. He might have a camera pointed at the van, but it's pretty dark so he won't be getting good visuals anyway. Unless he has extra fancy equipment."

"Press the cigarette lighter three times, then turn on the rear window wipers," Kevin said.

"I—what?"

Kevin's trademark impatient sigh. "Just do it."

Navy did as she was told. The rear window wipers didn't turn on. But she heard a lock click. A panel she hadn't even noticed opened on the floor where the second row of seats would be.

Kaitlyn pushed the panel to the side and took a deep breath. "Close quarters." She flashed a grin at Navy. "Pays to be small sometimes." Navy never would have fit where Kaitlyn had been hiding.

"This is a drug smuggling van, isn't it?" Navy asked.

"They're great for ops," Kevin said. "Already made to blend in and they have all sorts of secret compartments."

"Let's see what we've got here." Kaitlyn opened the zipper on the canvas bag slowly. The bag was full of shoebox-size packages taped with clear packing tape. "We have nine packages." She gingerly lifted one and weighed it one hand. "Feels like a Unabomber special."

Navy looked at Kaitlyn blankly.

"Half of these kooks are just copying the Unabomber's recipes," Kaitlyn explained. "Sometimes it's an honorary thing. Sometimes just to blend in so we can't tie the explosives to a specific group. I'll x-ray it and see what's actually in here."

"Get started on reading the directions," Kevin said. "One minute down already."

Navy tried to focus on the sheaf of papers in front of her. Nine addresses to visit in order. No names. An exact route to follow to each address. A place to leave each package. "There are nine dead drops," Navy said. "I'm not supposed to meet anyone. But he has a route and an order I'm supposed to visit the addresses."

"Use the phone to send me pictures," Kevin said. "How far out is the first address?"

"Eight, ten minutes," Navy said. "It's pretty close."

The portable x-ray machine hummed next to Navy. She wondered what sort of exposure she was getting just from being near it.

Kaitlyn studied the screen for a long minute. "I have good news and bad news."

Navy wondered if she was going to die as JaneOfTheJungle, the bitter and misguided former gym owner.

"The bad news is these are Unabomber-style pipe bombs."

"And the good news?" Kevin asked.

"The good news is they aren't assembled yet. Should be easy to sub out the explosive material and hide our trackers somewhere. But I'll need time. Ten minutes per package. If I'm not careful removing the tape, they'll see the boxes have been tampered with."

"Can you do it while the van is moving?" Kevin asked.

"Not much choice there," Kaitlyn said. "What's the timing between stops?"

"Some are long enough," a new voice said. Tom from Warren's team. "Some aren't."

"Okay, new plan," Kevin said. "Forget reading the directions. I'll be your GPS. You're going to help your stowaway get tape off the packages."

Kaitlyn dug into yet another compartment Navy hadn't noticed before. "Here's a hair dryer. I already plugged it in for you."

"You want me to heat up the packages with explosive material in them," Navy said.

Kaitlyn grinned. "Only the outside. Use the lowest setting. And just heat until the tape releases. Pull slowly and gently."

Navy stared at the package Kaitlyn had put in front of her. *Oh god oh god oh god.* Anxiety pressed on Navy's heartbeat. But she had learned to listen to the quieter instincts in these moments. The instincts that told her to look for what she should do instead of what she should fear. She ran her fingernail around the circle of tape until she found the beginning.

Now, heat. Kaitlyn had already turned on her hair dryer. Navy found herself wondering how the FBI had rigged the electrical on the van to handle two hair dryers at once. Not important, she told herself. Heat. At first, she could only get the edge of fingernail under the tape. Then the tip of her finger. Then it was time to pull. If she went too fast, the tape would take some of the decoration of the box with it. They would know she had tampered with their package. She couldn't deliver a tampered package. What excuse would she make?

Never mind. Focus. Slowly and gently, like Kaitlyn had said. Navy's hands were shaking when she finished pulling the last inch of tape off. She checked the time. Four minutes had passed. She could do one more.

Chapter 23

A roadmap of Des Moines had been taped to the conference room
wall. Kevin watched as Tom updated Navy's progress with a marker.
Warren's entire team had been there all night, just as Kevin had. Seven
packages delivered. Two more to go.

"I realize it's a last-minute request, Director," Alicia said from the
corner of the conference room. "But we need a few more people on
surveillance detail." Alicia's eyes narrowed as she listened to the response.
But her voice was calm and respectful when she replied. "I wouldn't disturb
you this late except we're getting a bunch of pressure from the governor.
They're nervous about these bombs ending up at the Capitol, even though
we've assured them that the bombs have been neutralized."

Alicia's eyes crinkled in what might have been a smile under her
mask. "I understand, sir. We'll get right on it. Thank you."

"Nice play with the director," Kevin said after she hung up.

"We've been fighting for funding and people for years," Alicia said. "And now I have actual proof that a cell of domestic terrorists are planning an operation here . . . and he wants to rely on the trackers we put in packages to find these assholes."

"None of the packages have moved yet," Warren said. "Tom, can get you the locations we don't have covered yet?"

X's on the map marked where Navy had dropped off a package with a sabotaged pipe bomb. None of the locations had been homes or addresses like Kevin had hoped. So far, they had only managed to identify two people in Derek's militia. They hadn't even located the farm Carrie kept talking about. Carrie insisted that she'd never been allowed to drive the last few miles to the farm. She'd always been blindfolded, with Derek driving.

Kevin unmuted his earpiece so he could speak to the field team again. "How's the assembly line, stowaway? On schedule?"

"Negative," Kaitlyn said. Two hours ago, she'd sounded unflappable. Now she sounded tired and stressed. "I need more time to disable the last one. You got that distraction ready?"

"We're in place," Jackson said. "Waiting on your signal."

Jackson meant Kevin's signal. Kevin wondered whether he could push Kaitlyn harder or take the risk of using Jackson and Mark. If Derek was one of the people watching Navy's route, he might recognize Jackson. Even with the dark and Jackson's disguise. And even using the distraction might scare off Snakecharmer. Snakecharmer had been insistent all night that Navy follow his directions exactly and on schedule.

On the other hand, rushing the woman handling explosives seemed like a bad idea.

Kevin turned his attention to the laptop tracking Navy's location. "Go." In the background, Kevin heard cars starting. Then brakes squealing. Then yelling.

"You were on your phone!" Mark's voice in Kevin's earpiece. "Then you rear-ended me."

"You think this is my fault?" Jackson's voice. Also yelling. "Have you ever heard of a turn signal?"

The little dot on the map that was Navy's van stopped in the middle of the block.

"You have two more minutes, stowaway," Kevin said.

Who are these people? Snakecharmer texted.

I don't know, Navy replied. I swear. I'll ask them to move.

No. Just honk.

If the roles had been reversed, Kevin would have said the same. Better not to make yourself identifiable. Kevin winced a little as Navy followed Snakecharmer's orders. He was getting the sound through Navy's earpiece and Jackson's and Mark's.

"Show wraps in one minute," Kevin said.

They're still not moving, Navy texted. I'm going to be late. I'm sorry.

I'll take care of it.

Shit. "Hostile incoming," Kevin said.

"Evening, gentlemen." A new voice. Not Derek's, thankfully. "Looks like you have a little fender bender here."

"This asshole—" Mark started.

"Probably something for the insurance companies to handle, don't you think?" the polite stranger said. "The damage looks minor. And you're holding up traffic."

Kevin really wished he could see this very polite domestic terrorist. "Stowaway, how are we doing?"

"Good." A pant. "I'm good."

"Wrap it," Kevin said.

"Whatever," Jackson said, still in character. "I'm getting pictures. And your insurance card."

"I'm getting my own pictures," Mark said.

When Navy's van began to move again, Kevin let himself breathe more deeply.

* * *

Last stop is just around the corner, Navy thought. Finally. She had only been driving for two hours, but Navy felt like she'd been up all night.

"Turnoff should be on your right," Kevin said.

"She's turning," Kaitlyn said. Still narrating for Navy because she couldn't be seen talking. Even on this country road after dark. "Now parked. Gravel driveway in a field. Gate is open. No signs of any buildings. Looks like someone's hunting land."

Kaitlyn's cheery attitude had faded around forty-five minutes in, and now she looked exhausted too. Navy didn't blame her. Replacing the explosives in ten packages in that time would have been challenging even without the added difficulty of trying to keep your hands steady in a moving car.

"Drop-off location is . . ." Kevin trailed off. "Shit."

What? Navy would have asked. If she could speak.

"Drop-off location is a hollow log next to the driveway half a mile in," Kevin said.

Hunting land. Once Navy left the van, she would have no cover. All the other locations had at least been close to other buildings or people. No one else was here, except for Kaitlyn who couldn't be seen. Beyond the windshield, the moon shone weakly through a cloudy sky.

"Do you think someone's going to make contact?" Tom asked.

"Or they're trying to get her away from the van so they can search it," Kevin said.

Navy turned around, as if rummaging in the back. "I should bring my gun. If anyone makes contact, they'll expect me to have one."

"You don't have to go," Jackson's voice was neutral. Not overly protective, as he had been on other operations.

"He's right," Kevin said. "Could be multiple people making contact. The whole goddamn militia might be out there."

"If I don't go, nothing we did tonight matters," Navy said.

"That's how it goes sometimes," Kevin said. But underneath his calm she could hear his impatience. This operation was personal for him. For her too, now. Maybe Carrie could find her way back, if her white supremacist friend club was locked away for a while. Maybe that would make up for Navy failing Carrie years ago.

But this wasn't just about Navy. If Navy left the van, Kaitlyn would be on her own to defend herself.

"What about you, stowaway?" Navy asked.

"Go get 'em," Kaitlyn said.

"We can't let them break into the van," Kevin said. "They'll see the x-ray machine. If you hear anyone coming, start the van and rescue the driver. Backup is coming your way."

The driver. That was her. Navy imagined all the things that could go wrong. If she were encircled in the field and her van started without her, would the militia shoot her? Or would Kaitlyn get there in time to ram them?

Navy held out her hand for the last package.

Leaves crunched under her feet as she stepped out of the van. A slight, cool wind raised goosebumps on her arms.

"Remember paradise," Kevin said. "If you need it."

Paradise, the word she had used in Hackerville to call for backup. She followed the patchy strip of grass in the center of the gravel road. *The road must see regular use,* she thought. Would Snakecharmer risk doing this on property they didn't own?

Before long, she had spotted the hollow log and almost wished she hadn't. The hollow log wasn't next to the driveway. It was in the middle of the driveway. No one would put an obstacle like that in a road they used. Unless they were planning to meet her.

There was no way she could tell her team without breaking cover.

Ten yards away. Three. Grass rustled behind her, in front of her, on each side of her. Five masked people in ghillie suits rose from the waist-high grass like shaggy forest creatures. Bright red dots, laser sights, danced on her chest. Each of the militia members had a semiautomatic rifle pointed at her. Presumably, two more bright red dots were dancing on her back.

"Stop."

But Navy had already frozen. She recognized the voice as the same man who had interrupted the fake car accident earlier. Must be Snakecharmer.

Navy held up her hands, the package still in one of them. Should she say something? What would the good employee say? Good employees asked questions to better follow orders. "Should I set the package down?"

"Slowly," said Snakecharmer.

As Navy set the package down, she risked a glance behind her. No movement near the van. She could talk her way out of this. As long as Kaitlyn didn't have to reveal herself.

"Now your gun," said Snakecharmer.

Navy released the snap on her holster and set her gun next to the package. She felt naked without it. But a handgun against five semiautomatic rifles was no contest. She would have to think her way out of this, not fight.

Be the good employee. While telling her team what was going on. "I don't understand." Navy let her voice waver a little bit. "Why are you pointing rifles at me? I'm just trying to do a job here. I followed your directions. I did everything you wanted."

"Backup is five minutes out," Kevin said in her ear.

Snakecharmer gestured at the package. "Rattlesnake, get the package and her gun."

Rattlesnake. The man she had been talking to online. Already she was cataloging details as she'd been trained. Five people. Snakecharmer, about her height, tan mask. Rattlesnake, a foot shorter, tattered black knit mask. The third militia member Navy could see wore combat boots with a heel. Shiny, like they were new. A woman?

Navy tried not to concentrate on the red dots wavering on her chest.

"One of the other packages is on the move," Tom said in Navy's ear. "But our surveillance isn't there yet."

"The car accident," Snakecharmer said to Navy. "What was that?"

Any explanation Navy gave might make her look guilty. Better to play the part of someone who didn't know why anyone would fake a car accident. "The people I honked at?" Navy asked. "That's what this was about?"

"This package looks fine," Rattlesnake said, examining each side. Her gun had been dropped in the long grass near Rattlesnake's feet. She would never find it before they shot her.

"What about the package we picked up in town?" Snakecharmer asked Rattlesnake. "Any sign of surveillance?"

"They're moving the package to test us," Kevin said. "Tell the surveillance team to give them space."

"Already on it," Alicia said.

"Nothing," said Rattlesnake. "Coast is clear so far."

"You think I would rat on you?" Navy's arms were starting to hurt from holding them up. Yes, backup was the way. But using it would blow the operation. "I'm on your side!"

For the first time, Snakecharmer seemed unsure of what to do. A red dot on Navy's chest flickered off as Snakecharmer lowered his weapon. He turned away from her, then back.

"We could just kill her," said a woman's voice from the ghillie suit wearing combat boots with heels.

"But what if she could help us?" said a man's voice behind Navy. "We could use one more."

"I told you we should just deliver the packages ourselves," said another man's voice behind her. His voice was gravelly and nasally. "You had to go and make everything complicated."

"License plate readers and cell phone records, Aaron," snapped Snakecharmer. "Now she's on the record, not us."

Aaron. A name.

"Could have used a car from the shop and a burner phone." Aaron said, apparently the one with the gravelly voice. "Done. And now she's seen Jim's face."

Jim. Another name. Undisciplined amateurs, Navy thought. Of course, that would be cold comfort if they shot her while they were arguing with each other. Also, her arms hurt. "Can I put my arms down now?"

Rattlesnake and Snakecharmer looked at each other, considering.

"It's not like I can run away," Navy said.

"I've got her covered," said the man behind her who wasn't Aaron.

"Fine, whatever," Snakecharmer said.

"I don't suppose you can get the rest of them to introduce themselves," Kevin said in her ear.

"Easiest thing to do is kill her," said the woman.

Navy calculated the trajectory of her shot and realized the woman would probably kill Rattlesnake at the same time. Definitely amateurs. "I used to onboard new employees at my gym all the time," Navy said.

Rattlesnake, Snakecharmer, and the woman stared at her.

Good. Surprised had been her goal. "What I'm trying to say is, I get it. I'm on your side, but you don't trust me yet. You don't know me."

"Are you trying to give me a reason to shoot you?" asked the woman.

"She has a point," Kevin said in Navy's ear. "Where the hell are you going with this?"

"That's what I would tell my new employees. I don't trust you because I don't know you," Navy continued. If this was the wrong play, she had already committed herself to it. "But I give them small jobs they can't fuck up too badly. And if they prove themselves, maybe I give them more responsibility."

Not Aaron laughed. "I like her."

"Are you saying you want more work?" Snakecharmer asked.

Play into his need for control. Offer him someone desperate. "I'll take small jobs, anything. I need the money, you can ask Rattlesnake," Navy said. "And you can see from tonight. I'm a hard worker. I'm good at following directions."

"But not the smartest maybe," said the woman. "You walked right into this trap."

If only you knew why I walked into this. But showing anger wouldn't help. "I was hoping I would meet some of you," Navy said. "It's so hard, being alone. Watching all these things happen that you know are wrong and not being able to do anything about it."

Navy could only read their body language with everyone's faces covered. She didn't know if she was convincing them or not. "Like I said, I'm on your side. I want to help. Especially after watching all those links Rattlesnake sent me."

A second passed. Then several more. Navy heard actual crickets in the field around her. Were they considering her or just deciding how to dispose of her body?

"We should see if her face matches her profile picture," the woman said.

The rest of the group made sounds of approval and nodded.

Navy was betting her life on the stylist's handiwork. She lowered her mask. Someone shined a flashlight in her eyes; she blinked away stars.

"It's her," Snakecharmer said. He tapped his gloved fingers on his weapon, closer to the trigger than Navy liked. "We see how the rest of the night goes," he said finally. "Any sign you screwed us over—"

"We will find you and we will kill you," finished the woman.

Navy nodded. "Can I-can I go now?"

"One more thing," Snakecharmer said. "Your phone. The one you used to communicate with me tonight."

Shit. Navy had sent Kevin pictures from that phone.

"He can't see that phone," Kevin said.

As if Navy didn't know. She flipped it open, dropped it on the ground and stomped on it. Before Snakecharmer could say anything. When Navy looked up, Snakecharmer still had his hand out to receive the phone. He looked equally startled and suspicious.

"That's what you wanted, right?" Navy said. *Like she was trying to help.* "Now there's no evidence to tie me to you."

"I—uh." Snakecharmer stared down at the smashed phone.

The woman scoffed. "We wanted you to give us the phone. Idiot."

Snakecharmer stepped in front of the woman in the ghillie suit and puffed himself up. "We'll be in touch." Then, perhaps realizing he didn't sound threatening enough. "Whether you're in or out."

They can't even decide who's in charge. What a shitshow. Still, Navy had to convince them she was a believer. "I'll do whatever it takes to earn your trust. I promise. You won't regret this."

"Whatever," the woman said. "Let her—"

"Let her go," Snakecharmer said.

Navy turned away from the battle of egos between Snakecharmer and the woman. The two men in ghillie suits who had been behind her now faced her. Aaron and Not Aaron lowered their weapons and she gingerly stepped between them.

"Backup team, hold your position," Kevin said.

Don't run, Navy thought. Walk normally. Breathe. The van seemed so very far away. She knew the sights of their rifles were trained on her back. She knew that with enough time and tech Snakecharmer might be able to resurrect the phone and reveal her duplicity. But none of that mattered tonight. Tonight, she would be walking away alive.

Chapter 24

Navy had never felt so lucky to walk into a conference room. She hadn't been shot last night. And she had tested negative this morning so she could actually sit at the table with Warren and Jackson.

"Welcome back," Warren said.

"Where's the rest of the team?" Navy asked.

"Everyone will be here in a few hours," Warren said. "They're all out running down leads. Well, everyone except Kevin and Dennis. They're with Carrie's FBI handlers."

"Did Tom ever find that officer the gun shop owner mentioned?" Jackson asked.

"The officer who knew Derek was at the Capitol on January 6 but didn't report it to the FBI?" Navy asked. Four days ago the possibility of a corrupt police officer allied with Derek's group had seemed like the biggest threat. That was before she had begun her adventures as JaneOfTheJungle, aspiring militia member. She and Tom had mapped out a network of online accounts. Like six degrees of Kevin Bacon, but with racists. The list of screen names was depressingly long. Navy couldn't even keep half of them in her head.

Warren nodded. "That's the one. We're close, I think. Hopefully Tom will have good news for us when he gets back. We'll debrief when everyone comes back together."

"Can I ask . . . where's Carrie? Has she made contact with the militia yet?" Yesterday Navy had watched Carrie leave with her FBI handlers. Carrie had agreed to meet Derek while wearing a wire.

"You're worried about her," Jackson said.

"Of course I am," Navy said. "Especially after meeting the incompetent clown posse last night."

Warren rubbed at his chin. "Derek's supposed to pick her up in an hour. But Navy . . . I'm going to tell you the same thing I told Sara. Don't look for justice here."

That was the last thing Navy had expected to hear. "Isn't justice why we're here?"

"Yes, but you need to understand . . ." Warren closed his laptop. "Carrie made some bad choices and she's trying to make up for that. And I wish I could guarantee her safety, but I can't. It isn't fair. It's just how things are."

Jackson squeezed her hand. "Warren's right, Navy. It's—"

"Could you not play professor today?" Navy snapped. She had been pleasantly surprised last night when Jackson didn't try to talk her out of walking out into the field. But she hated when he had this expression. Like a worried professor afraid his new student couldn't grasp today's lesson. "I get it, okay?"

Jackson and Warren exchanged a look in the awkward silence that followed. This, too, was familiar. Navy might have graduated to unofficial junior agent status, but she would never feel like she was on the team. Maybe she should be grateful she couldn't see Carrie as just an asset. Or Navy should stop asking questions when she didn't want to know the answers. Navy remembered something Jackson had said to her once.

We're—uh—not supposed to get involved with assets. Navy had been an asset when they met.

Jackson thought he understood everything. But he would never understand what it meant to be a pawn in someone else's game. To know that a group of faceless people had decided her life was worth less than achieving an objective.

"Been doing this too long, I guess," Warren said.

Navy wouldn't apologize. "You said we shouldn't be looking for justice. But Carrie deciding to risk herself to help Sara, that's some sort of justice, right?"

Jackson considered Navy's question for a long minute. "Never thought of it that way, I guess."

"What's our assignment for today?" Navy asked Warren. The conversation was veering dangerously close to a discussion on feelings.

"Following up on your lead to find Snakecharmer's den," Warren said. "I sent you a list of fiber runs requested by customers within the past five years around Des Moines."

"How many are there to go through?" she asked.

"Only a hundred or so." Warren smiled. "Congratulations?"

The distraction would be nice, actually. Navy's thoughts were full of dark fields and guns and graphs of overlapping starbursts. Each point was a person who might decide to pick up a knife or a gun or make a bomb and act out the plan Louis Beam had outlined in 1982 with a Commodore 64 and a BBS. Stochastic, provocative violence. Meredith had offered to help Navy. And there were no secrets left to keep—Carrie was already an FBI informant. "While I work on that, I have someone you might want to talk to," Navy said.

Warren raised an eyebrow.

"Before I came down here, I talked to someone in my office who maps terrorist networks," Navy said. "Meredith said these white supremacist groups use provocative violence. Violence that's designed to inspire other violence—whether against them or for them."

"Meredith the snake charmer?" Jackson asked.

Apparently Meredith had a reputation. "Yeah," Navy said. "And when Sara told me about her phone call with Carrie, I remembered what Meredith said about provocative violence. Carrie said she'd warned the group about attacking Sara's house. That attacking Sara's house would bring in law enforcement. But Derek didn't care. That's what Derek wanted."

They wanted the attention. They didn't care what would happen to me.

"I'm not following," Warren said. "Why would Derek's group want to get busted?"

"I don't completely understand myself," Navy said. "Maybe they're betting on not getting caught until after they bomb the State House and then embarrassing the FBI."

"Derek doesn't seem like a chess player," Warren said.

"White supremacists have made stupider plans," Jackson said. "Derek could be egotistical enough to assume we can't stop them. And there's that cop Tom is tracking. Maybe they think the cop will be able to get them proof the FBI knew."

Warren chewed on his lip. "It's a theory."

"Right, I know, just a theory," Navy said. "But Meredith had a lot of background on these groups. Like a history textbook full of background."

"And she trains snakes," Warren said.

"One snake. One time," Navy said. "Well, as far as I know. She might have escaped from more than one prison."

"Huh." Warren took the number Navy wrote down. "Well, should be an interesting conversation at least."

"I'll help Navy with those dig permits," Jackson said. "Enjoy your history lesson."

Navy grinned. "It's worth it, I promise."

Warren left the room with his phone on his ear.

"He said one hundred *or so*." Navy shifted her laptop so Jackson could see the folder listing 170 files. "This is almost 200. There's too many to go through one by one."

"What about the data you and Tom have gathered?" Jackson asked. "There must be something to filter this list."

"We could compare the list of addresses with property records for the people we've identified already." Navy switched to the Maltego window. Nodes representing people, places, and social media networks floated in starbursts that radiated out from Carrie and Derek. "I'll need to do some data entry."

"That'll give me some time to look up the records on that property from last night," Jackson said. "One of them might own it. Also, a few of the packages were picked up. I can research those addresses too."

"Ugh." Navy clicked on the first file. Messy handwriting on a low-quality scan. The second was the same. "These are images, not text. And the address isn't even in the same place on all the forms."

Jackson rubbed her hand. "We're out of the apartment together, and neither one of us is in mortal danger. Things could be worse."

"Are you saying I should think of this as a date?" Navy had to admit it had been a long time since they'd had anything resembling one.

"Once I get us some coffee, it's definitely a date."

Hours and addresses blurred together as Navy sifted through the documents Warren had sent her. When she'd proposed looking through permit records she hadn't expected there to be so many houses with fiber outside of the city. Maybe there were more rural gamers in Iowa than she thought.

Navy rubbed her eyes. She was done. Probably.

"Ready for some more addresses?" Jackson asked.

"Just need to double-check . . ." Navy ran a few commands on her terminal and compared the numbers. From 170 files she had pulled 170 addresses and names. Each file had been moved to a new folder once she'd visually confirmed the right address and name had been pulled out. She scanned the list one last time, looking for obvious typos. A couple small typos were okay. Her Maltego integration could do partial matches. "Yeah, we're good. I think."

"Why don't you let me type in the new addresses?" Jackson said. "You haven't left that chair in two hours."

Navy smiled. "Neither have you."

"Actually, I did. You didn't notice." Jackson pulled the laptop in front of him. "I even refilled your coffee."

"Which I also didn't notice?" Navy guessed.

"You're cute when you're focused. But you should probably take a break."

Navy felt her chair move. When she looked down she saw Jackson's foot pushing her chair away from the table. "Couldn't hurt to stretch a bit, I guess." Navy stood up and laced her fingers together, then stretched her arms over her head. She checked the clock on the wall. Correction, she hadn't moved for two and a half hours. She rolled her shoulders to loosen them. Hopefully there would be time for a sparring match when they got back to Mark's gym tonight.

"Done," Jackson said. "What do I hit next?"

"Nothing." Navy sat down, refreshed. "Time for me to drive." So often Navy felt like the junior agent or the trainee. She enjoyed the times when she could be the expert.

The graph was disappointing. None of the addresses she had spent hours pulling out of the permits connected to any of the nodes on her graph. None of the addresses Jackson had added connected either.

"Wait, there's something wrong with the data," Navy said.

"What do those red symbols mean?" Jackson pointed to a few red exclamation points in a sidebar.

"There are some invalid nodes. The data doesn't match the type."

Jackson's face was blank. "A what now?"

"Let's see what you entered." Navy skimmed the list of data Jackson added. "Some of these are names. They should be entered in a different section." As she was talking, Navy cut and pasted the names into a different list. She generated the graph again.

"Bingo," Jackson said. "We have a new connection."

"Maybe? Wait—" Navy frowned.

"What's wrong?"

"This new connection, it's not to any of the people we've been tracking. It's between two datasets we added today." Navy hovered the mouse over the thin line. "The person who owns the hunting land I drove to last night also pulled a dig permit for another address. Walton Stoppert."

"Walton? That's a name from another century. Can you look him up in the driver's license database?"

Navy double-clicked on the node. A small window popped up with more details. "Walton Stoppert. Lives at the same address he pulled fiber for. Born . . . that can't be right. There's no death certificate. He'd be—" Navy tried to do the math in her head.

"Almost 104 years old," Jackson said.

"Wait, that last name." Navy typed in the search bar. Three of the nodes highlighted when she hit enter. "Two Facebook accounts. Diane Stoppert and Aaron Stoppert."

"Wasn't there an Aaron in the group you met last night?" Jackson asked.

"And a woman wearing combat boots with heels. I wonder if it was Diane."

"They make combat boots with heels?" Jackson shook his head.

"For the paranoid militia fashionista in your life," Navy said. "I think we found Snakecharmer's den."

"Perfect timing." Warren walked into the room. "Time to debrief."

Tom, Dennis, and Alicia filed in behind Warren. While Warren connected his laptop to the projector, Tom settled in behind his nest of papers. Alicia sat in the corner next to her notepad, which she had neatly organized into columns with phone numbers and names. Dennis leaned back in his chair between Tom and Alicia.

The same seats they'd been in the day Navy met them. Had it really only been five days ago? Warren's laptop screen flickered on to the wall. The screen showed a list of emails organized into a folder—Operation Creek Rising.

"No slides this time," Warren said. "We don't have time. I'm just going to pull up links from what people have sent me. Mark and Kevin are still out in the field, so this is everyone for now. Alicia, you first."

"You asked me to find who had received all the bombs Navy delivered," Alicia said. "Unfortunately, I don't have names. The packages all scattered to different locations in the city. They're all storage lockers rented with a credit card. Surveillance footage was mostly useless. All I could see was a white male in a hoodie that could be Derek. Or any of his friends. The name on the credit card is Ethel Barnes. And . . . aside from these charges on this credit card, she has no financial activity over the past five years. Doesn't even have a driver's license."

"So the bombs are controlled by a ghost," Dennis said. "Great."

Another old name. Like Walton. Navy searched quickly on her laptop. "She's Walton's age."

Only Jackson understood. "Walton Stoppert is a name that came up in our property searches," Jackson said. "We'll explain later."

"I would really like this conspiracy to have fewer characters," Warren said as he scrawled some notes on his notepad. "Tom, you're up.

You said you found the officer who knew Derek was at the J6 attack but didn't report him."

"This is the service record for Officer Robert Harris," Tom said. "Forty-three years old. Been on the force for twenty years. He has one citizen complaint from several years ago but otherwise unremarkable."

The man projected on the wall did indeed look unremarkable. Slightly balding with short, light-brown hair. If anything, the photo reminded Navy of a DMV photo.

"Do we have any details on the citizen complaint?" Alicia asked.

Tom shook his head. "Too far back for me to dig up. The complainant was a white male, for what it's worth. Unlikely it was related to a race issue, but we don't know."

"Have you talked to his captain yet?" Warren asked.

"I wanted to talk to Alicia first," Tom said. "The only notable thing about him is he's currently assigned to the Capitol Police unit. I know Alicia's been in contact with the captain there."

"That's one more connection to the Capitol," Warren said. "What's your read? Is Officer Harris working with Snakecharmer's militia?"

"We don't know enough," Tom said. "At this point, he could be a sympathizer, an active participant, or just a useful idiot."

"I don't need to be there when you interview his captain," Alicia said. "I can just tell the captain you'll be in contact. I promised someone from our team would meet with them soon."

"I—" Tom shifted a pile of papers in front of him. "I'd rather have someone else with me. Someone white." Everyone else in the room was white. Navy hadn't thought about how it was for Tom to be the only black person in the room. She was often the only woman in the room. She never noticed until she had to point out something only she could see.

"What are you not telling me?" Warren asked.

"Officer Harris' captain used to be my captain when I was on the force here," Tom said. "All the rookies got harassed but I was getting the racist version of it. My complaints to him went nowhere. It's why I left that job."

Warren frowned. "Should we worry about the captain being sympathetic to Snakecharmer's militia?"

"Not that I know of. I . . . I don't know how to explain it exactly." Tom looked around the room, visibly frustrated. "The captain would run into a burning building to save a life. Anyone's life. But he'll also laugh when someone uses the N-word in a joke. I even heard him use the N-word once or twice."

Navy tried to put herself in Tom's place. She remembered all the times she'd heard misogynistic jokes and said nothing. And the times she had gathered the courage to actually call someone out. Sometimes people understood. Sometimes they didn't. "He said they were only jokes and you were being too sensitive. He thinks he's a decent person, and he's probably right, but he also doesn't understand how tolerating asshole behavior puts other people in danger."

"Yeah, basically," Tom said. "I mean, close enough."

Navy knew she could never completely understand. She had never needed to worry about whether one of her coworkers would show up if she called for backup. "Same zip code, maybe," Navy said. "But probably as close as a white woman who's worked a desk job for most of her life will get."

Tom smiled. Others laughed. Whether the laughter was uncomfortable or relieved, Navy couldn't tell.

"Jackson should go with you, Tom," Alicia said. "The captain's ex-Army, like Jackson."

Warren pulled up another email, this time from Dennis. "What'd you find out on those license plates, Dennis?"

"I was trying to identify the five people with Navy in the field last night," Dennis said. "Can you pull up my notes?"

A notebook page showed up on the wall. Six circles with the identifying information Navy had given to Dennis last night.

"So we had five people," Dennis said. "Snakecharmer, Rattlesnake, Aaron, Fashion Combat Boots, and Not Aaron. Six if you count the person Navy picked up the bombs from at Road Worthy Autobody. There's only one Jim working at Road Worthy Autobody. Jim Wallis. Can you—"

Warren pulled up the DMV records for Jim Wallis.

"Yeah, thanks," Dennis said. "This the guy you picked up the bombs from, Navy?"

Navy stared at the driver's license of the domestic terrorist who had offered to fix JaneOfTheJungle's van for free. "Yep, that's him."

"Fashion Combat Boots is probably Diane Stoppert," Jackson said. "And Aaron is probably Aaron Stoppert. Those are the names that came up in our property search."

Dennis scribbled on his notepad. "I think Not Aaron is Dave Sanders since the sedan that was seen at the gun shop and also seen at Road Worthy Autobody is registered to a Dave Sanders. Dave Sanders is also an employee at Road Worthy Autobody and an ex-Army mechanic. Dave

Sanders matches the height of Not Aaron, he's too short to be Snakecharmer, and too tall to be Rattlesnake. At least according to DMV records."

"What about Snakecharmer and Rattlesnake?" Warren asked, "Do we have IDs on them?"

"Maybe? Next link, please," Dennis said.

Another DMV record appeared on the wall.

"Jackson got video of a motorcycle dropping off a large canvas bag at Road Worthy Autobody," Dennis continued. "We think the canvas bag is the same bag Navy picked up the next day. That motorcycle is registered to a Chase Ferguson. Based on Navy's height descriptions, Chase Ferguson could be Rattlesnake."

"But we don't know," Warren said.

"We don't know," Dennis admitted. "I also don't know where Derek is in all of this. I doubt he's Snakecharmer or Rattlesnake. But if he wasn't with his crew last night, what was he out doing? Is there a second crew?"

"Well, let's hear some good news," Warren said. "Navy, you said you found Snakecharmer's hideout?"

Navy looked down at her notes for a reminder. "Yeah, we sent you a couple addresses."

Warren brought up records for two properties and put them side by side on the screen.

"That first location is the hunting land I was on last night. It belongs to Walton Stoppert," Navy said. "The second location is a house on some acreage an hour outside of Des Moines that ordered a fiber run recently. That house also belongs to Walton Stoppert. We think this is the farm Carrie kept talking about."

"Walton Stoppert had five children with three different, much younger women. The youngest two, Diane and Aaron Stoppert, are still alive and in their forties," Jackson said. "That's why I mentioned those names earlier. But we're not sure Walton is even involved. His driver's license says he was born in 1918."

Warren did the same math Jackson had earlier. "Walton is 104 years old. If he's still alive."

"Exactly," Jackson said. "There's no death certificate. His driver's license still lists his address at that house. I guess it's possible Walton Stoppert is still alive and living at that house. But seems unlikely."

"That's why I've been chasing ghosts!" Dennis slapped the table. "I was trying to figure out why I can't find financial records for this cell. Only a few vehicle registrations here and there. If Walton died and they just . . . didn't say anything . . ."

"They have the perfect cover," Alicia finished the thought. "They can use his accounts, file his taxes, collect his social security. Maybe they're using Ethel Barnes in the same way."

"I need to run all my records searches again," Dennis said.

Warren's phone rang and he shushed the room as he answered it. "Mark, you can give us your update on Carrie," Warren said. "Let me put you on speaker."

Static and background noise crackled in the room. "We lost her signal ten minutes ago," Mark said over the scratchy connection. "We're waiting near the meet. The other car is following a van that drove away from here. But we don't even know if she's in it. We might have to wait until she makes contact."

If she makes contact, Navy thought. "What do you mean you lost her signal?" Everyone was staring at her. Had Navy just yelled? She didn't know.

"Navy," Mark said. "Didn't know you were there."

How would Mark have sugarcoated the news if he had known Navy was there?

"Listen, I'm sorry," Mark said. "We gave her the cell phone with our bug in it. We dropped her off a few blocks away from the meet. They went inside the store, then into a back room, and we lost her signal."

"Did you hear anything before the signal dropped?" Warren asked. "Anything more about their plans?"

"Nothing useful," Mark said.

Warren looked at Navy, as if considering his next question. "Do they know she was working with us?"

"I don't think so, I'm not sure," Mark said. "Carrie stuck to the script—she told Derek she bought the cell phone to contact them. He seemed to buy it. There was some small talk and then . . . nothing. Like the cell tower dropped. But we still have a signal. We're checking with the phone company."

Navy's first instinct was to run out of the room to find Carrie. But search where? "Snakecharmer's den," Navy said. "We might have found the farm Carrie kept talking about. They might be headed there."

Warren pulled up a map. Navy could see three blinking dots on the projector screen. One was a question mark—Carrie's last known location.

Another dot waited near the question mark—the car with Mark and Kevin. A third dot was moving away—the car following the van Carrie might be in.

"Let's see if the mystery van is headed toward the farm," Warren said. A few keystrokes and all the locations they'd talked about appeared on the map—the shooting range, the autobody shop, all the package drop-off locations, where the bombs were now. And, of course, the farm. "That van isn't headed toward any locations of interest."

Such clinical language, Navy thought. What Warren meant was, Carrie was lost and on her own.

"No other vehicles have left the area," Mark said. "You think we should pull the team off that van?"

"That's your call," Warren said. "Just telling you what I know."

Earlier, Navy had considered the possibility Carrie might die. She had been able to think of it as a noble sacrifice. A sort of justice to make up for Carrie's mistakes. But the poetic logic didn't hold up in the moment.

"Navy." Jackson's voice. "Navy, your burner phone." Snakecharmer was calling Navy. Correction: Snakecharmer was calling JaneOfTheJungle, aspiring militia member.

"We'll have to call you back," Warren said as he hung up on Mark.

Get in character, Navy told herself. Maybe she would even hear something about Carrie. "Hello?"

"You said you wanted to prove yourself," Snakecharmer said. "You want to help us find the ballots?"

"I do, I want to help," Navy said. The same lines she'd used last night. Would they think she was a broken record? Did she sound eager enough? She hoped so. She kept seeing Carrie's face in her head. Imagining how they might be punishing Carrie right now.

"Call Blooming Spring Flowers and tell them there's a bomb in their shop. Right now."

"Should I—"

Snakecharmer hung up.

Everyone in the room stared at Navy expectantly. "He wants me to call in a bomb threat. He said it would help find the ballots."

"What else did he say?" Warren asked.

"Nothing." Navy wanted to throw the phone across the room. "Just the bomb threat. To Blooming Spring Flowers. And he said I had to do it right now."

"It's a loyalty test," Jackson said.

"Or a distraction," Alicia said.

Warren was typing again. When Navy looked back at the projector screen, the map was gone and her research was displayed again.

"What do I do?" Navy asked Warren. "What if they actually have a bomb there?"

Alicia was already on her phone in the corner, asking for the police captain.

"You let us handle this," Warren said. "I need you to go talk to Sara. She's expecting an update on Carrie. I promised I would call her."

Navy would rather call in a bomb threat.

Warren stood and put a hand on her shoulder. "Go be with Sara. You need each other right now."

Jackson tugged gently on her elbow. "I'll drive."

"No," Warren said. "I need you here."

Warren's usual easygoing manner had changed. Navy had never seen this side of him before.

"Navy," Jackson said. "Is it okay—"

"I'm fine," Navy said. "It's fine." She would not break down in front of this room of professionals. She would not be the emotional, fragile one. She would gather her things and go tell Sara they might have killed the person they had tried to rescue.

Chapter 25

Jackson watched Navy leave. Maybe no one else could tell, but Navy was definitely not fine. "What the hell, Warren?"

Warren ignored him and dialed the phone. Mark answered.

"Is Kevin there with you?" Warren asked.

"Yeah," Mark said. "I'll put you on speaker."

Warren switched back to the map he'd displayed earlier. Blooming Springs Flowers was now marked on the map. And the flower shop was right next to Carrie's last known location.

"Shit," Jackson said.

"I didn't want Navy to see," Warren said. "They might have sent Carrie in with a bomb."

"What bomb? Send Carrie where?" Kevin said.

"Snakecharmer called Navy and told her to call in a bomb threat to Blooming Spring Flowers," Warren said. "Because it would help find the ballots. But he didn't say how."

Mark made a sound. "We're staring at Blooming Spring Flowers right now. That's next door to the meet. Carrie's not in flower shop. At least not in the front where we can see her."

"That's good news at least," Warren said. "Alicia's coordinating a police response. I don't know if this is real, but we have to act like it. I just don't want them to send everyone."

"This could be a test of Navy's loyalty and a response test." Dennis pointed to the map. "The Capitol building is less than a mile away. They want to know how quickly the police will arrive if anyone calls them."

"Or this is a distraction," Warren said. "They're going for the ballots now. And they want the police focused on the flower shop while they hit the Capitol."

Jackson saw Warren's plan. The same plan he would have made. Until they knew more, they had to operate as if the bomb threat was both real and not real, a distraction and not a distraction. "You needed me to stay because you need someone to check out the Capitol while the police are busy at the flower shop."

Warren nodded. "I think Dennis is probably right—this is a response test and a test of Navy's loyalty. None of the bombs are in place. But I can't discount the possibility they're attacking the Capitol entirely. I don't want to send any additional police to the Capitol and tip them off."

"The police are headed to the flower shop," Alicia said. "I gave them Carrie's description as a potential hostage."

"Clever," Warren said. "Mark, pull your team off the mystery van. I want them to head out to the farm. Then I want you and Kevin to meet Jackson and Tom at the Capitol."

"You want me at the Capitol?" Tom asked. "Don't you want a bomb unit?"

"We need a lower profile." Warren frowned. "But we also need expertise. Alicia, can you get in touch with Kaitlyn? The bomb tech who rode around with Navy last night? Have her meet them there."

"Sure thing," Alicia said.

Jackson shook his head. Had Warren just done what Jackson thought he had done? "You just sent everyone on Carrie's support team to the farm or the Capitol," Jackson said.

Warren nodded. "If Carrie is still near the flower shop, the police will find her. If she's not, odds are Derek is taking her to the farm. Where half of her support team is headed right now."

"You're assuming Snakecharmer's den and the farm Carrie mentioned are the same place," Jackson said.

"Yes. That's what you and Navy said. And I think you're right."

"But we don't know for sure." Jackson was being too stubborn. And he knew it. So why say it?

Warren rapped on the table with his knuckles. Jackson had noticed it was Warren's way of stalling for time or changing the subject. If they were playing poker, Jackson would have said it was Warren's tell.

"Are you upset because you're actually upset? Or are you upset because Navy would be upset if she knew?" Warren asked the question with an equal mix of kindness and authority. Like an older brother trying to nudge him to the correct conclusion.

"It's the right call." Kevin broke the uncomfortable silence.

And you know it. Jackson finished Kevin's sentence in his head. "Yeah, you're right. I'm sorry."

Warren waved Jackson's apology away. "Tom, Jackson, I want you to interview Officer Harris' captain. Kevin—you remember those sketches you made of their training grounds?"

"Yeah," Kevin said.

Jackson couldn't get used to Kevin taking orders from someone else.

"See if you can find their likely entry points," Warren said. "You and Mark and Kaitlyn can look for where they might place explosives. Dennis and Alicia will stay here with me. Everyone get earpieces before we leave. Questions before we break?"

Everyone in the room shook their heads.

"Negative," Kevin and Mark said on the phone.

Jackson grabbed an earpiece and felt for his weapon. He wasn't wearing a holster. Because he'd come down here for vacation. And technically he was just a civilian assisting on a case.

"I can't give you a service weapon," Warren said. "Not as a volunteer."

"I have a personal weapon in the car," Jackson said.

"And I'm going to pretend you didn't tell me that," Warren said. "But you should definitely bring that weapon you didn't tell me about."

Jackson almost smiled. "Understood. I'll meet you in the parking lot, Tom." Outside, Jackson took of his mask. Fresh air felt good after being stuck in the conference room for hours. What would he tell Navy to do? Deep breaths. Focus. But thinking about Navy made him think of where she was right now. Probably pulling into the gym parking lot. Worrying about how to tell Sara that Carrie was lost. He shouldn't be thinking about Navy. *Focus on the work.* It had always carried him through before.

"You ready?" Tom had taken his mask off too—faint red lines were visible where the straps had been. He rocked back and forth on his feet slightly. Tom was more nervous than he'd let on in the conference room.

"I know why Warren wants you there to interview the captain—you did most of the research here," Jackson said. "But are you sure you're ready to confront the man who drove you away from your first job?"

Tom shrugged. "This is as good a time as any. I'll finally get to use that speech I've been practicing in my head for ten years. And I even have supporting evidence." He held up two file folders.

"I love a good revenge story," Jackson said. He put his mask back on, already missing the more human connection. He knew the masks were necessary. He was also looking forward to the day when he could actually see people's faces indoors again.

Outside the car windows, a normal weekday afternoon in Des Moines played out. Jackson passed school buses driving kids home and grocery stores with half-full parking lots before the evening rush. The normalcy was jarring. What would his life be like if he wasn't always between one crisis and the next?

* * *

Navy held her key just outside the lock on the gym door. What would she say to Sara?

Carrie met Derek and she has a team backing her up. Technically true, but also misleading. Mark was clearly worried that they'd lost Carrie's signal.

Carrie met Derek but we don't where she is now. Everything could be fine. Less misleading. Still true.

Still. Navy had lied to Sara before. When it had been necessary. She didn't want to lie now. Not just because lying had damaged their friendship. She was tired of pretending everything was okay. She was tired of pretending she could think of Carrie as an asset instead of a friend.

Navy opened the door. Sara was in the lobby about to put on her shoes.

"Just in time," Sara said. "Go for a walk with me. Warren's supposed to call but I haven't heard anything and I just . . . I need to get out or I'm going to go—" Sara cut herself off.

Navy felt both numb and exposed at the same time. What was Sara seeing in Navy's expression? Navy didn't know. Her muscles seemed frozen, as if she were a hollow porcelain figurine under pressure from all the emotions she couldn't control.

"Warren sent you," Sara said quietly. "That's why he hasn't called."

Navy nodded.

"Oh, god," Sara said. "What happened?"

Navy cracked. She hated crying in front of anyone, even Sara. "We don't know, they don't know." *We, they.* Was Navy part of Warren's team or was she Sara's friend? Why did it feel like she couldn't be both at the same time?

"Carrie met Derek and then they lost the signal," Navy said. "They don't know where she is or what's happening."

"But everything might be fine?" Sara asked.

Ever the optimist, Navy thought. But Sara's tone seemed more desperate than hopeful. "Everything might be fine. Or it might not. We might have—" Navy couldn't finish the sentence. "I wanted her to go undercover, but now . . ."

"I wanted her to go too." Sara dropped her shoes on the floor. "Navy, what if we killed her?"

"There's no justice here," Navy said, echoing Warren.

"No matter what we do," Sara said. "Someone gets hurt."

When Sara began to cry too, Navy realized why she couldn't have lied to Sara. Navy didn't want to walk through this pain alone. They would carry each other through. They didn't have a choice. Their work wasn't done.

Chapter 26

Jackson was glad the captain had agreed to meet outside. He could watch the grounds from their vantage point on the front steps, and meeting outside avoided any discussion around masks or no-masks. Best to minimize any potential flashpoints. A man in a blue uniform approached Jackson and Tom.

"I'm Captain Wallace, but you can call me Luke. Alicia said you're a fellow Army man." The captain held his hand out for Jackson to shake. Apparently not cautious about COVID at all.

Jackson didn't want to share germs, but he needed to establish rapport. "Once a soldier, always a soldier." Jackson shook his hand. "Glad you could meet us today."

"You had good timing, actually. You just caught me. The Capitol building is closing early today for some maintenance work."

"Tom." Luke nodded at Tom. "It's good to see you. I was glad to hear you landed on your feet after you left the force."

Tom's smile was strained. "Yes, I've been very happy there."

"We wanted to talk about Officer Harris," Jackson said. "How long have you worked with him?"

"I've known him for years," Luke said. "Trained him at the academy after he left the Army. I worked with him before I was assigned to the Capitol. I even encouraged him to request to be assigned here."

Great. They were interviewing Officer Harris' fan club. Jackson would have to push a little harder. "There's a complaint on his record. Did that happen before or after he was reassigned to the Capitol?"

"Oh, *that*," Luke said. "It wasn't anything." Luke's leadership wasn't inspiring confidence.

"Still, do you remember any of the details?" Jackson asked.

"Some guy's house was robbed. Harris took an hour to answer the call. The guy was pissed we didn't show up right away."

"Where was his house?" Tom asked quietly. So quietly Jackson almost didn't hear him.

"Sorry?" Luke said. "Where was what?"

"The robbery," Tom said. "Where was the house?"

"Don't quite remember, actually." Luke said. "That complaint was years and years ago."

"A long response time? That's all there was to the complaint?" Tom asked. "Are you sure?"

Between Luke's evasive answer and Tom's insistence, Jackson knew he was hearing an old argument.

"Tom, I like you," Luke said. "But I don't want to hear your speech about median response times again."

Jackson knew he was risking alienating Luke, but the details might be important. "What was the issue?"

Luke narrowed his eyes. "Some bullshit investigative reporter ran a piece saying our response times were slower in certain neighborhoods."

"The statistics were solid, Captain," Tom said. "I reviewed them myself."

"Christ, Tom. We talked about this. Not everything is about race."

"But a lot of things are," Tom said. "I saw it too. Officers were and are slower to respond to calls in poorer neighborhoods."

Luke threw his hands up. "So what if they are? It isn't about race."

"It just happens to affect non-white people more than white people."

"You said you wanted to talk about Officer Harris." Luke directed his statement to Jackson. "That's the only complaint he's had. And, as I said, it was years ago. Don't tell me you're here to accuse Officer Harris of being racist."

Not yet. "Has Officer Harris ever mentioned the name Derek Taylor to you?" Jackson asked.

"No, who's Derek Taylor?" Luke had crossed his arms over his chest. A defensive posture.

Jackson needed to disarm him somehow to get real answers. Could he lean on the Army connection? "Derek's an old Army buddy of Officer Harris, I guess." The casual language was deliberate. "Do you remember when you left the service? I was disoriented." Jackson hadn't been, actually. He'd left the Army for the CIA. But he needed Luke's sympathy.

"One day I had this purpose and someone to tell me what to do every minute of the day," Jackson continued. "And then . . . suddenly I didn't."

Luke put a thumb in each pocket. "Yeah, it can be. I went straight from the military to the police force."

"This We'll Defend," Jackson said. "That motto still sticks with me."

Luke, still wary, glanced at Tom. "It's why I became a cop. I trust you have a point with all of this."

"Some people like you and me left the service and kept our commitment to that motto," Jackson said. "We found other ways to do the same thing. Some people, like Derek Taylor, found their homes in less honorable causes." Jackson was haunted by the profiles he'd read; twenty-one people arrested for the attempted J6 coup were current or former military.

Tom opened the folder and showed Luke a page of Derek Taylor's known associates. "Derek Taylor's part of a local Patriot Front group now. We have reason to believe they're threatening violent action against the state Capitol building."

"The attack that Alicia's been warning me about," Luke said. "Okay, but what does that have to do with Officer Harris? Are you saying he's guilty by association?"

"Derek was with a group of Patriot Front members who breached the Capitol on January 6," Tom said. "And Officer Harris knew. Officer Harris was supposed to call in the tip to the FBI line. He never did."

Luke shook his head. "That's . . . not possible. How do you know that?"

"We have a reliable witness who also recognized Derek in the TV footage and discussed that footage with Officer Harris," Jackson said. "Officer Harris told our witness he was going to call the tip in. But nobody ever did."

"Well, it must be a misunderstanding."

Denial was a helluva drug, Jackson thought.

"We reviewed the footage and confirmed with cell phone records and social media posts," Tom said. "Derek Taylor was at the J6 coup attempt. And Officer Harris is friends with him on multiple social media sites. Officer Harris must have seen the posts too."

"I know my department," Luke snapped. "Officer Harris is a good man."

Jackson waited. Tom did too.

"Look, I know what you're doing." Luke directed this to Tom. "You've told your new friend that you overheard a few racist comments when I was your captain and I didn't care and that means I'm probably racist and everyone who works for me must be racist too."

"Let's not—" Jackson started, but Tom cut him off by raising his hand.

"I never said any of that." Tom weighed the folders he brought in his hands.

Jackson could see Tom choosing between two arguments: factual or emotional.

"I said you were providing cover for racists," Tom said.

"No one in my department was or is racist," Luke said. "People need to blow off steam sometimes, that's all."

"If someone were dangerous would you know?" Tom said. "You wouldn't. Because you allow them to be ironically racist or casually racist or whatever the fuck you want to call it. You don't even remember my complaint about Harris, do you?"

Jackson was caught by surprise. Tom hadn't mentioned knowing Officer Harris. Only knowing Luke, the captain.

"You complained about a lot of things," Luke said.

"I heard Harris say he didn't rush to reports of shootings in black neighborhoods because 'those N-words were always trying to kill each other' and 'why should I get in the way?' and then he looked directly at me and said I would probably get him in trouble by reporting him. And I reported it anyway and the next week I found a noose in my locker."

"I—uh—remember something about that." Luke scuffed the stones with his toe. "You didn't tell me about the noose."

"Because you didn't take any of my previous complaints seriously. I applied for a transfer instead. And then I took desk duty until I was accepted at Quantico." Tom held out the folders. "You should take these. And read them. Or don't. But don't say I didn't warn you."

Luke took them grudgingly. "That all you came to say, then."

Shit. Jackson knew Tom's complaints were valid. Jackson also knew that Alicia needed Luke's cooperation and they had likely lost it. "Look, Captain Wallace, we're just trying to prevent something bad from happening." Jackson deliberately used Luke's title to appeal to his authority. "I think you want the same thing. We don't know if Officer Harris is involved or if he's sympathetic or if he just didn't want to get his friend in trouble."

"But I should be careful with him." Luke sighed. "I can keep him out of the way for the next couple of weeks. So he won't jeopardize our response. I'll do the paperwork tomorrow. Right now, I'm headed home like everyone else."

Jackson was glad at least part of their message had landed. He waited until Luke was out of earshot before speaking again. "It would have been nice to know your history with Harris before we walked into this meeting."

"You're here because one of your friends was a victim," Tom said. "You want to lecture me about not being personally involved?"

"That's not what I meant. We were looking for evidence Harris was racist, and apparently you already knew he was."

"You weren't even listening to what I told the captain, were you?"

"I don't—" Jackson shook his head. "You called him out for not listening to you when you said Harris was racist."

"I said his leadership was flawed."

Jackson replayed the conversation in his head. "You said Harris used the N-word. Isn't that enough to say Harris is racist?"

Tom flung his arms out in frustration. But he didn't answer. He fixed his eyes on a cannon displayed at the bottom of the steps. "That's a civil war weapon. Any white Iowan will tell you proudly how many men from Iowa volunteered to fight for the Union and how we display a cannon used in the Siege of Vicksburg on the steps of the Capitol."

Jackson realized he'd never thought twice about what it meant to be black man hunting the modern KKK. What was it like hunting the groups that hunted you? Illuminating the threads of racism in every social network he searched, then listening to most of the world tell him that racism was over.

"What they don't brag about is how Iowa schools are still largely segregated. Because our neighborhoods are largely segregated. They don't like to talk about how differences in educational achievement, or healthcare, or police response, or the criminal justice system affect black people more than white people."

"I'm sorry . . . I still don't understand."

Anger flared in Tom's eyes. "Explain my trauma to you."

The fragmented sentence made no sense to Jackson. "I—"

"That's what you're asking for," Tom said. "You want me to explain my trauma to you. You have no idea how fucking exhausting these conversations are. How much you will never get because of the skin you walk around in."

"You're right." Jackson sat down on the steps while he considered his approach. He needed the information in Tom's head. But clearly approaching Tom like a colleague wasn't working. Treating Tom like one of the patients he counseled didn't seem right either. A friend? No, they weren't close enough for that.

"Every goddamn cop on the force used the N-word when I started," Tom said. "They were all a little racist. Could have been Harris who put the noose in my locker. Could have been any one of his asshole friends. You think of racism as a personality trait. I'm telling you it's a system. We all participate."

There was a lot Jackson didn't understand in this situation, but he knew guilt when he saw it. "You feel like you failed."

"I wasn't just a cop," Tom said. "I was a *Black cop*. You want to know why I didn't say I knew Harris?"

"You don't have to tell me." Jackson did want to know. But now the question felt like prying.

"I had a responsibility. I walked away from a fight I shouldn't have walked away from. I could have stayed. I could have made things better."

"That's a lot of pressure to put on yourself."

"Every police brutality case that's happened since, I wonder. If I had stayed, if I had persevered, maybe I could have prevented just one."

A warrior, Jackson thought. That's how he should approach Tom. "You're still fighting," Jackson said. "Maybe not in the way you thought you would. But that's worth something."

Tom leaned against a column. "You're trying to make me feel better."

"I'm telling you what I tell myself," Jackson said. "I know it's not exactly the same. But I feel guilty too. For all the compromises I've made." Jackson remembered all the women he'd seen in passing in his time undercover in Afghanistan. The times he hadn't challenged the rules about what they could or couldn't do. Because he needed someone's support. *It's a system. We all participate.* He'd told himself it would be worth it when the Americans won. But the Americans had only managed to support a fragile democracy for a limited time. And now he read the headlines of Afghan women suffering under the new-old rules the Taliban had put in place.

"Does it help?" Tom asked. His tone was equal parts bitterness and resignation.

"Sometimes." Jackson checked his phone. "Have you heard from Kevin or Warren? We should have heard something by now."

"No." Tom unlocked his phone. "Signal's still strong. The earpieces operate over the cell network too. We should have service."

The double doors opened as two people in suits left. Jackson caught a glimpse of a familiar face. "Moss is inside. What's Moss doing here when everyone else is leaving?"

"Something's wrong," Tom and Jackson said together.

Chapter 27

Sara's eyes were red from crying. At first, she thought she might be hallucinating the caller ID on her phone. "Navy, Carrie's calling me. From her old phone."

Navy's hand was clenched around a crumpled tissue. "The phone she left behind at the farm?"

"Do you think it's actually Carrie?" Sara asked. "What it they have her? What if it's them?"

"Either way, we answer," Navy said.

Sara let it ring once more before she answered. "Carrie?"

"Sara!" Carrie was whispering. "You answered."

"Where are you? Navy said they lost you."

"The militia figured it out. They stripped me and found the wire and . . ." Carrie's voice cracked.

"Did they hurt you?" Sara demanded.

"Quiet, they're coming," Carrie whispered. Metal clanked close to the phone. Farm implements? Indistinct voices clouded the background, yelling. Carrie's panicked breaths marked the agonizing seconds as they waited.

Text Warren. Navy should have texted Warren five minutes ago. Carrie calling Sara's phone now. Trace call. Warren's response was nearly instantaneous. Where is she? Don't know yet. Need to calm her down.

More agonizing seconds passed as the voices faded. "They're gone, I think," Carrie said. "Derek left me with them. He left me."

Good riddance, Navy thought. But, of course, Carrie wouldn't see it that way yet. "Where are you?" Navy asked. "We can send your team to you."

"I'm hiding." Carrie whimpered. "My ankle hurts. I don't know how far I can run."

Navy swallowed her frustration. "Hiding in a shed? Are you at the farm?"

"They took me in a van. In circles at first."

"To where?" Navy snapped. "Where are you?"

Sara shot Navy a look. "Carrie, take a breath for me," Sara said.

Navy heard Carrie take one shaky breath, then a second.

"Of course I answered," Sara said. "I'm not going to abandon you. But we need to know where you are. To send help."

Carrie sniffled. "In the machine shop. At the farm. But I don't know where that is. They blindfolded me on the way here."

"Does the name Walton Stoppert sound familiar?" Navy asked.

"I hear them talking about Walton's prescriptions sometimes. They sell his pain meds for cash."

Still circumstantial, Navy thought. "Anything else you've seen today that might help? Mail? A family graveyard? License plates?"

"I don't know, I don't know, I don't know." Carrie was almost wailing.

"Shhhh." Sara waved Navy away from the phone. "It's okay, we'll find you."

Navy wasn't sure. Her phone buzzed with an insistent message from Warren.

Update?

Carrie's heard the name Walton. She's hiding in a machine shop. Can't say for sure where she is. Navy wondered what else she could ask. When she turned back to Sara, Sara was halfway across the room. Navy couldn't hear what Sara was saying, only the rhythm. Slow and soft, like a lullaby. When Navy took a step toward Sara, Sara shook her head.

Sara was protecting Carrie from her.

Nothing else, Navy texted.

Carrie's team headed out to the farm we know of. Best I can do.

I know, she texted. Navy sat down on the mats and hugged her knees. She should be . . . what? Talking to Carrie? Navy had nearly made Carrie hysterical. Helping Jackson? Warren's actions had been clear; he wanted Navy out of the way.

"Everyone left? Even the computer guy?" Sara said. "This is good. You can search for something to help yourself."

The computer guy must be Snakecharmer. Why would everyone leave? If the farm was the central communication post, as Warren suspected, Snakecharmer wouldn't abandon it. Unless. Navy thought of the bomb threat to the flower shop. A loyalty test or a distraction.

"You found an address. Great!" Sara scrawled some notes on a piece of paper. "Did they leave any vehicles behind?" Carrie must have said yes because Sara smiled encouragingly. "Go inside the house and see if you can find the keys. Or a landline."

Sara muted herself then waved Navy over. "Carrie found some mail with an address."

Navy let out a relieved sigh. "We know this address. Help is on the way."

"Carrie's going to search the main house now," Sara said. "You can ask her questions. *If* you can stay calm and be patient with her."

Navy nodded. "You're right, we'll get further that way."

Sara unmuted herself.

"Do you know where everyone was going?" Navy asked. "Did you overhear anything before they left?" Navy had to find out what Carrie knew about the plot on the Capitol.

"The door isn't locked," Carrie said. "This door is always locked. They've never let me in the main house." A squeaky hinge complained in the background. None of that answered Navy's question.

Navy bit back her frustration. Sara shot Navy a warning look.

Patient and calm. "Can you tell me what happened before everyone left?" Navy asked. "Did they say anything? Were they packing anything into the car?"

"I was too far away to hear anything," Carrie said. "They were dressed for an exercise."

"Like the exercises they used to do at the shooting range?" Navy asked.

"What are you talking about?" Sara whispered to Navy.

"Yeah," Carrie said. "I don't see car keys. Just schematics for some flying thing, piles of paper, and electronic parts."

"I'll explain later," Navy whispered to Sara. Then, in a normal voice, to Carrie. "Did you see them loading up the cars with anything large?"

More rustling as Carrie searched. "Big canvas bags, I think. It was hard to tell from where I was hiding."

So what was in them? Navy thought. *You're not being a cooperative witness right now.* Carrie didn't sound upset anymore. But with everything Carrie had been through, maybe she wasn't thinking clearly yet.

"What the—" Carrie said.

"What did you find?" Sara asked.

"It's a printout of an email to Moss," Carrie said. "With edits. And notes."

"To Moss!" Sara said. "What do you mean they contacted Moss? He never said anything."

Navy motioned for Sara to calm down. "What do the notes say?"

"Case officer email from Harris," Carrie said. "What does that mean?"

Harris. Officer Harris. The Capitol Police officer Warren suspected might be involved.

"I have to call Moss," Sara said. "I'm going to hang—"

"No! Carrie, stay on the line." Navy took Sara's phone. "Call Moss on my phone. And after that call Warren."

Sara walked away with Navy's phone. Navy was alone with Carrie. The last time Navy had been alone with Carrie was at the campfire. That conversation had ended in yelling.

"Read me the email," Navy said.

"I would like to discuss your case with you today. Would you be able to visit the cap—"

"Spoofing," Navy said. *Shit. Shit. Shit.* "They asked Harris for the email address of the case officer so they could spoof the email to Moss. They're trying to lure Moss to the Capitol."

"I can't reach Moss," Sara said. "Or Warren."

"Oh god," Carrie said. "Moss. I never wanted him hurt."

Think, Navy, think. Carrie had said there were electronic parts. Schematics for something that flies. Mark had been confused about how they lost Carrie's signal. *We lost her signal ten minutes ago. Like the cell tower dropped.*

"Did the militia build a Stingray device?" Navy asked Carrie.

"A Stingray?" Carrie asked. "What's that?"

Navy tried to summarize all the thoughts racing in her head. "It's an electronic device. Looks kind of like a drone." She had piloted a fancy, expensive one in the waters off North Korea to record phone calls from a military base. But with a few thousand dollars the militia could have made their own bare-bones version. "It pretends to be a cell phone tower. They can intercept cell phone calls or block them within a small area."

"What do they have planned for Moss, Carrie?" Sara yanked her phone out of Navy's hands.

"I . . . I don't know. I don't even know where they went."

What would Warren do, Navy thought. "Carrie, I need you to look around. Is there anything that you see that can tell us where they went or what they have with them? Anything recently disturbed or empty boxes or—"

"There's an empty gun rack," Carrie said. "And open boxes for body armor and some small cameras."

Derek's militia was headed to the Capitol and they were going to use their homegrown Stingray to block emergency response. And if Moss and Warren couldn't be reached, that probably meant Moss and Warren were also at the Capitol. Carrie was safe at least, that would make Navy's next task easier.

"Carrie, we've sent help to your location. We have to go."

"Don't hang—"

Navy ended the call to Carrie.

"Navy, what the hell is going on?" Sara said.

Navy wondered how much she should explain. "Derek's militia is planning to attack the Capitol."

"Derek has a militia?"

Right. Sara didn't know any of that. "Yeah, Carrie's boyfriend is part of a bad group. And I think—." No, if she explained the bomb threat was a distraction, she would have to mention JaneOfTheJungle and going undercover. "I think the militia leaving the farm means they're headed to the Capitol. And they're using a Stingray device to block incoming calls. If we can't reach Warren and Moss, that means they're probably both at the Capitol."

As Navy spoke, she was calling Jackson on speaker. Navy and Sara listened to one ring, then two, then three. The phone kept ringing until it went to voicemail. Navy tried to call Mark and Kevin. She tried Warren again. Every call went to voicemail.

"They're all at the Capitol. Jackson, too," Sara said. "Oh, Navy."

"I don't have the numbers for anyone else on Warren's team," Navy said. "What time did Carrie say everyone left?"

"Thirty-five minutes ago," Sara said. "Do we have time to go by FBI headquarters and see if anyone from Warren's team is there?"

Navy shook her head. "I don't know if we should call 911. We know at least one local police officer is involved."

"We have to go to the Capitol," Sara said.

"We? Sara, you're—" Navy cut herself off. She didn't have to time to summarize everything she'd learned over the past week. Even the parts she could share.

"Pregnant?" Sara challenged her. "That doesn't mean you get to decide what risks I take."

"That's not what I was going to say." *These people are dangerous. Please just trust me.* "You don't know who these people are, Sara. I do."

"Navy Elouise Trent, you are not leaving without me." Sara drew herself up to her full height and blocked the door. "My child is not growing up without a father."

On the other hand, Navy knew that look. There was no way she could talk Sara out of coming short of physically restraining her. And they had no time for that. Navy sighed. "For the record, I still think this is a terrible idea. But we should at least get you a Kevlar vest from Mark's supply room."

"This is a very odd gym," Sara said.

In the supply room, Navy pulled her gun out of the gun safe and grabbed two vests. A box of radios was sitting on the floor. Navy grabbed those too. With a tank top, vest, and shirt on top, Navy was sweating before they'd even reached the car. Navy paused before unlocking the car doors.

"Are you sure you want to do this?" Navy asked. "I can find Moss and get him out."

"You're going to search the entire Capitol building? All by yourself? You need my help. You don't even know if the rest of the team is okay."

Navy frowned. Sara was right. The farm was an hour outside of Des Moines. By Navy's calculations, the militia was either already at the Capitol or very close. *If you get hurt, I'm never going to forgive myself.* "When we get there, take one of the radios with you. They work on a different frequency and the Stingray won't interfere with them."

"Let's go rescue our boys," Sara said.

Navy almost smiled.

Chapter 28

Jackson nearly had to run to catch up with Moss.

"Moss!" Jackson yelled across the Capitol rotunda. People were looking as they walked out, but Jackson didn't care. Something was very wrong. "Moss!"

Finally Moss heard him. "Jackson?"

"What are you doing here?" Jackson asked.

"I got an email from Officer Tellison," Moss said. "He said to meet him here to talk about my case because something important came up."

"That doesn't make any sense," Tom said, just catching up. "Tellison isn't assigned to the Capitol."

"He's with you?" Moss asked Jackson.

Jackson nodded. "Sorry, this is Tom. He's from Warren's team. And he's right. Tellison wouldn't want to meet you here."

Moss held out his phone. "But the email's right here. With the room number and everything."

Jackson clicked around on the email, then shook his head. "Navy would know how to check this email. We need to get you out of here."

"Could someone please explain what's going on?" Moss said.

"That email isn't from Officer Tellison," Jackson said. "It's from the Patriot Front group that's been targeting you."

Moss' hands trembled. "They're here right now?"

"If they told you to be here right now, they're probably close," Tom said. "We might walk right into them if we go outside."

Jackson glanced around the rotunda, trying to remember the map from Warren's briefing earlier that week. He needed a better map than his memory provided. "Well, we definitely shouldn't stay close to the meeting spot."

"Not too close to the rotunda either," Tom said. "That's where Derek's militia is planning to breach the building."

"Derek? Carrie's boyfriend?" Moss asked.

"We'll catch you up later, I promise," Jackson said. He pulled Moss down a nearby hallway, and Tom followed.

Jackson tried to call Warren as they walked. "I can't reach Warren," he said softly.

"Me neither," Tom said. "I've tried everyone on the team. No one's answering."

"Warren said the bombs hadn't moved," Jackson said. "But if Patriot Front is headed here?"

"They wouldn't show up without them."

"Bombs?" Moss asked with a rising tone. "They have bombs?"

Jackson should have stayed quiet. "Careful, we should keep our voices down."

He saw an elevator and scanned the walls near it. Yes, that's what he needed. A map to an emergency exit. He took a picture with his phone. *At least it's still good for something.*

Tom glanced at the map, then pointed. "This way to the exit."

Jackson and Tom fell into a simple bodyguard formation around Moss, Tom in front and Jackson behind. Jackson was glad to have someone who knew the layout of the Capitol with them. Soon, they saw a lit emergency exit sign at the end of the hallway.

There was no way of knowing what they would find on the other side of the door. Jackson pulled his weapon out and saw that Tom had done the same. Moss had stopped shaking but his eyes were still wide. Not coping exactly, but at least Moss wasn't panicking.

Tom put his back to the wall as they approached the door.

"Stay with Tom." Jackson positioned himself on the wall on the other side of the door. Tom began a count down with his fingers. Three . . . . Two—

Voices. "You messed up the fuse, dumbass."

"I didn't mess up anything."

"Then why didn't it explode?"

The bombs Navy had delivered with the explosive material switched out. One of them was behind this door. A few shells in the woods hadn't been enough to know Derek's plans after all.

"We have to find a place to hide," Jackson said.

"I know a spot," Tom said.

The emergency exit door rattled as someone yanked on it. Then the muted impact of a bullet against thick steel.

They ran.

* * *

Kevin ducked around a corner when he saw the men running up the front steps. Next to him, Kaitlyn pulled out her weapon.

"So we didn't find any bombs because they hadn't placed them," Kaitlyn said. "Yet."

"And the bomb threat on the flower shop was a distraction," Mark said. "Alicia sent three police units there for nothing."

"Doesn't matter now," Kevin said. "We need to figure out where Jackson and Tom are."
He tried to dial Jackson for the umpteenth time and got voicemail. He tried to dial everyone. "No one on the team is answering."

"Not even FBI HQ," Kaitlyn said. "We haven't heard anything over the earpieces for an hour. Comms are down."

"I counted seven leaving the van," Kevin said. "You?"

Kaitlyn nodded. "We might be able to pick a few off before they get in."

"But they'll still get in," Kevin said. "They'll get hostages."

"One of us could go for help," Kaitlyn said.

Kevin calculated the odds in his head. If all of them stayed, they could likely get in the building. Anyone leaving lowered the odds. "We should try to get in. Once we get in, we can find a working phone."

"Assuming they don't cut the phone lines," Kaitlyn said.

"So we get in quickly," Kevin said. "If you're game." Given the choice, he would always risk his personal safety for the mission objective.

"It's kind of the job," Kaitlyn said.

242

Kevin smiled. "If you're doing it right."

A red dot appeared on the pavement between them.

"Shit." Kevin brought up his weapon and scanned the horizon. Someone already had a weapon pointed at them. But the only thing close to them was a car fifty yards away. Further away, Kevin saw pedestrians. But no combatants.

"It's . . . blinking." Kaitlyn said. "The red dot is blinking."

Kevin kept his eyes on the horizon. "Sights don't blink. What the hell is going on?"

The door to the car slowly opened. Someone stepped out, hands up as if they were surrendering. Kevin squinted. Navy?

He peeked around the corner again. Two men and a woman were fumbling their way through setting up bombs near the door. The militia members weren't even looking behind them. How could such incompetent people cause so many problems?

"I think she's trying to get our attention," Kaitlyn said.

"To do an interpretive dance?" Kevin snapped. "We can't go to her and she can't get to us."

* * *

Once Navy had Kevin's attention, she moved on to the next step of the plan she'd come up with five minutes ago. With Kevin and Mark and Kaitlyn here, she could send Sara for help. And Sara might actually listen. Navy took one of the radios, made sure it was turned off, and clipped it to her belt under her sweatshirt. Her gun was in a side holster, also under the sweatshirt. The bulky sweatshirt hid the vest, her gun, and the radio. It was also too warm for a late spring-early summer day. At the rate she was sweating, the militia might smell her before they saw her. Navy wrapped the rest of the radios inside a T-shirt.

"Keep your radio on. Give these to Kevin and Kaitlyn and Mark," Navy said to Sara. "And—"

"Don't go inside the building." Sara rolled her eyes. "You've said that a billion times already."

Navy wasn't sure it mattered how many times she said it. Sara was going to do whatever she wanted to do.

"After you give them the radios, tell them exactly what we discussed." Navy searched in the back seat for something, anything, to add weight to the paper takeout bag she would have to carry. Her ice scraper? That would work. As long as no one looked inside.

"Kaitlyn is the one between Kevin and Mark?" Sara asked.

"Yeah." Navy kept forgetting what she knew versus what Sara knew. "Okay, I'm going in. Crouch behind the car. Keep your vest on and—"

"I got it," Sara said.

Navy should have thought to grab a better disguise from Mark's before they left. Her improvised disguise wouldn't hold up to close inspection. She could judge herself later. If this ploy didn't get her killed. On the bright side, stressed and harried was exactly the vibe she needed for this disguise to work.

First step, get across the lawn. Navy twisted the paper bag as she walked, for maximum noise. Kevin was waving his arms and mouthing what she could only assume were swear words. But Navy needed the militia at the front door to be focused on her, and not Sara.

Once Navy turned the corner, the three militia members at the main doors would be able to see her. Still twisting the bag, she stepped off the lawn onto concrete. Now she was completely exposed, the militia members could see her at the bottom of the grand steps leading to the entrance. She glanced up just enough to confirm the militia members were watching her approach. Then she kept her eyes down, on her phone. The receipt taped to the paper takeout bag was four days old. But from a distance, no one could tell. From a distance she was just a woman delivering food who was paying too much attention to her TikTok account.

Navy laughed, her signal to Sara.

* * *

Sara stayed in a crouch as she made her way across the lawn. Kevin didn't look happy to see her. Not that she'd expected him to.

"What the hell are you two doing?" Kevin asked in a whisper.

"These are radios. Use Channel A." Sara set the T-shirt bundle down between Kevin and the woman she didn't know.

"Good thing Navy knew about my supply closet," Mark whispered.

Sara counted on her fingers. Five things. "Navy and I talked to Carrie and—"

"How did you—" Kevin started.

"Don't interrupt." Sara felt the details waver in her mind. Why hadn't she typed everything into her phone? Oh, right, because she'd been doing Navy's hair as they drove. "Navy thinks the militia might have built a Stingray device. And they're using it to block cell service."

"That would explain a lot," Kaitlyn said.

"After I leave here, I'm going to drive out of the Stingray's range and call Alicia," Sara said. "Navy said I shouldn't call the police. Unless you said I should."

"Navy's right," Kevin said. "Alicia's a better contact."

What else am I supposed to tell them? Sara wanted to run in the front door and get to Moss. Wherever he was. "Moss was lured to the Capitol. We think he's inside." *My partner. My lover. The future father of my child. Is currently being hunted by assholes with guns. Focus.* Sara and Moss had made it through being kidnapped in Amsterdam. They could make it through this. "We think Warren and Jackson are close to the Capitol because we weren't able to call them earlier."

"How far out are they blocking service?" Kevin asked.

"Maybe a half mile?" Sara frowned. "Hard to tell. We were just trying to get here as fast we could. Anyway." *There were five important things to tell them.* "Let me finish." *One: Stingray and radios. Two: Sara was going to find Alicia. Three: Moss, Warren, Jackson. Four . . .* "Navy is pretending to deliver food. She has a radio and a gun on her and she's wearing a vest. She said not to intervene if you don't have to. Once she's inside and able to contact you, she'll turn on her radio."

"She's going to let them see her up close?" Kevin hissed. "But they—"

"I told you not to interrupt," Sara said. *Five: Tell them the entry points are different.* "Navy said to tell you the entry points aren't what you thought."

"Does she mean the entry points don't match what we saw on the range?" Kaitlyn asked.

Sara frowned again. "I don't know. I don't know about any of that. I'm just repeating her message. The entry points aren't what you thought. We circled the building before we parked. There's a team trying to break in one of the fire exits in the back. And another trying to break in a side door on the north end of the building."

"Oh, hello!" Navy's voice, pitched higher than usual, from around the corner. "I have a veggie korma—"

* * *

"Wrong time, wrong place, lady," the masked man said. His gun was pointed at Navy.

Navy recognized the voice as Rattlesnake's. She hoped a slight pitch change would be enough for Rattlesnake not to remember her voice. *Act scared and surprised.* "Oh my god." Navy dropped the bag near a column and froze, hands up. If she played this right, they would forget about the bag entirely.

"Harris said the building would be closed," said the second masked man. Snakecharmer. "I cancelled the construction work by pretending to be the building manager. Who's calling for food?"

The building was closed? Some cover she'd chosen. *Think fast, Navy.* "Oh-god-oh-god-I'm-so-dumb. I was running late and I thought, just show up anyway—"

"Well, she has to come with us now," the woman said. Another voice she recognized from the field. The woman they suspected was Diane.

Exactly what Navy had expected they would do.

"We said we didn't want hostages," Rattlesnake said.

Or maybe she'd be wrong and Kevin would get to yell at her after he saved her.

"We didn't want *hostages*." Snakecharmer again. "One hostage is perfect, actually."

Three masked faces studied her. They had seen JaneOfTheJungle three days ago. But three days ago Navy had been wearing colored contacts, a wig, and heavy makeup. As an added touch, Sara had used some hair coloring chalk they'd found in Mark's supply closet to put rainbow stripes in Navy's hair. She noted they were all wearing body armor. When she finally had her gun out, she would have to remember that.

"Hold your hands out," Snakecharmer ordered Navy. He wrapped her wrists in duct tape. But didn't search her, just as she'd hoped. Betting on an adversary's incompetence was always tricky.

Navy sweated some more while the trio set their explosives by the door. There were easier ways to get in a locked door. Surely, they knew. Maybe the explosives were for style points.

"Take cover like we practiced," Rattlesnake said, as he set the timers.

The bombs wouldn't explode. Or at least, Navy was pretty sure they wouldn't. But she would have to act just as surprised as the incompetent clown posse would be. Snakecharmer grabbed Navy's arm and pulled her several feet away. Diane's elbow grazed Navy's other arm. Navy's gun was inches from Diane's elbow. Still, as long as they didn't search her, they wouldn't find it.

Rattlesnake came around to the other side of Diane. "Ten . . . nine . . . eight . . ." All three of them stuck their fingers in their ears.

Navy would have if she could, but her hands were bound.

"Three . . . two . . . one." There was a pop and a fizzle.

Navy jumped a little, just like Snakecharmer did.

"None of them worked?" Snakecharmer said. "That can't be right."

"It's that bitch, Carrie," Diane said. "She sabotaged the detonators."

Carrie had said she didn't know what the militia's plans were. But she'd been close enough to the bombs to mess with the detonators. Navy hoped Kevin was still listening.

"We'll deal with her later. We can still get inside." Snakecharmer pulled a crowbar out of a black bag and went to work on the door. Navy followed Snakecharmer inside dutifully. She didn't want to give anyone an excuse to push her. They might feel the radio at her belt.

Now she had to play a waiting game. Navy had to take the first opportunity they gave her to free herself. She just didn't know when that would be.

Chapter 29

Jackson was hiding behind a desk in a senator's office. Tom was hiding behind the neighboring desk. If the senator had been important enough to have three aides instead of two, Jackson would have put Moss farther away from the door. But this was the best they could do.

If the militia came in, at least Jackson and Tom could get a few shots in. It might be enough to get Moss out alive. Tom had to break the lock to get them in the office at all. They'd managed to block the door with a short bookcase. But if the militia members decided to go searching office-to-office eventually they'd find them.

"You doing okay?" Jackson whispered to Moss.

"Aside from cramping in all my limbs, you mean?" Moss was squeezed beneath the desk in front of Jackson. It was a small spot for a tall person.

Jackson heard footsteps in the hallway. Not right outside their door. But close.

"He's here somewhere," a man said. "His cell phone is in the building."

How do they know that? "Get your cell phone out and turn it off," Jackson said softly to Moss.

"Well, he's not where he was supposed to be," another man said. "What does Snakecharmer expect us to do? Keep searching every hallway?"

"Every hallway, every door," the first man said. "Stop whining. This is for the cause."

Fuck.

"Through the door?" Jackson said softly to Tom.

Tom nodded.

Jackson heard bullets shattering wood. They were shooting locks to open locked doors.

"No one in here," the second man said. His voice was next door. Footsteps approached the door.

Jackson moved into the aisle between the desks, right in front of the door. The broken handle jiggled.

"Aaron! This one is—"

Jackson aimed for the chest below the voice and fired two shots through the door. A weight thumped against the wood and slid to the floor.

"Aaron—" the voice was weak. Jackson had injured him, but he wasn't dead.

"Get away from the door, dumbass," Aaron said.

Jackson heard a body dragging against carpet. The injured man, pulling himself away from the door.

"So you can shoot. Did not expect that." Aaron's voice from the hallway. "Won't save you, but I'm impressed."

Aaron thought Moss was alone. That was one advantage, at least.

"My chest hurts so bad," the injured man said.

"You're just bruised," Aaron said. "Your vest saved you. Shoot him if he comes out. I'm going to get Jim and Derek."

Not injured, Jackson thought. Just stunned. And soon there would be four automatic rifles against Tom and Jackson, who were only armed with pistols.

"We have to leave before reinforcements arrive," Tom said quietly, echoing Jackson's thoughts.

"We move the bookcase away together, quietly," Jackson said. "I'll open the door, then you shoot from behind the bookcase. He'll be focused on me."

"Moss, you'll stay behind me," Tom said.

Moss crawled out from under the desk. "Fine with me."

Jackson gripped one side of the bookshelf and Tom lifted the other. They moved it just far enough for the door to swing open. Jackson flattened himself against the wall and reached for the door handle. Tom was in position behind the bookcase.

Fast, like a Band-Aid, Jackson thought. Every second they waited was in the attacker's favor.

Jackson threw the door open. A spray of gunfire filled the opening, narrowly missing Jackson's arm. At the same time, Tom rose from behind the bookcase and fired two head shots. A small red circle appeared on the man's forehead and his body slumped against the wall.

They ran again.

* * *

Navy hadn't been in the Capitol building since a middle school field trip. The elaborate arrangement of red and tan tiles led her eye to two American flags, moving slightly from the open double doors. Snakecharmer had splintered the locks on the rich mahogany wood.

Crack. Crack. Navy heard two distant shots, quick and controlled. All the militia members were armed with silenced automatic rifles. Those were pistol shots. There was no way Kevin was inside the building yet. Was Jackson close?

Somewhere near Navy, radio static echoed. *Shit. Had she forgotten to turn off her radio after she tested it?*

"Snakecharmer, this is Aaron," a voice said on the radio.

Not her radio. Their radios. "We've pinned down Moss," Aaron continued. "Office on the ground floor. Going to let Jim and Derek in."

No one was paying attention to Navy. She took a small step toward the column closest to her.

"Pinned him down?" Snakecharmer asked. "You don't have him yet?"

"He had a gun," Aaron said. "Shot Dave through the door."

Moss didn't know how to shoot a gun.

"And why aren't Jim and Derek in yet?" Snakecharmer demanded.

The cool marble of the column felt good against Navy's sweaty back. No sudden movements, she reminded herself. Just turn a little bit. Enough that they wouldn't see what she was doing with her hands.

"The bombs didn't work." Aaron's voice over the radio again. "Ours didn't work either."

Navy felt for the razor blade she'd hidden at her belt. A trick Kevin had taught her.

"Fucking sabotaged," Rattlesnake said. "When I find Carrie again—"

"We don't know that it was Carrie." Defensive. A new voice Navy didn't recognize.

Not that it mattered. She'd nicked the duct tape holding her hands.

"Shut up, Derek," Snakecharmer said. "You're lucky you're still here. Your girlfriend screwed us over."

Still cutting the tape, Navy took another small step around the corner. Closer to cover.

"She messed up our whole plan," Aaron said. "We were supposed to have the ballots and Moss by now."

"We have a new plan," Snakecharmer said. "We have a hostage now."

"She was right here—" Diane looked around.

Shit. Navy's hands weren't free yet. But if they came closer, they would see she had cut the tape. Five yards to the hallway. She would have to risk it.

At least they didn't know she was wearing a vest. She ran for the hallway.

"Get her!" Snakecharmer yelled. "I'll secure the front door!"

Good luck, Kevin. Navy dropped the blade as she ran. She didn't look back to see how quickly they brought up their guns. She would know soon enough. Bullets sprayed the wall just after she turned the corner into the hallway. But she was still alive.

Another turn. Another spray of gunfire narrowly missing her. Two directions. Two choices. *Doesn't matter. Just pick one.*

"Which way did she go?" Rattlesnake yelled.

"I'll go this way, you go that way," Diane yelled back.

Navy spotted the men's bathroom. The door would be unlocked. An obvious choice for Diane or Rattlesnake to search. Except they didn't know she was armed. Five more seconds. That's all she needed. She ran into the last stall and stood on the toilet. When she'd practiced this maneuver, she'd been sitting on the floor not balancing on a toilet. *Never mind.* Footsteps pounded toward her as she raised her bound wrists up and away from her and held her elbows wide. Then she slammed her arms back as if she was trying to hit herself in the stomach. The weakened tape ripped, pulling skin and hair with it.

Navy pulled her gun out. She could see over the stall because of her perch on the toilet. *Aim for the head.*

The door flew open and a black-masked figure stormed in; Navy fired three precious bullets at the void of black fabric. The figure dropped.

No time to celebrate. Navy ran over to the corpse and pulled it into the bathroom so the door could close. She set the safety on the rifle and took it. His radio began to crackle and she hurried to switch it off. Diane would check the bathroom eventually. But Navy still wanted the element of surprise.

Your comms next. Navy shed the sweatshirt and pulled the radio off her belt. She connected the earpiece before she turned it on Channel A.

"K—" No names over unsecured channels, Navy reminded herself. But they hadn't settled on names for each other before because none of this had been planned. "Handler," Navy said into the radio. "Handler, come in." Kevin would know she meant him.

"Gadget Girl, you're alive." Definitely Kevin's voice. Even whispering, Navy knew. "After that stunt, I'm surprised."

"We're in the rotunda." Kaitlyn was whispering too. "The last one ran off chasing something a second a second ago."

"They're chasing me," Navy said. If no one was in the rotunda, that meant all three people were searching for her. Well, two people. She kept the rifle pointed at the door as she lifted the mask on the corpse at her feet. A male face. Presumably not Snakecharmer, since he'd stayed back to secure the door. "I killed Rattlesnake. Snakecharmer and Diane were with him at the front door."

"We'll make some noise to bring them back here," Kevin said.

"No, you should find Moss," Navy said. "I heard them talking. They said they had Moss pinned down in an office on the ground floor. Aaron was going to get reinforcements. I heard pistol shots."

"Jackson and Tom must be with Moss," Kevin said. "What's your position?"

"Defensible," Navy said. "And I have Rattlesnake's weapon now."

"We can split up," Kaitlyn said. "You two go help Moss. I'll go to Gadget Girl."

"Decent plan," Kevin said. "Agreed."

"Where are you, Gadget Girl?" Kaitlyn asked.

"Ground floor. East side. Men's bathroom," Navy said. "Diane will probably double back toward me soon. Watch out."

"Let's see how well those fashion combat boots work in actual combat," Kaitlyn said.

"Did you hear them talking about Carrie?" Navy asked. "They think Carrie sabotaged the bombs."

"That means—" Mark started.

"Carrie knew about their plan," Navy said. "At least, she knew they had bombs."

"There's a team headed out to retrieve Carrie from the farm now," Mark said. "They don't know she's hostile."

"Nothing to do but tell Warren first time we have comms," Kevin said. "I think I hear people ahead."

* * *

Sara was glad Kevin's instructions were simpler than Navy's. Still, Kevin had made her repeat them twice before he let her go. *Find Alicia and tell her what's going on. Give Alicia your radio and tell her to come to the Capitol.* She hated driving away from Moss, knowing he was in the building somewhere. Under attack. But Moss had the best chance if Sara could bring backup. And Alicia was the only person they could trust.

She called Alicia repeatedly as she drove. *Come on. Come on.* The signal had to go through sometime. Was the Stingray blocking her calls or was Alicia sending her to voicemail? Or was Alicia near the Capitol? She couldn't know. Her phone had shown five bars of service the whole time she'd been at the Capitol.

So test a number you know will answer. Sara dialed her favorite pizza place.

"Brick Oven—"

257

Sara hung up. Her phone finally worked again. She parked the car and called Alicia again. Voicemail.

Maybe Alicia would answer after she heard Sara's voicemail.

This time, when Alicia's voicemail picked up, Sara started talking.

"This is Sara . . . Sara Farmington."

Alicia would only know Sara from the police files.

"Kevin is at the Capitol and Patriot Front is too and Moss and Jackson and Navy and Derek's group has some sort of device to block cell phone signals so no one can call out or in from around the Capitol. Mark and Kaitlyn are with Kevin."

God, she couldn't even put a complete thought together. Maybe Kevin should have given her longer directions.

"Jackson and Tom might be with Moss inside, or they might be separated. We don't know. Navy, Mark, Kaitlyn, and Kevin were going in after them. Patriot Front is inside."

The radio. Sara couldn't forget the most important thing.

"Navy and I brought radios to Kevin's team. I have a radio for you. He wants you to come get it before you come to the Capitol."

So tell her where you are.

Street signs. Sara looked at the closest intersection. Somehow formed the right words.

"You have to send help," Sara said. "Before Patriot Front finds my husband. Please."

Sara hung up and fumbled for napkins, anything. She was crying, again. So cry, she thought. There was nowhere to go. Nothing to do but wait for Alicia to show up. The Kevlar vest that she'd needed at the Capitol felt like a vise around her chest. She was tempted to rip it off.

What would Navy say? *Pretend you're on a tough climb.*

Sara and Navy had taken on some tough ascents. Where they weren't sure of the route. Where they had to trust their gear to hold. A little faith and a little luck and they had made it.

When Sara counseled women at the shelter, she would remind them to take deep breaths. She would tell them everything would be okay. Not because every story ended well. Because you needed to believe your story might end well. A little faith and a little luck and you doing the right thing. And *maybe* everything would be okay.

A knock on the window. Sara jumped.

"Sara?"

Chapter 30

Jackson took the corner at a run, then jumped back and flattened himself against the wall. An open office door. Lights on. On a floor where all the other offices had been closed.

Tom pulled Moss back and crouched behind Jackson.

"We can't stay here long," Tom whispered as he kept his gun focused behind them.

"We can't go back," Jackson said. "They're not far behind us."

"What's going on?" Moss asked.

"Someone's in that office ahead of us," Jackson said. "Probably."

"We'll have to sneak past them," Tom said. "It's our only option."

"You ready, Moss?" Jackson asked. "Quiet, slow, and steady. Like you're playing hide-and-seek. And if anyone comes out of that office, you run. Don't worry about Tom and me."

"Sure, why not," Moss muttered. "This is fine. Everything's fine."

Jackson took a cautious step around the corner. Slow and steady, like he'd told Moss. No voices. No sounds of movement. That was good, at least. Five more steps. Something, cloth of some sort, was laid out in front of the door. Two more steps. Only a quarter of the way down the hallway.

Two more steps. He could see words on the cloth now. No, a T-shirt. *Butterfly Mixed Martial Arts Studio*. Mark's gym. Mark had been wearing the shirt this morning.

This was either a very good sign or a very bad sign.

Tom looked at Jackson, asking the same question Jackson was asking himself. Did this mean they had help? Or did it mean that Mark had been captured?

With a squeak, the door opened further and two familiar figures appeared. Kevin and a shirtless Mark, waving them into the office. Thank God. Once everyone was in the office, Kevin turned off the lights and shut the door.

This door actually locked. An improvement over their last hiding spot.

"How did you get in?" Tom asked. "And how did you have time to pick the lock?"

"I have good news and bad news," Kevin said. "But, first, put these on. Channel A. Remember, these are push to talk."

Radios. Like the ones Mark kept in the supply closet at his gym. "Are these from—" Jackson started.

"There's a lot to catch you up on," Kevin cut him off. "Get your earpieces in. No names on the radio except Moss." Then, while pressing transmit on the radio. "Stowaway, Gadget Girl, sitrep."

Gadget Girl? That's what Navy had been called on the op last year.

"Still alone in the men's bathroom with a dead rattlesnake." Navy's voice.

Navy was in the building?

"I couldn't get to you." Kaitlyn. Jackson recognized the voice of the bomb tech Navy had ridden with a few nights ago. "Diane spotted me so I ran. She and Snakecharmer are looking for me now. They think I'm you. Trying to lose them."

"Do you need me—" Navy started.

"You need to stay where you are," Kevin said. "You've made yourself enough of a target already. Good news—I found Moss, Secret Agent Man, and Ex-cop."

Kevin was giving them code names. Jackson wasn't sure he liked Secret Agent man, but there was no time to quibble. Ex-cop must mean Tom.

"I heard shots," Navy said. "Everyone's safe?"

"We killed one of them," Jackson said. "Then Aaron ran off—"

"To get help," Navy finished. "I know. I heard them on the radio when they brought me in the building."

"You were *with* them?" Jackson reminded himself to keep his voice low.

"My turn," Kevin said. "I need to get everyone up to speed. We saw seven hostiles exit the van. You two say you killed one, Gadget Girl got a second."

"Good news—that leaves five hostiles with semiautomatic rifles. Bad news—we found a set of keys the militia dropped in the rotunda. That means someone else on their team might have keys too."

So that's how Kevin and Mark had gotten into the office without breaking the lock, Jackson thought.

"I sent someone outside the Stingray's range to get the message out we need help," Kevin continued. "I also sent a radio with our messenger. But I don't know when we'll get reinforcements."

A Stingray? That explained a few things. "They were tracking Moss' cell," Jackson said. "That's how they knew he was in the building."

"They're not just using it to block our signal? That's a new wrinkle," Kevin said. "Everyone turn off your cell phones. They're useless right now anyway."

"Diane and Snakecharmer are getting close," Kaitlyn said. "What do you want me to do?"

"Lead them to us," Kevin said. "We'll be waiting."

"What about the other three hostiles? The ones not chasing Stowaway?" Jackson asked. "They could be anywhere."

"I can help with that," Navy said. "I have one of their radios. I'll monitor comms."

"Quietly," Kevin said. "I don't need you to be a target again."

"Got it," Navy said.

Jackson wanted to ask if she was okay. He hated the idea of leaving her alone while armed men stalked the hallways. But he knew Kevin's strategy was sound.

Best to focus on what he could actually do. Jackson scanned the room. There were three desks and a couple filing cabinets, plus the short bookcase currently barricading the door. The metal sets of drawers underneath the desks might hide a person, but they wouldn't stop a bullet. The filing cabinets might if they had enough paperwork in them. "If we're going to start a fight here, we should prepare. Moss, find a place to hide."

"This looks like a comfy closet," Moss said.

"We pick them off at the door," Kevin said. "Everyone, put the furniture in a ring formation around the entrance."

"They have vests," Jackson added. "Aim for the head."

"You have three minutes to redecorate," Kaitlyn said. "Running toward you in three . . . two . . ." Her last count was cut off by the sound of a door slamming against the wall.

"We'll leave the lights on for you," Kevin said, waving Jackson over. "Come on in when you get here. The center desk is yours."

Jackson turned the lights on. Kevin and Jackson moved the bookcase blocking the door into the ring of furniture Tom and Mark had started. They had already taken spots behind tall filing cabinets. Jackson crouched behind the bookcase. Kevin, predictably, had taken the most dangerous position. He would be the first target when anyone entered. And all he had to defend him was a couple thin layers of metal from the desk's built-in drawers.

Jackson was unnerved by the silence. Normally, they would have fancy earpieces that automatically broadcast any sound. He would be able to hear Kaitlyn running. And whatever was going on the background where Navy was. These radios only transmitted when someone held down the button. Surely, it had been three minutes already.

His watch told him otherwise. *Focus on the door.* More excruciatingly long seconds passed. He counted to fifty before he could hear a muted, fast pounding in the distance. Feet running. Hopefully, Kaitlyn's.

"Anything on comms?" Kevin asked on the radio.

"Nothing. They've gone silent," Navy said. "It's weird. They were chatty before."

That mystery would have to wait, Jackson thought. Someone was running down the hallway. Kaitlyn exploded into the room and vaulted over the center desk.

"How many behind you?" Kevin asked.

"Just two." Kaitlyn managed between panting breaths. "I think."

"The light's on in one of the offices!" a woman's voice yelled in the hallway. Must be Diane. "She ran in there."

"Lights?" A man's voice. Snakecharmer. "Hold up. Does she have help? Rattlesnake hasn't checked in."

"Shit," Kevin said softly. "They choose now to be smart?"

"Hey team," Snakecharmer said. His voice was echoed by Diane's radio. "Who else have you seen on the grounds? Anyone in the offices?"

"No one," came the reply.

"Back to radio silence, until I say otherwise," Snakecharmer said.

"I don't need help." Navy's voice, almost a whisper. Over Snakecharmer's radio. "I have Rattlesnake's radio and his rifle and I've been running circles around you this whole time. Come and get me."

"That bitch!" Diane ran into the doorway with her rifle up. Kevin fired first and Diane wilted. Her head bounced lightly on the carpet before her glassy eyes rested, staring at the expanding pool of blood.

"What happened!" a man's voice on Snakecharmer's radio. "Did you get her?"

"Diane's dead is what happened," Snakecharmer said into his radio. "Because she didn't listen to me. I said *radio silence.* No one else uses the radios but me. Stay on mission."

"Those weren't shots from Rattlesnake's rifle," Snakecharmer said. "Which means you have help. Somehow. And you're not in that office. And I bet you weren't really delivering food. I bet you're Carrie's friend, Navy Trent."

Snakecharmer's voice was getting softer. He was walking away. "But since you asked so nicely, I will come get you."

Jackson broke cover. "I'm going after him."

"I'm coming with you," Kevin said. "Everyone else, stay here."

* * *

"But since you asked so nicely, I will come get you."

Navy froze. Snakecharmer seemed very confident that he knew where she was. Her cell phone was off now. Had they recorded the location of everyone's phones before she turned it off? He was too far away to hear her. RF signals could be triangulated, certainly. But that took specialized equipment to measure the strength of a radio signal as you moved.

"Gadget Girl, two friendlies headed your way," said Kevin over her radio.

"What equipment did Snakecharmer have when you saw him?" Navy asked. "Anything to track radio signals?"

"We didn't see him," Jackson said. "He didn't run into the trap like Diane did."

"He knows exactly where I am, I'm sure of it," Navy said. "I just don't know *how*."

"Stay where you are," Kevin said. "Better not to run into the other group when you have a defensible position."

Navy weighed Rattlesnake's radio in her hand. It was heavy and had multiple antennas. The large display was brightly lit and had menus. A fancy, tactical radio for a group who liked war games. Was location tracking built-in? She almost turned it off.

No. If Snakecharmer was tracking her with the radio, that meant she could track him.

Steady, Navy told her shaking hands. She clicked through the menus, exploring. She had two minutes left, tops. Not settings. Not text messaging. There it was, GPS.

And not just her location. Everyone's location. Navy was looking at a screen with rings of concentric blue circles. She was a green dot in the center. Little green squares represented the other radios. And the dots were in an alarming pattern.

Navy pressed the transmit button on her much-less-fancy radio. "Their radios have GPS. That's how Snakecharmer knows—"

"Turn it off, already," Kevin said.

"*Listen*," Navy said. "There are three radios right above or right below me. Probably below me—that's where they think the ballots are hidden."

"The other three hostiles," Jackson said. "How do you know they're not right outside the door?"

"Too quiet," Navy said. "No one's here. *Now listen.* I can see two dots that aren't moving—the other two dead hostiles. And Snakecharmer. But there's a fourth dot. Probably fifty yards outside the Capitol building."

"Another militia member," Kevin said. "Now turn the radio off so Snakecharmer can't track you. We lost track of him. Fucking hallway combat. I hate this shit."

On the militia's radio screen Navy could see distances. But she didn't know how many hallways or turns Snakecharmer had left before he would get to her. And she didn't know where Kevin and Jackson were. They might not get there in time. And Snakecharmer wasn't as impulsive or reckless as the rest of his crew. He was fifty yards away.

If she was going to run, now was the time. There was no time to ask for permission.

"I should run," Navy said. "I know where to avoid. I'll leave Rattlesnake's radio here. I can get out."

"Not a bad idea," Kevin said grudgingly.

But Navy was already out the door, headed in the opposite direction of Snakecharmer. There was an emergency exit she should be able to reach.

"We'll take care of Snakecharmer," Jackson said. "Get out of the building if you can."

"That's the plan," Navy said. "I'm going to the emergency exit. You'll hear the alarm if I get out."

Three minutes later she was missing Rattlesnake's radio. She hadn't heard gunshots. Had Snakecharmer changed course? Had she guessed wrong? Was he tracking her some other way? Had she just made herself more vulnerable? Had Snakecharmer found Jackson and Kevin?

There it was, midway down the hallway. A bright red door. Navy stopped and listened. No sounds. The coast was clear. Or it wasn't. She couldn't know for sure and she couldn't wait.

Walk toward the door. Fast. Running would be too noisy. She looked down each connecting hallway as she passed. No one. She wanted to ask if everyone was okay, but she didn't want to risk speaking. Ten yards to the bright red door and safety. Three yards. Almost there.

"Don't go." A woman's voice. Carrie stepped out from around the corner. She was holding a rifle like the one Rattlesnake had. "You can't go yet. We're not done."

"We?" Navy was afraid of the answer, but she had to ask. How the hell had Carrie gotten all the way here? And how had Carrie even known where to go? When Carrie called them, Carrie had said she didn't know where the militia was headed. Carrie had also said her ankle was hurt, but she was standing just fine.

Carrie waved her arm at someone around the corner. "I told you to stay in front of me."

"Oh my god," Navy said. "Sara."

Sara moved in front of Carrie, as ordered. "Hello, Navy." Her voice was wooden and her face was pale. Sara was as frightened as Navy had ever seen her. *The pregnancy,* Navy thought. Carrie doesn't know how much Sara had to lose.

Carrie pointed the rifle at both of them. "Weapons on the ground, Navy."

Navy had no choice. Maybe if Sara weren't there. But Navy couldn't risk starting a fight. "Okay."

"And the headset and radio," Carrie said.

"Okay." Navy was unarmed and completely cut off from her team. And both she and Carrie were being hunted. On Carrie's belt, Navy saw a radio much like the one Rattlesnake had.

That's why Snakecharmer had called for radio silence. He saw one of the militia's spare radios appear on the location screen and didn't know who it belonged to.

"What's your plan, Carrie?" Navy asked. "These people aren't your friends anymore. They'll kill you when they see you."

Carrie tapped the radio. "We're staying away. I can see where they are."

"And they can see where you are."

"This is important!" Carrie gestured with the arm holding the gun; Navy flinched.

Maybe Navy could lead Carrie past the office where Mark and team were protecting Moss. They could help. "Tell me what's important," Navy said. "Why did you bring Sara here?"

"We have to find the ballots," Carrie said.

Navy had forgotten about the ballots. The stupid conspiracy theory in that video that she had watched what felt like years ago. "You still believe your friends?" Navy asked. "After they hurt you. After all the racist things they did."

"They're right about the ballots," Carrie insisted. "They're hidden in the basement. I didn't go through all of this for nothing."

If Carrie wanted to get herself killed over an imaginary conspiracy, Navy no longer cared. "Then go find the ballots," Navy said. "Let us go."

"No one will believe me," Carrie said. "I need Sara as a witness."

Ice sped through Navy's veins. "And me?"

"I need you to not warn anyone. The Stingray is working so far."

Navy was sorry she asked.

"Don't hurt—" Sara started.

"I don't want to kill her," Carrie said. Then, to Navy, "You're my friend."

Navy almost laughed. "Then what are we going to do?" She heard shots from a few hallways over, the rapid staccato of a rifle mixed with pistol fire. Navy wondered who had won.

The gunfire rattled Carrie. "We have to move."

"The basement is this way," Navy lied. She might be able to fool Carrie into walking past Mark's team.

"No tricks," Carrie said. "You won't delay me. I have the layout memorized."

Well, I tried, Navy thought.

* * *

Jackson dragged Snakecharmer's body next to Rattlesnake's. Honestly, Jackson had hoped to take Snakecharmer alive. The intel in his head was too valuable. But Snakecharmer had started firing first. They'd had no choice.

"Gadget Girl," Jackson said into his radio. "We're clear. Where are you?"

Silence.

"Gadget Girl, where are you?" Jackson asked again.

A longer silence. Each second made Jackson's stomach sink a little lower. They hadn't heard the emergency exit door alarm yet. Navy should be outside already.

"The other militia member she mentioned," Jackson said. "What if they found her?"

"Or she got out some other way," Kaitlyn said. "And her radio's out of range."

271

"We haven't heard anyone come by here," Mark said. "Can you get us a location check on the militia like Gadget Girl did? With Snakecharmer's radio?"

Jackson fumbled his way through several menus before he found the map Navy had. She was right. "The militia is where Navy said. Directly above or below us. And a fourth dot sixty yards away. Looks like they're in the building now."

"Snakecharmer told his team to stay on mission," Tom said. "I think he has those three searching for the ballots."

"And the other one?" Kevin asked.

"Someone who has one of their radios that he doesn't trust," Tom said. "I bet that's why Snakecharmer told his people not to use the radios. He thinks someone's listening in."

"Am I late to the party?" A new voice. Alicia's.

"We're sharing radios." Another new voice. Warren's.

Jackson felt a surge of relief. "Please tell me you have backup on the way."

"An FBI SWAT team," Alicia said. "Five minutes out. Ordered it soon as I got the voicemail."

"Voicemail?" Kevin asked. "You never talked to Sara?"

"We must have been in range of the Stingray when she called," Alicia said. "And once we had a signal again, we were dealing with what they found at the farm."

"We have news about Carrie," Kevin said. "She knew—"

"*I* have news about Carrie," Alicia said. "She wasn't there at the farm when her team got there. Looks like she stole one of their cars. We don't know where she went."

"Moss is safe," Kevin said. "Where is S?" S referred to Sara.

"We don't know," Warren said. "We found her car and this radio. No sign of a struggle."

"S and Carrie and Gadget Girl are all missing," Jackson said. "That can't be a coincidence. Gadget Girl wouldn't have shot Carrie—it would explain why Gadget Girl has dropped off the radio."

"And how S disappeared. S would have let Carrie get close," Alicia said.

"You think Carrie came back here?" Kevin asked. "That would be spectacularly dumb."

"Fuck." Tom's voice. "Not dumb, devoted. I listened to her last interview this morning. She rejected all the racist stuff, but she was still convinced the election was stolen. She was worried about the group's credibility. That if her former friends found the ballots, no one would take them seriously."

Kevin pressed two fingers to his temples. "We can psychoanalyze her later. Right now, we have four hostiles on site that should be considered separate groups. Three are in the basement. The fourth may have hostages and is likely headed to the same place."

"We'll pass that on," Warren said.

"If that lone moving dot is Carrie," Jackson said. "We can track her."

"But she can also track us," Kevin said. "She'll try to keep ahead of us. Here's the plan. We're going to the bring Snakecharmer's radio back to the office where everyone else is. Make it a command center. So Carrie won't see the radios moving."

"We can direct you," Tom said. "While we protect Moss. And we'll coordinate with SWAT when they get here."

Four bodies, Jackson thought. They had killed over half of the militia. But now they had two competing groups of hostiles on site. And Sara and Navy might get caught in the crossfire.

Chapter 31

The gun or the radio. Navy knew she needed one of them. The gun would be more useful, but Carrie would be expecting Navy to go for the gun. Jackson and Kevin might have Snakecharmer's radio by now. If they had survived the confrontation. *Don't think like that. Of course they survived.*

"Get that door," Carrie said to Navy. "Open it slowly." Carrie fumbled her weapon as she tried to point the barrel to the utilitarian door marked 'Basement Access.'

Christ. Carrie might just shoot them accidentally. She was trying to operate the radio while keeping them covered with her weapon.

Sara's steps, then Navy's, echoed on the concrete stairs. Navy was trying to keep herself between Carrie's gun and Sara. For what it was worth. The bulletproof vests they wore wouldn't protect them from close range rifle fire.

Get the radio, then. "I could watch that screen on the radio," Navy said. "Make sure we're staying away from the militia. If you wanted me to help."

Carrie paused on the concrete landing to consider the offer. "Why would you help me?"

"Because they'll shoot us too," Sara said. Gently, like she was negotiating with a child. "I think we all just want to make it out of this alive."

"It's not like I can call your friends for help," Navy said.

Navy knew that Jackson might have Snakecharmer's radio, but Carrie didn't. Getting a message to Jackson would be tricky because any other living militia members would hear her too. But an open channel was better than no channel.

"I guess so." Carrie fidgeted with the safety on her rifle.

Navy wished the militia had managed to fit in some gun safety training in between watching conspiracy videos.

"Yeah, okay." Carrie held out the radio. "The menu buttons are on the bottom, just below the screen."

Navy nodded as if she hadn't just used a radio like this one five minutes ago. "They're fifty yards ahead of us on the east side of the building. We should be able to avoid them if we stick to the western perimeter."

"They're wasting their time," Carrie said, sneering. "I watched all the videos and the numerology clues clearly point to the archives room below the rotunda. On the western side. But no one believed me."

"So that's where we're headed?" Sara asked.

Navy was glad Sara spoke; Navy had almost rolled her eyes when Carrie mentioned numerology.

"Snakecharmer, this is Aaron, come in." The radio in Navy's hand squawked to life. The scratchy transmission echoed off the cold, hard edges surrounding them.

"Snakecharmer, I repeat, this is Aaron, come in."

Carrie was staring at the metal door separating them from the militia members fifty yards away, as if she was having second thoughts.

"He said radio silence, asshole," another voice said.

"That's Derek's voice," Carrie whispered. "Derek's in the basement."

"We don't have to do this," Sara said. "We could just go."

"Stop trying to talk me out of this!" Carrie yelled. Too loudly.

Fifty yards. How many rooms, hallways in between them? Had the other militia members heard Carrie?

"He should know," Aaron said over the radio. "We finally got into the safe. There's nothing here."

"Took you long enough," a third voice on the radio. "I could have broken into the safe faster."

"Shut up, Jim," Aaron said. "Snakecharmer said I should do it."

"Get off the radio already," Derek said.

Navy wasn't sure if she was listening to a domestic terror group or the Three Stooges.

"Shut up, both of you," Aaron said. "We need new orders."

Shit. "Sounds like they'll be moving soon," Navy said. "We need to get out of this stairwell."

"Up or down?" Sara asked Carrie.

Up meant relative safety, where Kevin and team could find them, hopefully before the remnants of the militia did. Down meant going closer to the men who hunted them.

"They'll thank me later," Carrie said. "They'll see that I was right. *Everyone* will see that I was right."

Down, then. Navy wondered if anything could bring Carrie back to reality of this point. When they didn't find the imaginary ballots, how would Carrie take the news?

"Snakecharmer, what the hell?" Aaron again. "Answer us."

Navy could see the dot that was Snakecharmer's radio on the screen. Snakecharmer's radio was near where Mark and team were. Did that mean Jackson had Snakecharmer's radio? Or did that mean Snakecharmer had shot Jackson and Kevin and was going to attack the office where Moss was hiding?

"What if he's—" a voice in the background was cut off as the transmission ended.

The dots on the screen started moving. "They're coming toward us," Navy said. She needed Carrie's permission to move, either way.

"Down the stairs." Carrie gestured with her rifle. "We go along the western perimeter. Like you said."

If the militia doesn't kill her, I might, Navy thought.

Beyond the door, Navy found a concrete hallway with pipes running along the walls. Upstairs the décor was meant to impress. This area of the Capitol was clearly for the workers and the mice, judging by the black traps she saw in the corners. Navy didn't miss the fancy carpet and gilded columns. But any scrap of carpet to soften the echoes would have been useful. She turned the volume on the radio down a little more.

As they walked, Carrie alternated between directing them with her rifle and looking behind her. Each time her focus switched, she swung the rifle like a child's toy. As if this were some sort of absurd game. Play at being a soldier! Decode the conspiracy! You're the only one who can save the world!

Navy watched moving dots on a screen. The Three Stooges had stopped just past the stairwell. Odd that the Three Stooges weren't following the mysterious stranger with one of their own radios. Or going upstairs to check on their compatriots.

"There should be a room labeled 'Archives' in this hallway," Carrie said. "Room 807."

"This is Room 807," Sara said. "But the door says 'Office Supplies.'"

How was Carrie going to react when she didn't find her imaginary ballots?

"They must have changed the label to confuse us," Carrie said.

Maybe Bigfoot changed the label, Navy thought. The Three Stooges hadn't moved. Or maybe they had left their radios behind, like Navy had upstairs. Maybe they had been moving toward them this whole time.

"Ca—" Navy started.

"Open the door," Carrie told Sara. "Both of you inside."

Navy followed Sara inside. The room was larger than Navy had expected, more like a mini office supply store than a supplies closet.

"The fax machine!" Carrie exclaimed. "The ballots should be in the boxes under it." She forgot her hostages and ran to the corner with an ancient fax machine.

Not quite far enough for Navy and Sara to run. But far enough away Navy could ask the question she'd been wanting to ask since she saw Sara. "Did you reach Alicia?" Navy whispered to Sara.

"Only her voicemail," Sara whispered.

Nothing Navy could say would ease the worry lines on Sara's forehead. Moss had been alive ten minutes ago, but Navy didn't know if he was still alive. Navy couldn't lie and say they would be rescued. Navy didn't know if the small team upstairs was pinned down, and she didn't know if Alicia was coming with help.

"Get away from the door," Carrie said. "Come help me open these boxes."

Navy checked the radio again. The Three Stooges hadn't gotten any closer. Probably. Maybe. "Carrie, how long are we going to—"

"As long as it takes," Carrie snapped. "These boxes are it—see how heavy they are? Full of paper ballots. Navy, open that one."

Navy opened the box, as Carrie had ordered. It was full of paper . . . neatly stacked reams paper. "This is paper for the copier," Navy said.

"Dig below that," Carrie said.

One at a time, Navy dug out the heavy reams of paper. Carrie's confidence wavered with each ream Navy added to the stack. When the box was empty, Navy turned it upside down and showed Carrie.

"That must have been a decoy box," Carrie said. "Do the others."

Navy checked the radio again. The Three Stooges were five yards closer. But they had stopped again. They were waiting for something.

For what?

With Sara's help, Navy could finish this bullshit faster. "Sara, help me dump out these boxes," Navy said.

"Not dump," Carrie insisted. "We have to preserve the evidence."

"Fine." Navy was losing patience with this charade. "Sara, please help me *search* these boxes. As quickly as we can. Before the militia decides to kill us."

A second box. A third, fourth, fifth, sixth. All full of reams of generic white office paper.

"This can't be," Carrie said. She ripped one of them open. Blank pages cascaded down the small mountain. She ripped open another.

Navy checked the radio again. *Shit.* The Three Stooges had separated. One dot waited at the end of the hallway closest to the stairwell. A second and third dot were moving along another hallway parallel to them. Navy had underestimated them.

"They're moving to block both ends of the hallway," Navy said. "We have to go. *Now.*"

Carrie was still digging through the pile. She'd left the gun on the floor next to her. Navy couldn't get the gun and reach the door. But she and Sara could get out the door before Carrie could shoot them.

Navy grabbed Sara's arm. They both ran out the open door, down the hallway. Navy heard pounding steps behind them and looked back. Carrie was running too. Navy could feel the heavy radio bouncing on her belt, but she didn't dare stop to look. They might reach the end of the hallway before they were cut off. They might not.

But better to run for the stairwell than try to defend themselves with papercuts and highlighters. Right? Navy hoped, with each panting breath, that she wasn't leading Sara to her execution.

* * *

"We're in place next to the north stairwell," Jackson said into the radio. A gray, metal door and less than twenty yards stood between him and the hostages. *Not just hostages, Navy and Sara.* But he needed to think like a soldier now.

Better to pull Navy and Sara away while the militia was engaged with the SWAT team. And that meant waiting. Jackson hated waiting.

"SWAT team is almost in place on the south stairwell," Tom said.

"Give me a location check on the hostiles," Kevin said.

"Carrie's radio is just beneath the western edge of the rotunda," Tom said. "The other three radios are probably thirty yards away from her, on the southwestern edge of the rotunda."

That put Jackson and Kevin ahead of Carrie and the militia. At least for now. The stairwell door mocked them. One more minute and everyone should be in place. Kevin looked just as impatient as Jackson felt.

"They didn't come upstairs to find Snakecharmer," Jackson said. "They're going after Carrie."

"They've gone silent again," Kevin said. "I don't like it."

"S said Carrie was injured," Alicia said. "She can't run."

Would Carrie let her hostages go or make them die with her? Jackson didn't know.

"Someone with Carrie's radio is running," Tom said. "Go! Before anyone gets past you!"

Jackson slammed against the door to open it; pain shot through his shoulder. The door wouldn't open. Kevin tried next, with similar results.

Jackson kicked the door out of spite. The sound of his kick echoed in the stairwell beyond, but the door didn't move at all.

Fuck. Jackson could imagine, more clearly than he liked, Navy and Sara being chased down the hallway. They had found Navy's pistol and rifle upstairs. They had nothing to defend themselves.

Kevin grabbed Jackson's arm. "Focus," Kevin said.

"We can't get in," Kevin said, this time into the radio.

"What do you—" Tom started.

"The door's been disabled somehow," Jackson said. "Not locked. Disabled."

"SWAT team is going down the southern stairwell now," Tom said. "I'll see about getting some equipment to get that door open."

"There's no time," Kevin said. "We're going to the south stairwell."

As Jackson ran to the other stairwell, he played out the possible scenarios in his head. They had planned on getting Navy and Sara out before the militia found them and before the SWAT team started a firefight. Now the militia was likely to capture Navy and Sara before the SWAT team could engage. A labyrinth of tunnels, utility rooms, and maintenance offices wound through the basement. The militia had been planning this attack for months. Did the SWAT team know the terrain as well as the militia did?

Jackson knew the dilemma well. Defenders had to prepare for every possibility. Attackers only had to practice for one.

Chapter 32

Navy could tell from the way Carrie was running that Carrie's ankle was definitely not injured. Not even a little bit. *I should be grateful,* Navy thought. At least this meant Carrie wouldn't shoot them for getting too far ahead.

"There's another stairwell," Navy said. "We can get upstairs."

"No!" Carrie yelled. "It's blocked, we'll be trapped."

Navy stopped by the door, unwilling to leave their best escape route behind. "What do you mean it's blocked?"

"They welded the door shut. At least that was the plan," Carrie said. "That's why we came down the other stairwell."

And that's why the militia had followed them for so long, Navy thought. *They* had known once there was only one exit. They had planned for a standoff. "Would have been nice to know that half an hour ago," Navy snapped. "So what's your plan now?"

"I . . . don't know." Carrie looked lost.

Navy wanted to scream in frustration. Instead, she took stock of her surroundings. "Okay, follow me." She ran toward a bright red square on the wall. The bright red was, as she had hoped, the edge of an emergency cabinet. She smashed the glass with the metal hammer hanging on the wall. "Here's the plan," Navy said. "We run until we find a good spot to hide. When they walk by, I use the fire extinguisher to give us cover, and you fire on them."

Carrie fidgeted with the safety on her rifle again.

Worst fidget toy ever, Navy thought.

"I can't shoot them." Carrie said.

"They're not your friends anymore," Sara said. "I know you don't want to—"

"There's no ammo," Carrie mumbled. "I couldn't find any ammo before I left the farm. Did you really think I would point a loaded weapon at you? You were never in any danger."

"Never!" Sara said. "I'm in danger right now! We all are—thanks to you."

Apparently even Sara's compassion had limits. Navy had plenty she wanted to say to Carrie, but forced herself to focus on the task at hand. Navy turned the radio off so the Three Stooges wouldn't know exactly where they were.

"New plan," Navy said. "Carrie, you said you had the layout memorized. We need to find a maintenance room with supplies. Preferably somewhere with chemicals. Not too small, so we have room to maneuver. Where should we go?"

Carrie was breathing fast. Not the panting breaths of someone who had been running, but the short staccato of breaths of someone about to panic. *Lie to her.*

"We can fix this," Navy said. "I know you didn't mean for anyone to get hurt. I know you were just trying to do the right thing."

Sara looked so angry, Navy was afraid Sara would interrupt. Navy leaned in closer. She had to keep Carrie's focus on her. Navy was close enough to get the gun away from Carrie now. Not that it mattered anymore.

"We need your help," Navy said. "Where should we go? Somewhere with supplies we could use to defend ourselves?"

"J—Janitorial Services," Carrie said. "Their offices are close."

Navy kept the fire extinguisher as she followed Carrie. A mediocre weapon was better than nothing.

"Can't fucking believe this," Sara muttered under her breath, low enough Carrie couldn't hear. Hopefully.

Navy was about to warn Sara to be quiet when Carrie pointed. As Carrie had promised, there was a door labeled 'Janitorial Services.'

Navy lifted the extinguisher with both hands. "Stand back." One, two, three solid hits and the lock broke. Inside was an office about thirty feet square. Navy looked past the piles of paper and schedules and counted up what might be useful. Furniture. Objects on the desk that could be weapons. And there, another door in the corner.

"They store extra cleaning supplies for the whole building in there." Carrie pointed where Navy was looking. "We marked it as a fallback position too."

We. As if she was still part of the militia. After everything.

"Block the hallway door with the heaviest furniture you can move," Navy said. "I'm going to see what else we have to work with."

Navy broke the lock on the supplies closet. The pungent smell of chemicals was promising. Navy skimmed the labels on the shelves. Kevin had called the lessons urban survival training. Things you could find in just about any building that could help you in a fight. Caustic chemicals and anything with a long handle might be useful in close quarters. But not against semiautomatic rifles.

Unless Navy could weaken the person holding the rifle. From afar.

Yes, that might work. Navy hadn't seen gas masks in Snakecharmer's gear or on Rattlesnake after she killed him.

"Carrie!" Navy yelled out to the office. "Did your plan include gas masks?"

"Our plan?" Carrie asked blankly.

"Derek and his friends," Navy said. "Do you think they're carrying gas masks?"

"No," Carrie said. "Why?"

She grabbed some large plastic bottles, clear plastic tubing, and a roll of duct tape. She glanced at the radio on her belt. How far away were the Three Stooges? How much time did she have before they found the broken glass in the hallway and the door with the broken lock? She couldn't find out without also revealing their location. She couldn't plan on help coming. They would have to rescue themselves.

Navy ran back out to the office. Sara and Carrie had barricaded the hallway door with a desk. Perfect. The gap where a chair would normally sit was a great spot for a chemical weapon. As long as the Three Stooges weren't prepared.

"Are you becoming a serial killer?" Sara gestured to the supplies at Navy's feet. "And can I help?"

Navy grinned. "Actually, probably better if you stay back. I'm going to smoke out the hallway so they can't get close to us without fainting."

"Bleach and ammonia," Sara said. "I see."

"Can you look in the supply closet for anything we can block the bottom of the door with? Like a towel or something? There are some masks in there you should grab too. Respirators for cleaning with toxic chemicals."

"What can I do?" Carrie asked.

Navy was loath to trust Carrie with anything, but she needed Carrie calm and trusting for now. "Use this duct tape to seal the plastic tubing to the empty bottle. We need a tight seal or we're going to smoke ourselves out too."

Rubber gloves first, Navy reminded herself. The smell of bleach burned Navy's nose as soon as she opened the bottle. Sara handed them two respirators and backed away while putting on her own. Even with the respirator on, Navy could smell the bleach. She took the empty bottle from Carrie and wiggled the plastic tubing to test the seal. Seemed good.

Was it her imagination or were there footsteps in the hallway?

Navy poured bleach into the empty container until she thought it was half full. Then she filled the rest with ammonia. She coughed from the stench, even with the respirator. She capped the open end of the plastic tube with a rag.

"Close those open containers," Navy told Carrie. Still holding the tube closed, Navy crouched under the desk. She threaded the tubing under the door then stuffed the towels Sara had found around it. Not a medical seal, but good enough. Hopefully.

Now to spring the trap. The Three Stooges would find them in the next ten minutes. Navy needed the Three Stooges to arrive while the fumes were concentrated in the hallway. She unclipped the radio from her belt and turned it on.

"Are you looking for us?" Navy said into the radio. What could she tempt them with? What would they want so much they would keep walking into a gas cloud? "We have the ballots you were looking for. And we're going to destroy them. You lost. Run away while you still can." She should warn Jackson—if he was listening. "Or breath in the fumes and we'll kill you on our way out."

A long minute passed.

"Who the hell are you?" Aaron said. "Who's with you?"

"It has to be Carrie's fault," Jim said. "She must have brought them here."

Carrie reached for the radio, but Navy held it out of her reach.

"What are you going to say?" Navy asked her.

"I'm not a traitor!" Carrie said. "I wouldn't destroy the ballots."

"*It doesn't matter,*" Navy hissed. "There are no ballots. I just need them to hang around long enough to pass out so we can leave."

"But I don't want them to think—"

"They're assholes," Sara said from across the room. "They're all racist, stupid assholes, and you shouldn't care what they think."

"We're coming for you, Carrie," Derek said. "I shouldn't have walked away before. I should have helped them finish you off."

Shit. Navy should have expected that the militia would use the radio to manipulate Carrie. Navy and Sara were locked in the room with someone who could turn any minute.

"We've got both ends of the hallway covered, Carrie," Aaron said. "You help them destroy those ballots and we'll never forgive you."

Death threats alternated with forgiveness. *You're the one being difficult. I wouldn't have to threaten you if you weren't being difficult.* The abusive cycle was too familiar. Navy squeezed her eyes shut to fight the memories.

"I have to tell him." Carrie was in tears now. "I have to tell him I would never."

He doesn't love you. None of them cared about you, they never did. Not in any way that mattered. Navy wanted to tell Carrie all these things. Psychological manipulation was what tied the abuser to the abused. But could Navy break a connection that had been forged over months in just a few minutes? Navy turned off the radio.

"No!" Carrie said. "Turn it back on."

Navy heard coughing from the hallway. The door rattled as someone kicked it. She had turned off the radio too late. They could talk to Carrie through the door.

"Let us in, Carrie," Aaron said, coughing between each word. "Let us in and we can show the world what really happened."

Navy positioned herself in front of the door, just in case. "We don't have any ballots, Carrie," Navy said softly. "They're not your friends. If you let them in, they will kill you. And me. And Sara."

"We could be together again," Derek said. He sounded weak.

Carrie only had to hold it together for another two minutes and they would pass out.

"If you can be good, we can be together again," Derek said.

Carrie lunged for Navy.

Rotate the arm and throw. Navy countered with an arm bar, step, throw, and pinned Carrie to the ground. The door rattled. The desk shifted. Carrie was still struggling; Navy couldn't reinforce the door with her weight.

"I've got it." Sara ran toward the door as the desk moved an inch, then an inch more.

Too late. The door exploded inward. The bleach-ammonia mix tipped over and flooded down the tube into the hallway. Acrid fumes bloomed from the doorway. A tall, heavyset man with a thick, dark beard entered the room. Definitely outside of Navy's weight class. At least the fumes had weakened him.

"Derek!" Carrie screamed. "Help!"

Navy rolled away from Carrie. There was no way Navy could fight Derek and keep Carrie pinned down.

"Oh, god, it burns!" a man screamed from the hallway.

Derek had accelerated Navy's chemical attack by dumping the bottle into the hallway. He was coughing hard. He looked at the tipped-over bottle, realized what he'd done.

Another man was crawling, almost at the door. "Help," he said weakly.

Derek tossed the now mostly empty bottle into the hallway and barricaded the door again. He was sacrificing everyone on his team to save himself. "Seal the bottom of the door, babe," he told Carrie in between coughs. He fell to his knees while Carrie scrambled to seal the crack at the bottom of the door. Each cough sounded like phlegm and sandpaper. His red eyes leaked waterfalls of tears.

Sara was coughing some too, even with the respirator. Navy had gassed her own friend. Her own pregnant friend.

"It's okay, honey, it's okay." Carrie hovered over Derek, rubbing his back as he tried to catch his breath. "There's no ballots there. I wouldn't destroy them. She lied to you. She trapped you."

Disgust or anger, Navy couldn't decide which feeling was stronger. They would have been fine if Carrie hadn't turned. Even the men in the hallway would probably have been fine without the megadose of chlorine gas Derek had unleashed when he kicked down the door.

Never mind. Could Navy get his gun while he was trying to recover? With Carrie fighting her?

"Get in the supply closet," Navy told Sara. "Block the door."

"Fuck no," Sara said. "I'm not leaving you alone."

Sara wasn't wrong. Navy had a better chance of disarming Derek with help. And Sara had the Kevlar vest, right? Wouldn't protect her from everything, but the vest would probably stop a ricochet from Derek's rifle.

"You take Carrie," Navy said softly. "I take Derek."

Sara leapt with a guttural scream Navy had never heard from her before. Carrie looked up just as Sara tackled her. They rolled against one of desks, against the legs of a chair. Had Navy miscalculated? If Carrie knew how to shoot, did she know how to fight? Sara was an athlete, not a fighter.

Navy couldn't afford to think about it. She had to take Derek while he was still weak. Derek stood, wavering, still coughing. But stronger, now that the chlorine gas was isolated in the hallway. Navy couldn't afford to be cocky. He was stronger and weighed more. And he had a loaded rifle slung at his back.

"You must be Navy Trent," Derek said in a raspy voice. "A government agent would be a fine prize. With or without ballots."

Fake him out. Before he gets his rifle up. Navy closed the yard between them and pretended to come in with a punch. His block found empty air, as Navy spun and grabbed his punching hand. She twisted the arm behind him and kicked behind his knees. He fell down to his knees again but shot his free hand out to keep from face-planting.

Of course he wouldn't be as easy to take as Carrie was.

Navy locked her free arm around his neck. He wouldn't be upright long if he couldn't breathe. He clawed at her arm, digging out stripes of her skin. The rifle she could feel between her stomach and his back was all the motivation she needed to hang on. Just a couple minutes. She could breathe through the pain. The blood dripping down her forearm didn't matter. Derek was weak right now. If she relented, he would have time to recover.

"Let him go!" Carrie was on kneeling on top of Sara's waist.

Oh, god. Sara. Sara's face was scratched and bruised. She was moaning softly. Conscious, but not fighting back as much as she should.

"I'll punch her and I'll keep punching her," Carrie threatened. "Until you let him go."

Derek thrashed against Navy's aching muscles, dug deeper in the wounds he'd already made.

"I'm not going to kill him," Navy said. "Just put him to sleep. That's more mercy than he'll show us."

"He wouldn't hurt me again," Carrie said.

Keep her talking. Just one minute more. "Maybe, maybe not," Navy said. "But he'll hurt Sara. And he'll hurt me. Do you want that?"

"I . . ." Carrie looked down at Sara. Finally seemed to see the marks she'd left on Sara's face.

"You said you wouldn't point a loaded weapon at us. Do you really think Derek won't?"

"You're hurting him," Carrie said.

Abusive relationships were a hall of mirrors Navy knew too well. Carrie wasn't hurting Sara *right now*. If Navy could just keep Carrie talking long enough for Derek to pass out.

"He's almost asleep," Navy promised. "Then I'll let him go."

Derek was fading. Navy could feel his pulse slowing against her inner wrist.

"You can stay with him if you like, if you think he really loves you," Navy said. "I'm just trying to keep us safe."

"C–c–aa—" Derek's speech was more of a croak. "H–h–h–elp."

Carrie's face hardened. "You asked for this." She raised a fist. "Let him go."

"Don't listen," Sara said softly.

"I'm sorry." Navy channeled her anger into holding the grip on Derek's neck. Sara was right, again. If Navy let Derek get away, they lost. She could take on Carrie after Derek was down. But she would have to watch Sara get beaten until then.

"Fine." Carrie brought her fist down; Sara swung a leg over Carrie's and flipped Carrie. Now Sara had Carrie pinned, but more effectively. Sara had her knees on Carrie's thighs, and her hands holding down Carrie's. Where had Sara learned that?

Derek finally slumped. Navy counted ten painfully long seconds before releasing him. Now she needed something to restrain him. The duct tape. She taped his hands behind his back and then his ankles for good measure. Then his mouth, just because. He would wake up with a hell of a headache. But he would probably wake up.

Sara climbed off Carrie. "Go to him," Sara said. "Or don't. I don't fucking care. But if you touch either one of us again, you'll be duct-taped like him."

Navy turned the Patriot Front radio on. The cloud of gas in the hallway was still protecting them. Maybe she could get answers from upstairs.

"Gadget Girl here," Navy said into the radio. "All of the assholes down here are neutralized. Anybody listening who's not an asshole?"

A long beat.

"SWAT and Jackson and Kevin were trying to get to you," Mark's voice. "But the gas was too strong. We're waiting for the fumes to clear."

No code names? That must mean all the militants upstairs had been neutralized. "Yeah, sorry about that," Navy said. "We didn't know if Sara's message had gotten out. Or how things were going upstairs."

"We're all good," Mark said. "Some minor injuries but everyone's alive and accounted for."

"Same here," Navy said.

"Sara's with you?" Mark asked.

"Yeah." Navy glanced at Carrie, who was sitting near Derek. Not touching him. Just near him. "Carrie too. We have Derek tied up. Everyone else is in the hallway."

"Hang on, I have someone who wants to talk." Mark sounded like he was smiling.

"Sara!" Moss' voice. "You're okay?"

Sara grabbed the radio from Navy's hand. "Moss! I was so worried. Are you hurt?"

"A couple bruises, that's all. Are you okay?"

"I'm . . . okay." Sara looked at Carrie, who was still focused on the unconscious Derek. "I had to fight Carrie. And the gas got in here a little bit. But we had respirators. They didn't."

"Is the baby okay?" Moss asked.

Sara touched her stomach. "I don't know. I guess we'll see."

So much pain condensed into so few words. Sara had lost pregnancies before. To the nameless, faceless struggles with infertility. But never because of a person. Carrie had brought her here at gunpoint. Navy had released the gas. If Sara lost this pregnancy, who would she blame more?

"Oh, sweetheart," Moss said.

"I'm so sorry," Navy said. "Maybe I shouldn't have—"

"Your plan was better than being shot to death," Sara said.

"You're pregnant?" Carrie asked. "I—I didn't know."

Oh, now you're paying attention? Navy thought.

Carrie stumbled to her feet. She was crying. For Derek? For Sara? For herself? Carrie opened her arms and took a step toward Sara.

As if Carrie was going to hug Sara.

"Don't *fucking* touch me," Sara said. "I tried to help you. And this is the thanks I get? You dragging me here? If I lose this pregnancy today, it will be because of you. And I will never forgive you."

"I didn't mean—" Carrie started.

Navy stepped between them. "Leave her be, Carrie."

"Can you put Navy on?" Mark's voice on the radio.

Sara handed the radio to Navy and then curled up in the corner farthest from Carrie. Carrie returned to crying over Derek.

"Here," Navy said into the radio.

"We've got fans coming to clear the hallway," Mark said. "We should be able to reach you in twenty minutes."

Navy chose a spot between Carrie, who was quietly sobbing over Derek, and Sara, who was lost in her own world. Derek's chest was rising and falling, ever so slightly. He would live.

"Twenty minutes," Navy said into the radio. "Okay. I wasn't trying—"

She wasn't physically exhausted. Emotionally, maybe. Navy had felt guilty for sending Carrie back to the lion's den. Then relief and sympathy when Carrie had called, because Carrie was still alive and supposedly injured. Then anger because Carrie had lied to them and taken Sara hostage. And now? Navy didn't know.

"Wasn't trying to what?" Mark asked.

"Wasn't trying to create that much concentrated gas," Navy said. "Derek forced his way into the room and dumped the bleach-ammonia mixture in the hallway. I'm not sure what you'll find there."

I may have killed them all. In the most painful way possible.

"You had to defend yourself," Mark said.

That had never quieted her conscience before. A roar like a small jet engine came from the hallway. The fans Mark had mentioned. Navy checked her watch. Eighteen more minutes. Eighteen, watchful, tense, very long minutes. Navy didn't trust Carrie not to turn on them again, especially after Sara's outburst. Not that Carrie hadn't deserved it.

"I guess so," Navy said. "Carrie's rifle had no ammo. And they were between us and the exit." As if Mark had accused her of something. When he hadn't.

She was accusing herself.

"Navy," Jackson's voice on the radio. He was panting. "Had to run back to Mark before we could talk, we couldn't carry a Patriot Front radio with us."

His voice brought relief and weakness. He was the one person in the world she would break down in front of, and she had to stay strong. For a little bit longer. Still, she was happy to hear him.

"We tried to reach you, from the other stairwell."

"Carrie said they welded the door shut." Navy pulled her knees close to her chest.

"My shoulder discovered that," Jackson said.

She was starting to feel her own bruises now. And the scrapes, no, more like gouges on her arm. "We'll be quite the pair tomorrow."

"Just ten more minutes," Jackson said.

Navy pushed the talk button down, then released it. He was injured, but fine. She was injured, but fine. What more was there to say? Especially in front of Carrie. And Derek, who was awake now and groaning. She'd been told waking up from a headlock felt like having a hangover. She hoped Derek was feeling the worst hangover he'd ever had.

"Navy?" Jackson asked. "You still there?"

"Yeah." Navy was thinking about that other time she'd been waiting for him. That other time she'd been stuck in a room with a man trying to kill her and won the fight, barely. Before she and Jackson had been committed to each other. She would ask Jackson for the same thing now she had asked for then.

"Just . . . keep talking," Navy said. "Keep me company."

"You told me once about a bar you liked here," Jackson said. "After we get cleaned up, we're going out for your favorite. Burgers and beer."

Navy smiled. "Promise?"

"And then we're going to talk about this habit you have of ending up in basements with psychos."

Navy surprised herself by laughing. The fans continued to roar in the hallway. She stopped listening to his words. Instead, she held onto the familiar timbre of his voice like a lifeline. This was how they worked. How they had always worked. Navy fought her own battles, and Jackson helped her find a way home afterward.

Chapter 33

The nurse wrapped Navy's lower arm in gauze and tape. "Those are deep scratches. Use petroleum jelly on them and change the dressing daily." His advice was muffled by the medical mask he wore. "You might avoid getting scars."

"Thanks." Navy twisted her arms to see her new gauze sleeves; the newly disinfected wounds underneath stung. Next to her, Jackson had an ice pack on his shoulder.

"Ice that shoulder every two hours for twenty minutes." The nurse handed Jackson two pills. "And here's some ibuprofen for the pain. Would love to ask what the story is, but I know the drill. When Warren brings people in, we don't ask questions."

The small clinic Warren had brought them to was tucked in a strip mall close to the Capitol. They hadn't even arrived in an ambulance. They had carpooled like coworkers heading out to lunch. It looked like any other clinic Navy had been in, but the staff hadn't been surprised to see Warren or the exhausted crew who had arrived with him.

"Much appreciated," Jackson said. "It's been a long day."

The nurse rolled his chair back. "Maybe just blink twice if it has something to do with that story on the news about an attack on the Capitol building? The guy they have in the hospital downtown with chlorine gas poisoning? And his girlfriend—the bomb maker?"

Carrie. The bomb maker. Derek's girlfriend. Navy's friend?

"Can't say I know either of them." Navy could feel that her tight smile hadn't reached her eyes. With Navy's mask, her expression must seem blank. She had watched the paramedics load Derek, moaning, into the ambulance. A second ambulance had left with bodies stacked inside, no lights, no sirens. No reason to hurry.

"The pregnant woman who came in with us," Jackson said. "Do you know what room she's in?"

"End of the hall," the nurse said. "Look, sorry about the questions. It's just . . . they're saying the guy at the hospital was there on January 6."

How had that leaked so soon?

"He was one of them and he grew up here," the nurse continued. "One of my friends went to high school with him."

"Everyone's a little scared," Jackson said. "It's understandable."

"I have a family," the nurse said. "How am I supposed to keep them safe if—" He stopped himself and stood. "I'm keeping you from your friend. I'm sorry. Again."

As the door closed, Navy's phone buzzed against her leg.

Heard about some excitement in Iowa. Need an exit counselor?

"It's Meredith," Navy said. "What's an exit counselor?"

"Someone who tries to de-radicalize people," Jackson said. "A specialized therapist."

Was there a possibility of bringing Carrie back? Did Navy care anymore? "Does it work?"

"Sometimes."

How am I supposed to keep them safe. The nurse's unfinished question and Carrie's possible futures tangled themselves in Navy's thoughts. Navy's possible futures too. The eye chart directly in front of Navy came into and out of focus. "What if the coup on January 6 had worked?" Navy said.

"We would have had some hard decisions to make," Jackson said.

"Stay on and be accessories or leave and be replaced by worse people," Navy said.

"I think we'd be a great power couple in the resistance." Jackson tried to lift his arm and winced. He moved his hand over to covers Navy's instead.

The warmth of his hand couldn't push away the day's fear. "We both had some close calls today," Navy said.

"No closer than usual," Jackson said.

"This feels different," Navy said.

"Because it's home?"

"Yeah, I think so." Navy thought of the long flights home after Amsterdam, Romania, North Korea. Thousands of miles across an ocean separating her from anybody who might have a leftover grudge. Anyone here with a car and some time to kill could reach her apartment in two days. "Derek knows my name. And he's still alive."

Jackson nodded. "Good thing you have a friend who works for the FBI tracking domestic terror cells."

"Always the optimist."

"Makes it easier to play the game," Jackson said.

"I'm excited to get back to my nice, boring desk job," Navy said. "You can have all the exciting workdays in Afghanistan or wherever they're sending you these days."

"We could apply for an overseas assignment together," Jackson said. His smile told her he was joking. "One of those ambassador positions where your partner is also a spy."

"I'd make a terrible ambassador's wife," Navy said. "I don't do mani-pedis or cocktail parties."

"Oh, you'd be the ambassador," Jackson said. "I would be the lazy one learning everyone's secrets over brunch."

Navy laughed. "You'd have to learn golf to fit in."

"Won't be doing much of anything with this shoulder for a while." Jackson rolled his shoulder and winced. "I did not know they made welding machines you could fit in a backpack."

"Look on the bright side, you get some extra time at home." Navy rubbed his back. "I'll even do all the driving on the way back."

"No more stalling." Jackson pushed her gently with his good arm. "You should go see Sara."

"Yeah, I know." Navy kicked the exam table with her heels. "I'm not sure what to say. 'Sorry I miscalculated and gassed you while you were pregnant because I didn't move fast enough?'"

"What do you mean?"

"I froze," Navy said. "For just a second. When they started working Carrie through the radio. I knew she was on the edge. Maybe if I'd turned it off sooner—"

"There's a thousand maybes on every op, Navy. Don't torture yourself."

"Someday I'm going to remind you of this advice," Navy said, as she stood.

Jackson smiled. "Alternating emotionally supportive roles. Almost sounds like a relationship."

Infuriating and loving, that's how Navy would describe her best days with Jackson. Infuriating how often he knew exactly where her insecurities were. Loving because somehow, despite both of their flaws, she had been with him for three years now and had no good reason to leave.

The door to Sara's room was open. Navy could see Sara in her hospital gown and Moss perched on the edge of the bed. His arms were wrapped around Sara. They weren't speaking. Had the doctor given them good news? Bad news? Maybe they didn't know anything yet.

Navy knocked lightly on the open door. "Hi."

Sara looked up and waved her in. "Come in. You can take off your mask, no one else is here."

"The ultrasound—" Navy couldn't finish the sentence. *Try again.* "Do you have the results from the ultrasound yet?"

"Everything's fine." Sara's eyes were brimming with tears. "At least for now."

"Thank God." Navy let the corner of the bed hold her up. "So that's it? Everything's good?"

"The gynecologist and the doctor decided Sara should stay overnight for observation," Moss said. "Just because we've had other complications."

"Moss, I need real food and my favorite tea from my favorite coffee shop," Sara said. "You know what to do."

"Indeed I do," Moss said. "See you in an hour."

"Come hug me already," Sara told Navy.

Navy did as she was told. "I guess one night here isn't so bad."

"Probably comfier than the floor of Mark's gym," Sara said.

Right. The house. The noose and the threats that had started this whole thing. "Do you think you'll go back to your house?"

Sara grabbed her phone and held up a picture of their house, where Patriot Front had left their threatening message. The graffiti was gone. "Our neighbors handled it already. They won't even let us pay for it. Every house on our block has a 'Black Lives Matter' sign now. We're talking to neighbors we haven't even met before."

"You have people watching out for you," Navy said.

"I think we'll stay," said Sara. "Warren told me they think they found everyone in the local cell. Everyone except Derek is dead. And we have community where we are. That's a kind of protection."

Navy would have left for a place where no one knew her. But she and Sara had always been opposites that way. Sara ran to people, built connections. Navy ran to high ground.

"I have a friend who might be able to help Carrie find her way back to normal," Navy said.

Sara twisted the sheets in her hands. "I guess that's good."

"Yeah, that's about how I feel. But if someone can help."

"Then you should probably connect them." Sara sighed. "I just can't . . . I can't care anymore. It's too exhausting."

"I know it's how abuse works," Navy said. "But it doesn't make it any easier to watch. Victims leave then come back, they make excuses for their partners. I did."

"You left and you didn't look back," Sara said. "You're not Carrie."

"I could have been." Navy said softly. The secret fear that she had never shared with anyone but Sara. "If I had grown up with a different family. Had less support. Fewer options." Navy straightened. "I don't mean you should worry about Carrie. I just mean . . . maybe I shouldn't judge her too harshly."

"After everything she did. Jesus, Navy. You can't take a minute to be angry? Carrie's a terrorist."

"She's *our* terrorist," Navy said. "She's one of them and one of us. I don't know how to wrap my head around that."

"It doesn't have to make sense, Navy. It just is. Maybe your friend can help Carrie. Maybe not. But I'm done."

"We're here for a couple more days," Navy said. "Whatever you need, name it."

"You and Jackson and Mark, at our favorite burger place tomorrow night. We're eating on the patio. You have to call for reservations. Even that asshole Kevin can show up if he wants."

"Patio reservations." Navy smiled. "I'm on it."

"I need to thank Mark," Sara said. "Never would have made it through that fight without his help."

"Mark taught you that self-defense move you used," Navy said. "When Carrie was sitting on top of you and you threw her off."

"The lessons helped with the boredom," Sara said. "I didn't think I'd actually use of any of it. Much less against . . ."

"Against a friend," Navy finished.

Epilogue

Navy wore long sleeves despite the warm night. Two days after Derek's nails had left gouges like tiger stripes on her arms, her wounds had faded from an angry red to a pale pink. But they still stung anytime she moved her arms. Even small movements, like opening the menu in front of her.

Next to her, Jackson opened his menu only using one hand. He was putting on a good face, but she knew his shoulder was still hurting him.

"They still have their peanut butter burger," Sara said, grinning. "That's what I need."

Moss grimaced. "Ew."

"I don't think you get to judge," Navy said. "You're going to order the jalapeño blue cheeseburger."

"Which is clearly superior," Moss said.

Navy wanted something simpler. A plain cheeseburger. A good beer. Sara and Moss' ability to bounce back always amazed her. Navy knew she wouldn't sleep well for the next week.

"This patio is my favorite," Sara said. "This is the only restaurant we actually eat at anymore. Everything else is takeout."

Navy did like how the patio overlooked a pond and was surrounded by greenery. Felt more like a picnic than eating next to a parking lot.

"And they gave us their biggest table," Sara said.

"Kevin said we would need a few extra chairs, but didn't say why," Navy said.

"No matter how many times we asked," Jackson added.

Navy saw Mark and Warren headed toward them. Kevin hadn't arrived with Warren?

"Sara, good to see you again," Mark said. "Heard you used some extra special secret ninja moves."

"We really can't thank you enough," Moss said. "For letting us stay at your place and. . ."

"Glad to be of service," Mark said. "Certainly spiced up my post-pandemic life. I think I've been living too much like a hermit."

"Do you know what Kevin's big surprise is?" Navy asked Warren. "He said we needed three extra seats."

Warren shrugged. "He wouldn't tell me either."

"Is that—" Jackson said.

Navy looked where Jackson was staring. Erin and Byron had just come through the patio gate with a young man following behind them. Kevin was last in line.

"They were in Amsterdam?" Sara asked. "Well, not the kid. But the other two."

Jackson nodded. "Yeah."

Erin sat down on the other side of Navy. "I have no idea why you had to fly us all down to Iowa. These burgers better be good."

"Ditto," Byron said.

The youngest of the new arrivals looked like he was about to run away. Navy remembered something about a mentoring program Jackson had badgered Kevin into joining. "You must be Irving," Navy said.

"Why am I here?" Irving asked Kevin. "What's so important I had to leave my mom for the weekend?"

Kevin rubbed his face. "Just sit. Please." He almost seemed nervous. Odd for Kevin. He put a hand on Irving's shoulder. "I want you all to meet Irving. He's my little brother from the Big Brother program."

Irving squirmed as all the eyes at the table looked at him. "You brought me all the way here just to say that?"

"His dad died several years ago. His mom's in chemo now and it doesn't look good." Kevin spoke without looking at Irving. "He doesn't have any other family. You're his family now."

Warren broke the silence first. "Welcome to the family, Irving."

Navy was still scrambling to process Kevin's announcement. If Kevin felt the need to introduce Irving to everyone that meant . . .

"What's going on, Kevin?" Byron asked. "Why are you doing this now? Are you in trouble?"

"Could be," Kevin said. "It's not important why."

"I don't need your pity." Irving almost spit out the words. "Fuck this."

"From one orphan to another," Erin said. "Don't be so quick to walk away."

"He starts at Georgetown in the fall," Kevin said. "On a full scholarship." There was obvious pride in his voice. "Jackson and Navy live in DC too. They'll be close."

Navy's concern for Kevin surprised her. She was still angry at him for so many things. But Kevin wouldn't want her sympathy. And whatever kind of trouble he was in, she probably wasn't qualified to help. "I remember how college was," Navy said. "Irving, anytime you want to do your laundry for free, you're welcome at our apartment."

* * *

Navy sat down on the hard stool bolted to the floor. Thick glass separated her from a featureless concrete block wall. If she craned her neck to the side, she could see the mirror image of her seating arrangement beyond the glass. A long stretch of beige countertop punctuated by plastic dividers and stools bolted to the floor. Above the glass, another section of wall stretched all the way to the ceiling. The small creaks of her stool echoed in the empty room. Navy ditched her mask.

Once upon a time, she had expected her parents would visit her in a jail much like this. Instead, she was visiting someone she had helped put here.

A prison guard escorted Carrie to the seat across from Navy.

Navy and Carrie reached for the phones mounted on the wall. Navy had the eerie feeling she was seeing a reflection of herself as they both put the receivers to their ears.

"I wasn't sure you'd actually show up," Carrie said.

Navy hadn't been sure, either. But she'd made a promise. "I said I'd be here."

This is going to be hard. Harder than you can imagine, Tali, the exit counselor had said. *Don't agree to it unless you're serious.*

"You had them all fooled when you delivered those bombs," Carrie said. "You're good at lying."

Navy felt the edges of the phone digging into her palm. "You want me to leave, I'll leave." She forced herself to relax her grip. "I'm here because you said you wanted a friend."

"And are you? A friend?"

Navy couldn't blame her for the question. What had the exit counselor said? *Be honest.* "I'm not sure. But I'll help with your recovery if you want me to. And I won't use you or manipulate you like Derek and the Patriot Front did."

"They moved him to a different jail," Carrie said. "Where we can't even send each other letters. I thought I'd miss him. But after the first week . . . I didn't."

That's progress, I guess. "Here are the ground rules," Navy said. "Tali will arrange video calls between us semi-regularly. You can tell me anything you want but I'm not your lawyer. You tell me you're going to do something illegal or dangerous, I'll report you. You should assume our calls will be monitored."

Carrie nodded slowly. "What if I tell you to fuck off?"

Navy shrugged. "Would probably be easier for both of us if you did."

"I thought I had all these friends online." Carrie chewed on a cuticle until a tiny, bright red spot of blood appeared. "They said they had resources to help me if we got in trouble. But the only people I've seen are you, my lawyer, and Tali."

Are you really surprised? "I'm sorry," Navy said. "We'll talk soon." She hung up the phone. Her heart was beating too fast. She had faced down terrorists on multiple continents and this made her nervous?

Tali was waiting for Navy as she left the jail.

"Did the conversation go like I said it would?" Tali's dark brown curls bounced as her shorter legs tried to keep up.

Navy was walking too fast. *Relax.* "Yeah, pretty much. She's still angry with me."

"We're playing the long game," Tali said. "Remember?"

"I don't know why I agreed to this." Navy stopped and crossed her arms. On her right, the imposing structure of the jail cast long shadows. On her left, a fence topped with razor-wire and the checkpoint she'd have to pass through to leave. "I'm probably the worst person you could have chosen."

Tali shook her head. "You learned how to fight. You can learn how to heal." She released an impatient breath as she looked past Navy. "What I do isn't magic, you know."

Navy wondered what Tali, the Jewish woman who reformed neo-Nazis, saw in the cloudless, blue sky.

"Everyone wants to complain about how COVID tore us apart. How social media is going to destroy us. No one wants to do the work."

"I'm here, aren't I?" Navy's anger sharpened the words.

"You're here for Sara's sake," Tali said. "Not for Carrie's."

Navy couldn't deny it. "Does it matter? I don't want Carrie to threaten Sara and Moss again."

Tali smiled slightly and narrowed her eyes. "You want to help people. You want to save the world, or at least a small corner of it."

"There's nothing wrong with that." Why did Navy feel like she was being interrogated?

"No, there's not," Tali said. "But you need to understand Carrie felt the same way when she was making packages with pipe bombs."

"And she was wrong!" Navy threw her hands out wide. "She was wrong and she could have hurt a lot of people. She nearly killed us."

"*This is the work*," Tali said. "Get your anger out of your system and find some empathy. Carrie is a very flawed human being, not a monster."

"Semantics." Navy almost spit the word.

"More than semantics," Tali said. "If animal control finds a rabid bobcat, they kill it. Why?"

Counselors and their games. "Because it's dangerous," Navy said.

"And?"

"And what? It's not complicated." Navy bristled at Tali's know-it-all demeanor.

"The bobcat can't become less dangerous. There's no blame. There's no cure. Just practicalities."

Navy didn't like where this was leading. "We don't treat humans like animals. Your metaphor doesn't work."

"Oh, I think it does. You understand the distinction. Carrie is responsible for her decisions and their consequences. She can become less dangerous. Monsters don't change. Humans can."

"You have more faith in humanity than I do."

"What's the alternative?" Tali asked.

"I—" Navy scraped at the pebbles in the parking lot with the toe of her shoe. She was thinking of all the people locked up for attacking the capitol. All the people like Derek, who were more committed to their homicidal fantasies than Carrie. "I don't know. Lock them up for life."

"In solitary?" Tali challenged her again. "Toxic ideas are like viruses. They spread through contact."

Navy struggled against the inevitability of Tali's logic. You can't put down humans like animals. You can't lock away their ideas without depriving them of human contact. What was left?

"Have you read any Arendt?" Tali asked. "She lived through two world wars, fled from Nazis twice. Wrote the authoritative book on totalitarianism. Reported on a Nazi war criminal's trial and after all of that . . . she didn't believe in demons or monsters."

Navy dug for her keys in her pocket. She was ready for this conversation to be over. "So what did she believe in?"

"Human frailty," Tali said. "You're still judging Carrie for falling for such a stupid, toxic lie."

Navy pressed her lips together. Again, she couldn't deny it.

"The lie could have been anything. The lie isn't special. Believing in the lie made Carrie feel exceptional, it gave her a purpose. It gave her a community."

"Follow the emotional truth," Navy said. A line Meredith had used when they spoke. Had it really only been two months since that conversation?

"Exactly. I think you're the perfect candidate to help Carrie. *If* you can stop thinking of her as a monster."

Navy weighed her car keys in her hand. She could just walk away from this whole thing – from Tali and her philosophical riddles and Carrie and her problems. "I'm completely unqualified for this."

"You understand the fight isn't over. That makes you more qualified than most."

"What would Arendt say about Carrie?" Navy asked.

Tali's smile reached her eyes. "That she was guilty of 'the crime of not thinking things through.'"

"That's so . . ." Navy searched for the right word.

"Unsatisfying?" Tali offered. "You're right, of course. That was Arendt's point when talked about the banality of evil. I'll be in touch."

Tali's words sat like stones in Navy's stomach as she walked to her car. What if evil was a question of circumstances and human frailty? Was she just as capable of being a monster? Years ago, the first time she had killed, she had felt disgusted and revolted. The last time, weeks ago, she had been calm. If she could find empathy for Carrie, would that keep Navy human? No, Navy corrected herself, humans could do monstrous things. That was Tali's whole point. The fight wasn't between us versus them. The fight was us versus ourselves.

Acknowledgments

Every book takes longer than I'd like. The last book suffered from the COVID-19 pandemic. During the final stretch for this novel, my leg was broken in a car/pedestrian accident. I'd like to say I handled my sudden loss of mobility with grace and equanimity. Truthfully, I struggled to find joy in the activities still available to me during the long recovery period. I wasted too many hours raging against circumstances I could not change.

So if you were wondering what was taking so long—that's my excuse.

I have been lucky in many ways. Aside from a permanent metal plate in my leg, I will get my life back. These last several months will be remembered as a difficult period in an otherwise good life. And also, five books. I have to repeat that to myself—this novel is the fifth book that I've published.

Once again, the cover art is by John Bell Art—I swear I wasn't trying to pick out the same artist twice. I guess he's just that good.

I was sad to lose Dara Syrkin as an editor – her work shepherded the first three Navy Trent novels to publication. Her friend and editing colleague, Heidi Peterson, has carried this novel to the finish line.

Bad luck delayed this novel, but good luck has pushed it along. Somehow, I've collected a group of friends who have been my critics and my cheerleaders over the years: Chris Gales, Bridget Kromhout, Ry4an Brase, and Kelly Stahlberg. Even if you never read another word I write, you have my eternal gratitude.